STAGED LIES & DECEIT

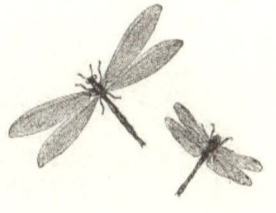

A NOVEL

ADDILYN PRESCOTT

ISBN: 9781735949680

Printed in the United States of America

JD BROYHILL

DEDICATION

A HUGE thank you to our talented artist,
Anthony Conley, for the beautiful book cover!

To my best friend and confidant – thank you
for your unconditional love and support.

ACKNOWLEDGMENT

Thank you to the outstanding police
officers, firefighters, and all first
responders
who keep us safe daily.
God Bless you!

CONTENTS

CHAPTER 1   3
CHAPTER 2   32
CHAPTER 3   58
CHAPTER 4   84
CHAPTER 5   103
CHAPTER 6   131
CHAPTER 7   151
CHAPTER 8   171
CHAPTER 9   199
CHAPTER 10   221
CHAPTER 11   253
CHAPTER 12   281
CHAPTER 13   302
CHAPTER 14   327
CHAPTER 15   351
CHAPTER 16   371
ABOUT THE AUTHOR   397

CHAPTER 1

Brexley Sinclaire squinted her eyes, reading the newspaper article. She wondered if her best friend, Devvyn, had already read it. Now, inspecting the photograph, she felt the black suit made her look stiff and non-approachable. Maybe she should have worn the navy dress instead. She regretted wearing the black outfit. She wished

3

she had listened to Devvyn and chosen the navy dress paired with the red and gold designer scarf. Why did she not request to see the photograph before publication? She felt frustrated.

Brexley ran her pointer finger around the rim of the coffee cup, focusing on the photo, biting her lower lip. Her cell phone rang, bringing her back out of her daze. Shaking her head, Brexley picked up the phone from the kitchen table, looking at the number on the screen. It was Maddison, her assistant, or Maddie, as she preferred to be called.

"Good morning, sunshine. You are at it early," Brexley joked, answering the phone.

"Brexley, we have a problem. The artwork and several other items did not arrive at the warehouse. We cannot stage the Campton estate today without them. What do you want me to do?" asked Maddie frantically.

"Did you call the vendor to find out why there is a delay? I called them yesterday to confirm delivery, and they verified the items were in transit, due to be delivered to our warehouse by 8 a.m. this morning!"

"Yes, I called them. For some reason, there is an issue with the delivery company. The plane carrying the items arrived late this morning, coming into San Antonio. They informed me they will deliver them tomorrow morning."

"Well, that will not do. Please, send me a text

with all the communication information. I will call the delivery company myself. If necessary, I will drive to them and speak with the supervisor in person. We must have the items today, not tomorrow. I am not losing such a valuable staging contract because someone is not competent enough to do their job correctly," replied Brexley. Irritated, Brexley slammed her fist on the table, causing her coffee to spill.

"Listen, I am not mad at you. I am angry because Mrs. Campton has zero patience for delays. I made her a promise, and I plan to honor it. We will stage the estate by this morning. Please, let me call you back. I need to try and fix this. Thanks for letting me know, Maddie." Brexley swiftly hung up the phone, feeling super annoyed. She worried about the the potential consequences.

Maddie gazed at the phone. She knew Brexley was mad and could hear it in her abrupt tone. Expeditiously, Maddie scrolled through her phone, looking for phone numbers and other information to text Brexley. She did not want this day to get any worse.

Brexley stood up and ran toward the sink, grabbing a sponge and towel. She cleaned up the mess on the table, annoyed with herself. She should not have given the responsibility for this contract to Maddie.

She was competent but not ready to handle the contract with minimal supervision. This staging job was important, giving Brexley's staging company — *Sinclaire Premier Staging*, free publicity, including a write-up in the local newspaper. It was considered a big deal to lock in the contract of the Campton estate. It was one of the largest estates in the area, and several other staging companies vied for the contract simultaneously.

Brexley was eloquent and presented herself in such a way that she won the contracts she pursued most of the time. Brexley had a powerful way of speaking and a smooth voice with a bit of huskiness, gaining attention. Her ex-boyfriend, Carlton, said her husky voice was rather sexy, especially when she whispered into his ear right before making love to him.

After cleaning up the mess on the kitchen table, Brexley made her way to the refrigerator to find something to eat. She was hungry and wanted to raise her energy level before heading out for the day. Realizing there was nothing in the fridge besides some leftovers and almond milk, she opted to make a protein shake, which she could take with her. After tossing a frozen banana, the protein powder, and ice into the blender, she made her favorite drink flavor — Salted Caramel. She took a sip, approving of the taste in her mouth, proceeding to walk down the hallway toward the bedroom to dress for the day.

Once in her bedroom, she removed the fluffy

pink robe, tossed it onto the bed, and strutted naked into the sizable, illuminated walk-in closet. She stared at the clothes, which were carefully color-coordinated and meticulously hung in a proper order.

She was a bit obsessive about hanging them in a color-coded way — whites on the left followed by yellow, orange, pink, red, and so on. Black was always on the right side of the closet. Yes, she liked her wardrobe orderly. Her color-matched shoes were displayed on racks below the clothes, with purses resting on the top shelves. Brexley liked order. Some would say she was too OCD, but she did not care what others thought. Carlton enjoyed walking into her closet, mixing up the colors of her clothes, hoping for a reaction from her. He thought it was funny, ever the prankster. Brexley, however, hated it. She became increasingly annoyed by his continually childish behavior and eventually cut off their relationship. She felt his mocking her was more than just annoyance. It was a sign of total disrespect. If she wanted to color-coordinate her closet, so be it.

After a few minutes of rummaging through her wardrobe for the perfect outfit, she decided on white slacks with a pale-yellow blouse. The blouse had tiny embroidered white roses, nothing gaudy or tacky by any means. She purchased it on a trip to New York City last year when she met with her new publisher.

While window shopping on a rainy fall day, she found the blouse in an upscale designer boutique. It cost way more than she ever paid for a blouse, but she wanted it to be the piece she brought back home, remembering her trip to New York.

Brexley fondly recalled staring at the blouse displayed on the mannequin in the store's window for a while, desperately wanting the blouse.

Finally, she gave in and entered the store to purchase it, regardless of the cost, which she recalled almost gave her a heart attack when she looked at the price tag. Never, ever, had Brexley spent that kind of money on clothing. However, she thought it was an exquisite blouse and quickly handed the sales associate her credit card, finalizing the purchase.

Today, she would wear her hair up, probably pulled into a loose bun. Her long, blonde hair always looked stunning, no matter how she wore it. She walked to the wall-mounted jewelry cabinet in the back of the walk-in closet, taking out large, dangly earrings. Brexley did not believe in under-stated jewelry. She liked bold, statement pieces of jewelry. Brexley had always been an audacious woman. She also had a refined taste, something her clientele appreciated.

Thus, her staging and décor business was quite successful. She knew how to bring out the best features of properties and homes, making them pop visually. Her company was well-known throughout the San Antonio and Austin areas of Texas.

Less than ten years ago, Brexley started her staging business. With rapid success, she built a multi-million-dollar empire. She enjoyed the challenge of taking a home that lacked style and turning it into a showpiece.

Most of the time, she personally interacted with her clients. Lately, though, she reluctantly placed Maddie in charge of projects as she was too busy with her new love — writing.

Writing became her new passion. She kept it hidden from her family and friends for a long time. It was her private outlet — a way to relieve stress and put down ideas. Recently, she signed a lucrative contract with a publisher in New York City. Now, she faced publishing deadlines, and it was becoming increasingly challenging to run her staging business at the same time. It occurred to her that she had to train Maddie to handle all aspects of the company to ensure things continued to run smoothly. Starla, a new hire and an assistant stager, needed to be trained to take on more projects.

After getting dressed for the day, Brexley headed to her study to read emails and call the delivery company to find out what they could do to ensure the delivery of items would still happen today. Brexley did not want to contact Mrs. Campton to inform her the estate would not be staged today, on the promised and scheduled date. Plus, the staging crew would arrive at the warehouse shortly to load the trucks. Everything was in place to stage the Campton estate. It seemed like an eternity before Brexley finally had the opportunity to speak to a supervisor at the delivery company.

On the other end of the phone line, the loud and obnoxious woman reassured Brexley that the delivery company would send a truck to the *Sinclaire Premier Staging* warehouse, delivering all items within the hour. Brexley hung up the phone smiling and called Maddie to relay the new information. Once she finished making phone calls, she realized it was time to head to the warehouse.

Brexley looked at the empty dog bed by the back door. She stood by the door leading to the garage, feeling sad. She dearly missed Jovanna, her mini, white Schnauzer. Every time she walked out the door, it broke her heart to see the oval, red velvet bed. Perhaps she should toss the bed out or put it in the garage? It was too difficult to see the bed, realizing her beloved pet was gone.

Jovanna died months earlier from old age. Still, it was a tragic loss for Brexley. She stared at Jovanna's picture, which hung over the dog bed, looking at the beautiful white dog with large brown eyes. Brexley felt her eyes well up with tears. Quickly, she sprinted out the door and locked it. Brexley did not want to cry and mess up her makeup before the staging. She unlocked her SUV and climbed into the front seat, feeling the cold and stiff leather under her butt. Starting the vehicle, she turned on the seat warmer as she shivered. 'The fall weather is here,' she thought. She opened the garage door and backed out of the driveway. Just as she was about to close the garage door, she noticed something odd — a white envelope taped on the left side of the garage door gained her attention. Brexley placed the SUV into the park position and quickly jumped out.

She approached the garage door, pulling the taped envelope off the door. Without reading it, she jumped back into the driver's seat of the SUV, feeling the heat blowing into her face. She looked down at the small, white envelope. On the front, it read: Brexley S. She carefully turned the envelope over to see if there was any other kind of writing. Since there was nothing else on the envelope, she decided to open it.

Brexley pulled the white piece of paper out of the envelope and looked at it, wondering what the dark-red smear was on the back of the paper. She hoped it was not blood and wondered…'Why did I automatically assume it was blood on the envelope?' The note read: *"You will not get away with it… Drop the Campton contract, or die!"* Stupefied, Brexley dropped the paper. It fell into her lap, the wording face-up. She looked down, contemplating if it was a joke. She instructed the car's Bluetooth to dial her ex-boyfriend, saying, "Call Carlton."

"This is Carlton," he answered the phone on the first ring, sounding chipper.

"Umm, Carlton, it is Brexley. Do you have a minute for me?" she asked, hoping he was not busy.

"Of course, I know it is you. How are you, Brexley? What can I do for you?" he replied courteously. He had not heard from her in months and wondered why she called.

"I have a problem. I found an envelope taped to my garage door containing a threatening message. I am not sure if I should take it seriously. My first instinct was to throw it away. Then, I thought maybe I should take it to the police. I am on my way to the warehouse. Can you meet me there?"

"Oh my gosh. What does the note say? Are you okay, Luv? Of course, I will meet you at the warehouse. Let me get ahold of Janice and cancel my appointments for the day. I will meet you in twenty minutes."

"Thank you, Carlton. I could not think of who else to call. I will let you read the note when we meet. See you shortly," Brexley responded. She ended the call with Carlton and reversed her SUV, closing the garage door. She quickly punched the Activate Alarm key on her phone, turning on her house alarm. She backed out of the driveway, still anxious and eager to get to the warehouse.

On the other side of town, Maddie looked at the items on the list. Everything seemed in order. Nothing was missing. "Thank you. Where do I sign?" she asked the delivery person happily. Brexley would be relieved to see the missing staging items had finally arrived at the warehouse.

"Right here, Miss," he pointed to the line on the tablet, handing her a stylus. "I am sure sorry about the mix-up. I am glad we could get a truck to deliver the items to you. Please, tell Miss Sinclaire our company is sorry about the delayed delivery. Hopefully, it will not happen again." He took the tablet and stylus out of her hand and then headed to the truck.

Maddie instructed several warehouse employees to place the items onto the right side of the loading dock, out of the way. She wanted Brexley to inspect them when she arrived to ensure she was happy with the accessories and furnishings before the crew loaded them onto the trucks.

Brexley pulled up in front of the warehouse, still feeling edgy. She was glad Carlton was on his way. Though they were no longer a couple, they remained close friends. She missed him sometimes, especially on weekends, when she was curled up on the couch by herself watching television. Now that Jovanna was gone, it was even more lonely. Brexley sighed, feeling somber. Now, she wondered about the threat. She glanced at the loading dock, noticing the two trucks pulled up to the warehouse loading dock next to each other. The black trucks, with gold lettering, displayed the name of her company, *Sinclaire Premier Staging*, with the tagline, *"Turning your Vision into Reality is our PRIORITY!"*

The right side of the truck displayed Brexley's picture. She looked amazing, wearing a pale-pink suit with a white blouse. Her long blonde hair was loose, spilling over her shoulders, down the front of the blouse, with her arms crossed. Her wrists showed off her signature designer bracelets. She wore nude-colored, four-inch heels, emphasizing her long, toned legs. Brexley's head tilted to the side, making her appear mischievous and sexy.

Maddie approached Brexley's SUV. She wanted to inform her the missing items had successfully arrived at the warehouse.

"Well, I made it," said Brexley, getting out of the SUV, clutching the paper from earlier.

"I instructed the team to place the items on the loading dock. I also informed the crew not to load anything until you inspected them. I wanted to confirm you liked the colors and designs of the pieces. I am so happy they delivered them in time," added Maddie, looking at Brexley holding the note. "What are you holding?" she asked inquisitively, noticing she tried to hide something.

"It is nothing. Is Carlton here yet? He is supposed to meet me at the office."

"No, I have not seen him. Are you sure you are okay? You seem a bit off or preoccupied."

"I am fine. Show me the pieces so the crew can load them into the trucks," Brexley responded, not wishing to elaborate.

After carefully inspecting the items, Brexley finally approved them. She wanted the trucks ready to head out to the Campton estate within the hour. Brexley entered the building, heading toward her office to wait for Carlton, leaving Maddie in charge of the warehouse. In the office, she impatiently sat on the white, plush leather sofa, waiting for Carlton. She pushed aside one of the grey faux fur pillows and let out a huge sigh. She wondered what was taking Carlton so long. She wanted him to read the note, eager to hear his opinion and determine if he believed it to be a serious matter.

Suddenly, the door opened, and Carlton Chastain appeared. He stood in the doorway wearing a dark-gray suit, a pale, baby-blue shirt, and a dark-blue tie embellished with white and dark-gray lines. It was a tie Brexley gave him last Christmas and was one of his favorites. Carlton held his briefcase in his right hand. His thick, dark-brown hair looked flawless, as always. He grinned at Brexley, exposing his perfectly white teeth. His blue eyes sparkled. Carlton certainly was a hunk of a man. Brexley missed his tight, round butt and his six-pack abs. He knew he was handsome but not egotistical. Carlton was the real deal.

"Hello, gorgeous," he said as he entered the room. He approached Brexley, leaning down to kiss her on the cheek. Brexley sat rigidly on the couch, holding the note as if it were toxic. She held it between her thumb and pointer finger, motioning for him to take it from her.

"Carlton, thank you for coming," she replied, wishing he would hurry and grab the dreaded item.

"Is that it?" Carlton asked. He noticed how uncomfortable she looked, holding the memo.

"Yes."

Carlton dropped his briefcase on the floor near the sofa. He sat down next to Brexley and looked at her face. She appeared to be on the verge of crying.

"Here, let me see," Carlton said as he took the note from her fingers, reading the message. After he finished, he placed it on the coffee table in front of the sofa, his head tilted. "You don't think this is something to worry about, do you?" he asked, trying to sound upbeat. He noticed her flinch, which told him she was frightened.

"Of course I do! I would not have asked you to come if I thought it was a joke. I am about to head to the Campton estate in an hour. I am nervous. You know me. I usually do not get anxious, but this scares me," Brexley said. She rubbed her hands fretfully.

Carlton grabbed Brexley's right hand. He smiled, trying to act like everything was okay. Truth be told, Carlton was nervous as well. He wondered why someone would do this to Brexley. Yes, she was headstrong and competitive. However, she was not mean or conniving. She was ethical and intelligent, earning the respect of her competitors.

"Listen. I will stay with you today. I have nothing on my calendar. I will accompany you to the staging. You have nothing to worry about, I promise." He smiled with that boyish grin, which always melted her heart. He wanted her to relax. "Hey, I brought my gun with me," he pointed to his suitcase. "Nothing will happen to you." He winked at her.

"You brought a gun? Why?" she asked apprehensively. Brexley hated guns. "I know you are right, and everything will be fine. I feel frustrated. I am grateful you came so quickly to meet me. Do you want to place your briefcase and jacket here? You won't need them at the staging," she asked, pointing to a spot in the room.

"Fine, I will leave them here, but I am

bringing my weapon," Carlton responded, removing his suit jacket and tie. He draped the jacket over the back of the chair. Next, he placed the tie on the desk. Quickly, he removed the gun from the briefcase, sliding it into the holster. He covered the firearm and holster with his dress shirt, kicking the briefcase under the desk.

"Come on, let's head to the loading dock and see what is happening." He wanted to show Brexley that everything was on schedule and moving along smoothly. He did not want her stressed out, especially since he knew this was a high-profile contract for *Sinclaire Premier Staging*. Brexley had called Carlton the moment she found out she had won the staging contract for the Campton estate. She was thrilled and wanted him to be the first to know. To Carlton, she sounded like a kid about to go to an amusement park, her excitement evident.

The two walked out of Brexley's office, Carlton leading the way. She closed her office door and locked it. Once on the loading dock, they observed Maddie giving instructions on what items required loading. Maddie was efficient and forceful. She stood near one of the trucks, wearing black jeans and a white collared blouse. Maddie's jet-black hair was in a ponytail, and she wore black and silver flats. Her glasses rested on the tip of her nose, almost falling off. She looked down at the clipboard in her hand while she checked items off the list as they were loaded. As always, she was on top of her game. Many times, Brexley attempted to persuade Maddie to use an electronic tablet, which she provided her. However, Maddie insisted there was nothing as good or reliable as the old-fashioned paper and pen method.

Once the truck loading was complete and all items checked off on the inventory list, Brexley, Maddie, and Carlton jumped into Brexley's SUV and quickly drove toward the Campton estate in Boerne. Both trucks with the movers following. It was less than an hour's drive.

Maddie sat quietly in the back of the SUV. She looked at her phone, reading and responding to emails while snacking on a protein bar. Carlton chose to drive, allowing Brexley to answer emails on her phone. He knew her mind was not on driving.

Watching her made his heart skip a beat. He missed her, not able to see her much anymore. Looking at her now, sitting next to him, he smiled. She was stunning, and he could smell her perfume. It was an intoxicating smell that always made him want to ravage her body. Carlton still loved her dearly, missing intimacy with her, feeling her soft skin and voluptuous breast against his body. Thinking about it made him hot, and he desperately tried to think of other things.

Sometimes, Carlton wondered why they

were no longer together. On many occasions, Brexley called him and asked if he wanted to come to her house. She needed someone there with her to watch movies. She hated being alone in the house.

Carlton usually agreed, showing up with snacks and a bottle of Chardonnay from her favorite vineyard in Washington state. He loved sitting on the massive L-shaped sofa with her, cuddled up under a fluffy blanket, watching a movie with a burning fireplace for ambiance. She usually lit a plethora of candles, wanting the warm glow in the room.

Brexley looked beautiful in the romantic candlelight, which illuminated her body. He blinked, shook his head, and tried to stop thinking about her romantically as he drove silently.

Arriving at the Campton estate, Carlton pulled up to the gate. He stared at Brexley, waiting for the gate code. "Hey…I need the code. I assume you have it? Or should I ring the house?" he asked, waiting for a reply.

"No, there is no one here. Punch in *799631#," Brexley replied as she read the gate entry instructions from her phone.

"Got it," Carlton replied as he punched in the code on the keypad. The massive gate opened slowly. He drove the SUV through the opening and noticed a camera mounted high up on one of the tall trees by the entrance, probably taking pictures of all vehicles entering and exiting the extensive estate grounds. The two moving trucks followed. Once they were inside, past the gate, it closed.

Carlton drove around the large, concrete, circular driveway, stopping in front of the house. A tall, modern water fountain graced the circle's center, surrounded by green plants and yellow and orange roses. Water flowed out of the top of the big, round ball on the fountain's top, cascading down. At night, the fountain lit up in a cool light-blue color. The bottom of the fountain featured iridescent blue and white tiles. They sparkled like precious gems as the sunlight hit them during the hot Texas days.

Carlton jumped out of the SUV and walked to the passenger side to help Brexley out of the vehicle. She took his hand and jumped down, proceeding to step to the back of the SUV, pulling out a large crate filled with numerous small items.

"May I help you with that?" he offered, standing beside Brexley.

"Yes, thank you," Brexley handed the crate to Carlton as she reached inside the vehicle to retrieve a large tote from the backseat. She smiled at him, grateful he was there for protection.

Maddie emerged, holding the checklist and clipboard. She smiled sweetly at Carlton and Brexley.

"Wow, what a gorgeous house!" declared Carlton looking around. He was impressed, just realizing the massive size of the estate. *'Everything really is bigger in Texas,'* Carlton said to himself, feeling amused. He held onto the crate as they headed toward the front door.

"It is stunning," replied Brexley as she turned to walk toward the first truck. She approached the driver and gave instructions. Two other men jumped out of the truck with moving dollies and headed to the back, attaching a ramp, ready to begin unloading.

Brexley headed to the second truck and instructed the other driver and his team. When done, she proceeded to the front door and punched in the code to open the massive, wrought iron and glass front double doors. Once inside, she disarmed the alarm system with yet another code. She opened both front doors, allowing the movers to quickly bring the furnishing and accessories into the estate.

"I think we will set up in the kitchen. It has a great view of the rest of the house, and we can keep an eye on the movers. That would be the best. What do you think?" Maddie declared, looking at Brexley and Carlton.

"I agree. We should also open the large, sliding accordion glass doors leading to the backyard so the team can place the outdoor furnishings around the pool," added Brexley, admiring the glistening pool.

It looked inviting as the water poured into the pool from a tall, modern, and concrete waterfall. The outdoor patio area featured an enormous, covered outdoor kitchen. The outdoor bar was attached to the front side of the kitchen by a long, white quartz counter. Eight barstools stood lined up in front of the bar. There was a tall, stone outdoor fireplace to the bar's right. Part of the fireplace was under the covered part of the outdoor kitchen, featuring a 75"outdoor-mounted television. It was an entertainer's paradise.

Brexley noticed the guest house near the end of the pool. It was 1800 square feet, including three bedrooms and two full bathrooms. It featured an open floor plan design with a spacious furnished living room and kitchen area. Brexley did not plan to stage it. Instead, she would add a few accessories, such as artwork, toss pillows, and plants.

Brexley wondered why Mr. and Mrs. Campton wanted to sell this gorgeous estate. It seemed absolutely perfect! It featured a whopping 12 acres of privacy. A tall stone wall enclosed the first two acres, which she assumed cost a small fortune to build. Several observation towers were in the distance, and she presumed they were there to monitor for intruders. Brexley could not help but wonder why that was necessary. It seemed a bit extreme to her. In fact, the observation towers seemed odd. *'Maybe they are fake and just for show?'* She wondered. The main house was slightly over 11,000 square feet, featuring six bedrooms, six bathrooms, two studies, a media room with ten reclining seats to watch movies, a kitchen, a formal living room, a family room, a panic room, and a full two-lane bowling alley.

The maid's quarters were large and accommodated up to four personnel located on the south end of the building. The house was nothing less than spectacular. Behind the pool was a driving range for the golf enthusiast and a tennis court in the backyard.

Brexley waited for George, the head mover and supervisor, to bring in some chairs. She wanted to rest. Her feet were already killing her. She regretted wearing a new pair of shoes.

Carlton stood beside Brexley, watching her every move, looking extremely protective. Maddie observed Carlton. She liked him and could not understand why Brexley and Carlton broke up. It made no sense to her. They made a beautiful couple and a powerful team. Maddie assumed they would get married one day. She was shocked when Brexley told her they had broken up and no longer lived together. Maddie did not pry. Instead, she told Brexley she was sorry and hoped she was okay. Brexley acted stoic, although her red eyes gave away the fact that she cried a lot over the breakup.

That day, Maddie spent many hours catering

to Brexley, bringing her lunch and snacks, hoping to keep her mind off Carlton. In the evening, Brexley sat on the sofa in her office, hunched over, head in her hands, crying. Maddie heard her loud sobs from her office. She left and went home without speaking with Brexley, assuming she wanted to be left alone to wallow in her sorrows. It took Brexley months to get over her breakup with Carlton. It did not help that they still saw each other socially and through common friends and family. Thus, in time, they decided it was best to remain friends.

"Brexley, do you think we will be able to complete the staging by tonight?" asked Maddie, noticing the project's progress. They had been staging for hours, and everyone was getting tired.

"Without a doubt. The majority is complete. We would be staging for days if we had to fill the entire house with furnishings. Thankfully, the owners have left many items behind. I am going outside to ensure everything is correctly placed. I want to get this done so we can all head home. Please ensure the bedrooms look perfect. George informed me he had placed the linens and steamer on the table in the laundry room. I'll join you in a few minutes. We can put the rest of the accessories up. George and his team have already hung all the artwork. I have not seen the toss pillows, have you?" Brexley did not wait for an answer. She walked off quickly.

Brexley stepped out onto the patio, ensuring the perfect outdoor setting. Carlton followed her, continuing to keep an eye on her. He still felt uneasy about the note and threats against Brexley. She acted stoic, but he did not buy it.

After several more hours passed, Maddie, Carlton, and Brexley sat on the bar stools in the kitchen, admiring the living room. The house looked magnificent. It was dark outside, and the moving team was loading trucks with moving blankets, empty boxes, crates, and more. Everyone was exhausted, but the job was complete.

"Maddie, let's conduct a quick final walk-through of the property. Do you have the checklist? I hope we didn't miss anything," Brexley announced, jumping off the barstool.

Carlton yawned, rubbing his eyes. He looked tired. Brexley felt bad about keeping him out late but was grateful for his company. He looked tired. His loyalty meant the world to her. There weren't many people she could count on. He was one of the only ones she trusted.

"Sure, where do you want to start?" asked Maddie, ready to finish the final steps of the staging.

"Let's begin outside."

"Okay," Maddie replied as she followed Brexley outside. Carlton stood by the door, leaning against the door frame, watching them.

He was glad they were about ready to leave the estate. After more than an hour, the three made their way to the front of the entryway, prepared to return to the warehouse, feeling exhausted.

"Another successful staging job," announced Brexley smiling.

"Indeed, it looks fabulous. I love the end results. When do the photographers arrive?" asked Maddie. She admired the completed staging job.

"They will be here tomorrow at ten in the morning. The realtor, Ms. Kline, will meet them here. I offered to be here, just in case, but Mrs. Campton said it was unnecessary. So, once we leave here, we are done until the de-staging day." The three exited the home. Brexley stopped by the front door, securing the house. Finally, they climbed into the SUV to head back to the warehouse, Carlton driving. The two trucks and crew members followed closely behind.

"See, nothing to worry about," said Carlton, gently touching Brexley's hand. "I told you the note was a hoax." He smiled reassuringly.

"Shhhh, we will talk about it later. We don't know either way about the note," replied Brexley, turning around and seeing if Maddie was still awake. She didn't want her to know about the threatening message. It would upset her.

"Okay, Luv." He drove quietly, keeping his

thoughts to himself the rest of the way. Brexley reminisced about the staging job and wondered about the mysterious note. She twirled her hair nervously, hoping the letter was just a joke and that all would be okay. But her gut told her otherwise. Thankfully, the staging had gone off without a hitch.

Everything at the house looked spectacular, and nothing unusual or scary happened. Arriving at the warehouse, Brexley turned around and gently tapped Maddie on her legs. She had fallen asleep and was lightly snoring.

"Maddie, we are here. Wake up!"

"Ah, okay. Well, I am going to head home. You two have a good night and safe travels home," she said as she jumped out of the SUV, dashing to her vehicle.

Carlton and Brexley stayed behind, talking with the warehouse personnel. The trucks were now backed up against the warehouse for security purposes. The warehouse members left, leaving Brexley alone with Carlton.

They entered the building, heading to her office. "Here, take your suit jacket and tie. Don't forget your briefcase under the desk," Brexley added as she looked around her office. She felt something was wrong, though she wasn't sure what it was. Carlton noticed she took a visual inventory of the room and stood beside her, watching.

"What is it?" he inquired.

"Oh, it's probably nothing. It just feels like something is wrong. Do you see anything obvious missing or odd in the room?" Brexley asked, still looking around. She began to worry.

"No, not really. Your office is tidy as always. What are you looking for, babe?"

"Not sure. I feel like something is missing. Maybe I am just tired. Oh well. Shall we head out?" She shook her head, the pit of her stomach telling her something was wrong.

"Sure, let's get out of here. I am exhausted. I will follow you home to make sure you are okay." He touched her back, gently guiding her to the office door. Brexley turned off the lights. She proceeded down the corridor leading to the main entrance, Carlton following. Once outside, he walked her to the SUV.

Brexley smiled at Carlton as he opened the door for her. She was about to get into the SUV when she saw the piece of paper on the driver's seat. She spun around to look at Carlton.

He immediately tried to peek over Brexley's shoulder, craning his neck to look inside the SUV. He picked up the note, wanting to be the first one to read it. It said, *"You have been warned."* He noticed this note, as the first, was typed and not handwritten, which seemed odd. *'How did someone get into her SUV? Did she leave the vehicle unlocked?'* He wondered.

"Brexley, I think it is time to take the two notes to the police. I am not sure this is a joke anymore," he said, alarmed. He could see she was getting scared, as she chewed on her lip.

"I think you are right. Let's do that in the morning. I want to get home and shower. I am exhausted. It has been a very long day," Brexley replied. She was not in the mood for more drama.

"Fine, but I am staying with you tonight. No Arguments. I will sleep on the couch and keep an eye on you. I don't like the idea of you alone at home. I am serious. This is not negotiable," Carlton helped her into the SUV. "I will be right behind you. Head Straight home, please!" She nodded.

Brexley drove home, speculating why someone would be leaving her threatening notes. She decided to try and forget about the threats until the next day. For now, she wanted to get home, shower, and crawl into bed. She was tired and frightened. Knowing Carlton would be in the house with her was a huge relief.

It would allow her to sleep without worry. They arrived at Brexley's home in less than ten minutes. The outside and inside lights were on since they were on timers. Brexley did not like coming home to a dark house.

Carlton parked outside and walked into the garage, following Brexley. She closed the garage door. They entered the mudroom, locking the door to the garage, grateful they made it home safe.

Carlton took her purse from her hand and dropped it onto the tile flooring. He gently took her into his arms and held her tightly, realizing she was shaking. Brexley started to cry as Carlton held her.

Oddly, he found himself becoming aroused. She smelled wonderful. However, he knew Brexley was vulnerable and did not want to take advantage of her. Yet, she looked sexy. Her long blonde hair cascaded down her back. Her pouty lips looked kissable. Carlton wanted her badly. He felt her warm breath on his neck.

Brexley noticed Carlton was breathing hard as he whispered into her ear. "Babe, let's go to bed." Without hesitation, she led him to the bedroom. He smirked as he followed her.

CHAPTER 2

Brexley woke up as the sun beamed through the blinds. She rolled onto her side, feeling comfortable and happy, looking at Carlton. He looked peaceful, curled up under the fluffy comforter. His thick hair looked curly and unruly, which made her heart melt. Brexley loved the way he looked in the mornings. She reached over and ran her hand through his hair. Carlton looked up, grinning.

"Good morning, beautiful," he said as he took her hand and placed it under the blanket on his body.

"Well, someone is up and happy," she teased, gently rubbing him.

"Stop that, or we will spend all day in bed."

Brexley removed her hand quickly, and lightning-fast jumped out of bed. She awkwardly wrapped the top bed sheet around her waist.

Confused, Carlton sat up in bed. "Did I say something wrong, babe?"

"No. I have a lot to do and must get ready. I cannot stay in bed all day. I am off to shower." She swiftly left the bedroom, closing the bathroom door, perplexing Carlton. She turned on the shower water and stood in front of the mirror inside the bathroom. She allowed the sheet to drop onto the floor, looking at herself in the mirror. *'Not bad,'* she thought, with a smirk on her face. Feeling cold and shivering, she entered the steamy shower stall, wondering if Carlton got the hint. She wanted him to leave.

Last night was a huge mistake. She let her feelings get in the way and allowed herself to give in to the temptation. Their lovemaking was incredible, but it was a distraction. She would not let herself to fall back into the same old situation and routine. They would start dating and go right back to the way things were. Sure, things would be great for a while, but in time, it would all end up as a big pile of shit. Most likely, they would fight and argue about stupid stuff. In the end, she would tell him to get the hell out, and things would get awkward between them. She liked their current situation and relationship. She was not ready to return to any romantic relationship or commitment. Carlton would remain in the friend-with-benefits zone.

Carlton heard the water flowing in the bathroom. He wanted to jump in the shower with Brexley but contemplated why she acted so strangely. Last night was incredible. He felt like things between them finally clicked again. Carlton yearned to touch Brexley and make love to her again. Somehow, he felt as if she regretted last night. The way she ran to the bathroom and slammed the door shut quickly, was nothing less than strange. It made him livid. He felt used. It almost felt like before when he was at her beck and call. Always ready to be there when she needed him. He wanted more and told her so on many occasions.

After a while, Brexley grew frustrated. She ended the relationship without offering him any kind of explanation. Brexley made it clear in the past that she didn't want the responsibility of a romantic entanglement. When she broke off their relationship, it almost killed him.

Carlton bought a diamond ring and hid it in

his jacket pocket when she met him for a well-thought-out dinner. He planned to propose marriage. He recalled the night clearly. Carlton sat across from Brexley, enjoying a glass of wine at their favorite steak house in San Antonio while soft, romantic music played in the background.

She looked stunning in the dimly lit room. Brexley wore a hot pink maxi dress tied at the waist with a thick, black, braided satin belt. Her hair cascaded down her back in long, spirally curls. She wore magenta-colored lipstick, accentuating her luscious, full lips.

He remembered thinking about how much he loved her and how badly he wanted to make love to her. He reached across the table and gently took her hand into his. Just as he was about to get out of his chair and propose, she dropped the bombshell.

"Carlton, I love you. I hope you know this," she said, looking away.

"Of course, I feel the same, Luv," he responded, smiling at her.

"I feel we are headed in different directions right now. I suppose what I am trying to say is...I want to break up," Brexley abruptly announced. She looked down at her lap, embarrassed. Her face looked flushed.

"What? Did you just say you wanted to break up? Seriously? Right before Christmas!? WOW, Brexley!" Carlton yelled in frustration. He could not believe Brexley wanted to end their relationship. His hands began shaking, and he felt nauseous. It was not the reaction he had hoped for.

"Darling...I love you. I am just not ready for a huge commitment. It is unfair to you, and it is better to set you free to find your lady love. I want you to be happy. I really do," she continued. "Please don't be mad. I think this is best for us."

"Bullshit! It is best for you. I love you, Brexley. I am ready to live the rest of my life with you." Infuriated, he pulled the teal-blue ring box out of his jacket and slammed it on the table.

"What is that?" she asked apprehensively. She felt her hands quiver and suddenly felt the urge to puke. *'Is Carlton going to ask me to marry him?'*

"What do you think it is? Dammit, Brexley, what the hell?" he stared at her.

Brexley reached across the table and took the box. She gently opened it and stared down at the glistening rock. It was large. She estimated at least 2.5 to 3 carats of a flawless diamond. She felt tears start to run down her face. The maître d' brought another bottle of wine and began filling their glasses.

"No, we just need the check," Carlton said as he continued to glare at Brexley.

"Of course, Sir," he placed the bottle of wine

on the table and expeditiously strode off to retrieve the check.

"Carlton, I am so sorry. I had no idea," Brexley said, embarrassed. She closed the box and pushed it toward him, feeling like crap. Carlton grabbed the box and shoved it into his coat pocket. By now, other diners in the restaurant directly stared at the couple, shaking their heads.

"Well, I guess I totally misconstrued the last few years of our life together, huh?" he said, hurt and confused. He was also embarrassed. Carlton was utterly shocked. He could not believe what she said to him.

"No, not really. I think I want this, but I am just not ready. I feel it is better to let you go. I don't want you to feel like I lead you on, giving you hope. I am not sure when and if I will ever be ready to commit to marriage. I am so sorry if that hurts you. It is not my intention to upset you ever. Please, don't hate me," Brexley tried desperately to control the tears. She did not want to cry in the middle of the restaurant, as others were already watching them. She did not know what else to say to him.

"Whatever," Carlton responded. The maître d' handed Carlton the check. Immediately, Carlton gave him a credit card. "Please hurry. We need to leave."

"Of course. I will be right back."

"Carlton, let's talk about this. Can we go

home and talk, please? I feel awful," Brexley pleaded, tears dripping down her face.

"What is there left to talk about? You made your feelings quite clear. You want to break up. Now, looking at the ring, you realize I want marriage. So, what changed? Nothing. You still do not want me. Why do you give a shit about how I feel? Let's get out of here and head home."

Brexley lowered her head and remained silent. She knew he was deeply hurt, and nothing she could say would make him feel better. She screwed things up big time!

Carlton placed the receipt in his pocket and rose out of the chair to help Brexley. He was a gentleman, no matter what. He stayed behind her as they exited the restaurant. Carlton had no idea what to say or do. He walked with his head down, utterly perplexed and hurt. On the way home, neither said anything in the car while Christmas songs played on the radio.

Brexley sobbed quietly, wishing she could fix everything. Hearing her favorite Christmas song made her feel worse. Christmas had always been her favorite time of year. The holiday season was ruined, and she felt utterly responsible. She knew he would never forgive her. Her heart ached.

Now, as Carlton listened to the water running in the bathroom, he continued to reminisce about that dreadful night. He recalled the feeling of emptiness. Staring at the bathroom door, he wondered what she was thinking. Nausea hit him. Was she ending things with him before they even started again? He loved her deeply. Carlton approached the chair by the window, picked up his clothes, and proceeded to get dressed.

Although he wanted to shower, it would be better to do that at home. Carlton heard Brexley blow-drying her hair. Instantly, the only thing he wanted to do was to leave. His gut feeling told him Brexley wanted him gone. He had to go, not ready to deal with another abrupt dismissal by Brexley.

Brexley sat on the stool in the bathroom, brushing her hair. She wondered if Carlton had left. She had no idea what she would say to him if he were still there when she finished. It was an awkward moment.

After a few minutes, she stood up and snuck to the bathroom door. Slowly, Brexley opened the door and walked out. She looked around, but Carlton was not there. Relieved, she strutted to her closet and picked out clothes to wear, still speculating if he was in the house.

Carlton sipped a cup of coffee in the kitchen, waiting for Brexley to appear. He wanted the opportunity to speak with her before leaving. To him, it felt best to confront her and outright ask about their relationship status.

If she wanted to remain *'friends,'* he would

not push her as before. It made no sense to him to continue fixing their relationship. He loved her, but it was getting tiresome chasing after her. In a way, it was as if she was a beautiful ghost, unattainable and unreal.

When she entered the kitchen, Carlton sat on a stool, reading emails on his phone. He could smell her before he saw her. That familiar smell always made his heart race.

She took a mug from the glossy, white kitchen cabinet and poured a cup of coffee. "Thanks for making coffee," she said, placing the coffee mug on the quartz counter and walking toward the refrigerator. She pulled out the creamer and poured some into her cup. Brexley looked at Carlton as he sat on the stool, ignoring her.

"Are you okay?" she asked hesitantly, hoping he was not mad.

"Sure, why wouldn't I be?" Carlton responded.

"Okay." That is all she managed to say as she pulled a Cream Cheese Danish from the bread box. "Do you want a Danish for breakfast?" she offered.

"No, I am about to leave. I just wanted to drink a cup of coffee and talk to you before I left."

"Oh? What did you want to talk about?" she asked, damn well knowing exactly what he wanted to discuss.

"Well, for starters, what happened this morning?" he placed his phone on the counter and glared at her, crossing his arms.

"I am not sure I know what you mean?" she responded, trying to deflect.

"Really? That's how we are going to play this?"

"Seriously, Carlton, what do you mean?" Brexley asked, her eyes wide.

"You ran to the bathroom when I tried to entice you into another round of sex. What...you no longer want me? You sure seemed to like it all night long!" he sarcastically responded. Carlton shook his head. He knew she was trying to push him away again.

"Oh, that...I see."

"Yes, that," Carlton replied snarkily. He was blown away by her attitude, wondering why she chose to act so nonchalantly.

"I needed to shower and get ready for the day. What's the problem, Carlton? Last night was amazing. I greatly enjoy our lovemaking. You know my body all too well, and our time together is always spectacular. What do you want me to say?" Brexley watched his facial expressions and knew he was getting very pissed. His right eye twitched, and he ran his right hand through his thick hair, staring at her.

"If you want to play games, I am not in the mood. I thought we were getting back together. Things have been so good between us. Better than ever before. Now, you are acting like I have the plague. What gives?" Carlton rolled his eyes.

"I believe I have too much on my mind. Please do not take it personally. The threats have me agitated. You know how much I adore you. I am not ready to move ahead in our relationship. Why can't we keep it the way it has been? It has been great, no?" she asked, hoping he would agree. Though she doubted he would go for that. He wanted to get married and spend the rest of their lives together. She was unable to commit.

"Oh, Brexley, you really are blind," he made his way to her. Carlton gently kissed her on the cheek and then placed his empty coffee mug into the deep kitchen sink. "I will call my friend, Detective Johnson, at the police department and get his feedback about the notes. I will let you know what he says."

Carlton slammed the door on his way out of the house, hoping to make a point. Brexley stood in the kitchen, shaking her head. *'Why does he always want more?'* She wondered. *'Why can't we leave things the way they are? Dammit!'* She placed her cup in the sink and walked to the garage to head out. She opened the garage door and started her SUV. Her heart felt heavy, and she wanted to call him but knew it was best to leave it alone for now.

Carlton drove off in a hurry. He sped down

the road, infuriated. Why did he allow her to do this to him over and over again? What was wrong with him? He had to let her go once and for all. She was like a disease with no cure. He could not stay with her. Their relationship was doomed to die. He realized she was not ready for a commitment, and sadly, he wasted four years of his life chasing after someone who did not want to be pursued. It was time to call it quits. There was no way he would continue to throw himself at Brexley. It was embarrassing and beneath him.

Carlton thought about the job offer in Seattle and wondered if he should look into it. It would allow him to get away from Brexley. Maybe he needed a fresh start away from her. It hurt him to think about it, but it was time. Minutes later, he pulled into the driveway of his house, picked up his cell phone, and called Sam.

"Hey, Carlton, how are you? Still thinking about my offer?" Sam teased.

"Actually, that is why I am calling. I will accept the position if it is still available. How soon can I start?"

"Wow, are you serious? The position is yours anytime. You know that. How about January 2nd? That gives me time to prepare things here and allow you a few weeks to get your things in order in San Antonio?"

"Great. Listen, let me call you later this week. I will start making arrangements for my move. Thanks, Sam. I appreciate it."

"I am grateful to have you on board. How does Brexley feel about you leaving? I thought you two were finally getting married."

"No, Brexley and I are done. I need to get away from here and start fresh. Let me fly into Seattle next week, and we can chat in person. I have to start house hunting while I am there."

"Sounds great, Carlton. Let me know when you arrive in Seattle. Hey, I am very sorry to hear about you and Brexley. Talk to you soon. Have a great day, friend." Sam hung up the phone.

Carlton looked out the car window. He felt awful—such finality. He stepped out of the vehicle and walked inside his house, deciding to call his friend Becker to discuss listing the home for sale.

Brexley arrived at the warehouse, feeling upset about her conversation with Carlton. She still needed to call and ask him to join her for lunch, allowing them time to talk. She had no idea how to proceed.

Maddie approached and began babbling about the fabulous feedback on the Campton estate staging and how much everyone loved it. The photographer stated it was *'magazine-worthy' staging*.

Brexley heard Maddie speaking but was not paying attention. Her mind was on Carlton and their brief argument this morning.

"Maddie, I am going to my office. I must make some calls. Please handle things," Brexley turned around, opened the office door, and slammed it closed. Maddie stared at the door, confused, wondering what was happening with Brexley. Maddie shook her head, sitting at the desk, deciding to call Mrs. Campton for feedback regarding the staging. She knew it was imperative to determine if she was happy with the results.

Brexley plopped down on a chair and stared at the computer screen. *'Should I call Carlton? Why is he so darn mad? Why does he always blow everything out of proportion?'* She felt as if she should call him to explain her feelings. But then again, maybe that would start another fight. Perhaps it was best to let it go? Her gut told her she needed to try and fix the situation ASAP!

Brexley could not concentrate on work. She pulled up her work calendar and schedule on her computer to see what she had to get done today. Maddie could handle everything on the calendar. Good, she could leave and surprise Carlton at work. Maybe she could fix things before they got out of hand.

Carlton showered and changed into jeans and a dress shirt. He rolled up his sleeves, picking up his cell phone. He sat on the couch in his living room, dialing Becker's number.

"Becker Wright, Wright Elite Realty Services of San Antonio, how may I help you?"

"Hey, Becker, it's Carlton. Do you have a few minutes to spare?"

"Hello, Carlton. How are you? Of course I do. What can I do for you, friend?" Becker responded.

"I need to list my house for sale. I am moving to Seattle. I want to do it right away. When can you come by to check out the house?" Carlton asked, looking around his home. It was immaculate. Brexley decorated it years before. There was no need to hire a different stager.

"I have some time now. I can come by in about an hour if you are around. Are you still at the same address? I can run comps and bring them with me if you like?" Becker offered.

"Yes, same location. You might as well bring a contract as well. I am ready to list the house today."

"Okay, then! I will see you soon." Becker hung up the phone.

Carlton dropped the phone on a pillow and stood up. He walked to the fireplace and looked around the house. Initially, he bought the spacious home, hoping someday Brexley would move in with him. Carlton wished to raise their children in this house and celebrate holidays with family here.

Now, he knew none of that would happen. Reluctantly, Carlton decided to look up movers on the internet using his phone. He would have them come immediately to pack up his personal things, putting them in storage until he found a house in Seattle. He would leave the house staged with furnishings and accessories for now. Feeling grim, Carlton collapsed on the couch and closed his eyes. This day was one of the worst of his life. He could only pray it would get better in the future. Leaving San Antonio and living far away from Brexley would be difficult, and he felt ill-prepared.

Brexley grasped her purse and left her office, heading to speak with Maddie. When she approached, she found her reading something at her desk.

"Hey, I am leaving for the day. I have an emergency I have to deal with quickly. Can you please handle everything on the calendar today? I will be back tomorrow. You can reach me by cell phone if need be."

Maddie stood up quickly. "Are you okay? What's the emergency? Can I help?" she offered.

"No. I am okay—nothing for you to worry about, I promise. Please handle things here. That is how you can help me. I have to run. I'll call you later." Brexley walked out of the warehouse, heading to her SUV. She hurried to find Carlton, hoping to salvage their relationship.

Brexley dialed Devvyn, thinking it was time to ask her best friend for her feedback on Carlton. Devvyn was her good friend and confidant. They had known each other for too long to let things interfere with their friendship.

Devvyn, a plus-sized, gorgeous redhead, ran a very successful Medi-Spa. She was a dermatologist, single, and a free-spirit, something Brexley adored about her. Devvyn was also driven, passionate, and happy with all aspects of her life. She radiated pure happiness and success. Brexley always felt better after meeting or speaking with her. Devvyn had a way of relaxing her, making her feel that anything bad would turn out fine.

After speaking with Devvyn for an hour, sitting in her car, she felt confident with her decision to talk with Carlton.

Devvyn knew Carlton and suggested smoothing things over before the situation got further out of hand. Brexley agreed. She became more anxious about speaking with him as she drove toward town, unaware of Carlton's new plan for his life.

"So, where do I sign?" Carlton asked, looking at the contract. Becker showed him where to sign. After twenty minutes, Becker shook Carlton's hand and left the house, placing the For-Sale sign in the front yard.

It was official. The house would be in the MLS—multiple listing service, by the end of the day. Now, with the movers and packers scheduled and the home officially on the market, Carlton's entire life drastically changed.

He wished to call Brexley but figured it was best to wait, planning to phone her just before departing for Seattle next week. He knew the right time would never happen.

Brexley called Carlton's assistant, Janice, to determine if Carlton was in the office. She informed Brexley that he took the day off for personal reasons, which he chose not to disclose. Janice assumed he was at home. Brexley thought this was odd and very unlike him. Carlton hardly ever took days off. She drove her SUV toward the other side of San Antonio to meet Carlton at his home, planning to surprise him.

Carlton looked through boxes in the garage. He could toss out a lot of things. Maybe he should make a donation pile, too. There was no need to store some of the items. It made no sense. He thought about hiring someone to help him separate things. Or, maybe he could call his sister Cherina. Though she lived in North Carolina, she would come to Texas to help him if he asked her. But then he would have to explain his sudden departure. That would piss her off — wanting retaliation against Brexley. Carlton decided he would hire someone who was not family to help him. He preferred to keep things uncomplicated.

Brexley pulled up to the gate and punched in the entry code. The large metal gate to the neighborhood opened, and she drove toward

Carlton's home. Minutes later, she pulled into the driveway, immediately noticing the small, black and white For-Sale sign with Becker's face on it. Instantly, nausea hit Brexley. She placed her left hand over her mouth. 'When did he list his house? Why did he not tell me about this?' She wondered, somehow managing to get out of the SUV, her legs feeling weak. Brexley made it to the front door and rang the bell. It took less than a minute, and Carlton opened the door, appearing confused about her presence at his house. She swallowed hard and looked him in the eyes.

"What are you doing here?" he asked, holding onto the right side of the double doors.

"Why is your house for sale?" she quickly replied, getting to the point.

"What?"

"I said,…why is your house for sale? You never told me you planned to sell it?" Brexley yelled, mad he would list his house for sale without speaking with her about it. It seemed cold and underhanded.

"I made the decision today. This morning, after I left your house. Why are you here, Brexley?" He stared at her, wondering why she would bother to show up at his home. He could tell she was taken aback by his decision to list the house. Frankly, he did not care what she thought. He was too hurt.

"May I please come inside? I would prefer

we talk in the house. I do not want to chat out here." She waited for him to invite her into the home. Carlton stared at her for a minute and then moved aside, allowing her to enter the house. He led her to the living room. Brexley sat on one of the two couches and waited for him to join her. He sat next to her, keeping his distance.

"So, why are you here, Brexley? I have a lot to do. I do not have time for drama today."

"You did not answer me. Why are you selling your house, Carlton?" she asked nervously.

"It is time," Carlton responded, sitting next to her, his hands folded in his lap. He was looking down, his eyes puffy. His eyes were also red and bloodshot.

"I did not feel good about how we left things this morning. I wanted to speak with you about it," explained Brexley.

"There is nothing to discuss. I got your message loud and clear. I am done chasing you. I have accepted a job in Seattle with a good friend. I am moving. That is why I put the house on the market today so quickly. The movers will come Friday to pick up my personal belongings. I plan to leave the home staged to sell. I am flying to Seattle the following Monday to start my house hunting. I believe there is nothing else to say, Brexley." There, he had said it. Though, it did not feel so good to him now that he had heard the words. In a way, he felt awful. But then, he remembered why he was doing this and instantly felt better about his choice.

Carlton stared at her, feeling empty. Brexley began to cry. She didn't want to, but the thought of him moving halfway across the country devastated her. "What can I do to convince you to stay?" she begged. The idea of Carlton moving away made her want to puke.

"Nothing. It is done." He got up and stood in front of her. "Here, let me walk you to the door," Carlton offered as he took her hand to help her stand. She slapped his hand away, rising quickly to her feet, almost running to the door. Brexley turned around briefly to look at him. Emotionless, he stood glaring at her with his hands in his jeans pockets. Brexley knew he was hurt and done with her. He had never responded like this before, acting out of haste. She realized he meant business.

"I am sorry, Carlton. I love you. You mean the world to me. I wish you nothing but the best," she ran out the door before he could reply. Brexley drove off quickly, tears pouring down her face, making navigating difficult.

Carlton closed the door and returned to the living room, feeling crappy. He hoped to break the news of his move to Brexley in a better way, preferring to talk with her over dinner. That did not happen. Her unexpected visit ruined his plans.

A short time later, Brexley entered her home, still crying. She felt like someone had just ripped her heart out of her chest. She could barely breathe. How could she live without Carlton? He was her rock and confidant. Brexley could not imagine a world without him. She ran to the bathroom, barely making it to the toilet, throwing up.

Feeling weak, she dropped down to the ground and curled up in front of the toilet, crying. She pounded her fists on the cold tile floor beneath her. Brexley cried and shivered, all alone in the bathroom.

Back at the warehouse, Maddie looked at the note. She wondered if she should open it. Who dropped it off? It said, *Brexley S.* on the front with no return address or other identifiable information. *'Would Brexley want me to open it? Should I call her and ask?'* Maddie decided to open it. She would call Brexley if it were important. She pulled the piece of paper out of the envelope and stared at the message. *"You have been warned more than once. Now, you die!"* the note read.

Panicked, Maddie dropped the paper, watching it as it floated down, landing on the desk. Her heart and mind raced. She knew she had to call Brexley!

Brexley managed to pull herself up off the floor and sit on the toilet. She felt awful. Her head hurt. Maybe she should take a hot shower? She undressed and placed her cell phone on the bathroom counter, the ringer on silent. Brexley turned on the hot water and waited for the water to warm, then she stepped inside, sitting on the bench in the shower, letting the hot water pour over her aching body, still crying. She leaned up against the back wall of the enclosure, exhausted.

Maddie dialed Brexley's cell phone. It rolled over to voice mail three times. Panicking, she decided to call Carlton. Maybe he knew where she was hiding. Carlton answered on the second ring.

"This is Carlton. How may I help you?"

"Carlton, it is Maddie. Have you seen Brexley? I must speak with her right away. Something awful has happened," Maddie relayed in an excited voice. She was terrified.

"No, she left my house over an hour ago. I assumed she would either go home or to the office. What has happened?" he asked, getting worried.

"I found a note. It is a threatening message. I am scared."

"Maddie, what does it say?" Carlton asked, assuming it was a note similar to the previous two. Instantly, his mind raced.

"It said, *'You have been warned more than once. Now, you die!'*" Maddie read out loud.

"Oh my gosh, not another one!" Carlton

responded, now fearing for Brexley's welfare. Instantly, he wondered how he could move and leave her alone. She was vulnerable. Abandoning her now made him feel awful.

"Umm, what do you mean by 'not another one?' What are you talking about? Brexley never mentioned other notes," interrogated Maddie, sounding furious.

"This is the third note. There were two others. Brexley did not want to worry you. She figured it was nothing. We should have gone to the police earlier. This is no longer an idle threat," explained Carlton, tying his shoes and looking for his car keys. "I am heading to her house. I will call you once I arrive." He hung up the phone and ran outside, quickly jumping into the car, feeling anxious.

Brexley showered and dressed in her pajamas. She planned to spend the rest of the day watching television and relaxing. Suddenly, she smelled something. *'Is that smoke?'* Before she could react, the fire alarms blared in her house.

Panicked, Brexley ran down the hallway. She could see flames at the other end of the house. She searched for her phone and realized she'd left it on the bathroom counter. Speedily, she ran back to her room, desperately looking for a pair of shoes to put on her feet.

She could hear the fire. It was growing quickly. She dashed down the hallway, running toward the front door. The door would not open. *'Why is it stuck?'* She panicked, trying desperately to open it. Realizing it would not open, she refused to waste precious time. Scared, she sprinted toward the back door, hoping to get out. The kitchen was on fire.

Terrified, she realized the only way out was through the garage, forcing her to run through the burning kitchen to get out. Bravely, Brexley closed her eyes, prayed, and ran toward the garage, dodging the hot flames, feeling the heat on her face and body, wincing in pain.

Carlton approached Brexley's house and saw the tall flames shooting out of her home. He could hear sirens off in the distance. His mind raced — *'Oh my God! Brexley's house is on fire!! Lord, please, let her be okay!'* Carlton pulled up to the house and saw the garage door opening. Brexley ran from the house, her face red. She spotted Carlton running toward her.

Brexley collapsed, falling into his arms. He pulled her away from the burning home. Carlton helped her sit in the car. The fire trucks arrived, and firefighters rushed to extinguish the fire, which now engulfed the majority of the house.

Brexley sat in the front seat, coughing, trying to catch her breath. Carlton saw the ambulance pull up next to them. He ran to the EMTs and informed them that Brexley struggled to breathe. Immediately, they placed her on a gurney, providing her with oxygen.

They rushed Brexley to the Trauma Center downtown, Carlton sitting beside her in the ambulance, holding her hand. Brexley closed her eyes, praying her house was not a total loss.

CHAPTER 3

The sky was dark and grey. It was gloomy, and rain was imminent. It made the day worse, in Carlton's opinion. He preferred the sunshine and heat. Texas usually graced him with it, but today was not a warm or beautiful day.

Carlton watched Brexley as she dozed in the hospital bed. She received pain medication for the burns on her left hand.

An oxygen cannula and tubing were attached to her nose, providing oxygen and aiding her breathing. Brexley looked tired, her face red and her hair messy.

Carlton gently touched her right hand, avoiding the burned one. A doctor entered the room with two interns. He looked at Carlton and motioned for him to step outside the room so they could talk.

"So, she received superficial partial-thickness second-degree burns, as previously discussed. I do not think she will require plastic surgery to correct this. I believe it will heal nicely on its own. It will involve daily bandage changing because of the few blisters on the hand. I suggest she follow up with me at my office in three to four weeks. I can reevaluate the burns, then. I will provide you with a checklist of things you must do to keep the wounds clean and dry. Do you have any questions for me?" asked the plastic surgeon, Dr. Hargrave.

"No, I believe that I understand. Thank you for coming in to see Brexley. We will make an appointment with your office tomorrow and see you in a few weeks," Carlton shook his hand, turned around, and opened Brexley's hospital room door.

She was awake, sipping water, when Carlton entered the room. "I see you are finally up. How do you feel, beautiful?" he asked, concerned.

"I feel like I swallowed a steel-wool cleaning pad. My throat is scratchy and burns."

"The emergency room doctor said it is normal. You were very close to the flames. Lucky for you, your throat did not get burned, just irritated from the heat and smoke. I am sorry about your hand. Dr. Hargrave, the plastic surgeon, and I just spoke. He reassured me it would heal fine on its own. We are supposed to see him in three to four weeks for a follow-up visit," explained Carlton. He felt grateful. Things could have ended up much worse for her.

"Okay, that is good to know. Thank you. I am so tired. When can I go home? I hate hospitals. " Brexley's voice sounded raspy and irritated to Carlton.

"Ummm, I wanted to speak with you about that. I talked with the police and fire department. I am so sorry, Brexley. Your home is a total loss. The Fire Marshal assumes it was arson. A preliminary investigation has the Fire Marshal believing an accelerant was used to start the fire since it spread quickly and throughout. There will be a thorough investigation to find out for sure. It could take some time. I think you should come home with me for now. We will figure out what to do about your living situation later."

Carlton sat on an uncomfortable chair by her bed, looking at her. He squirmed in his seat. She was crying, looking sad, making him feel awful. Regardless of what had occurred between them in the last few days, Carlton loved Brexley and felt compelled to protect her.

"Okay. When can I go home? You never answered me," she asked again.

"You may leave tomorrow. The hospital staff wants to monitor your oxygen levels throughout the night to ensure all is okay. I will head home and get things ready for you. What can I get you? I will shop for some clothes. Provide me a list of items you need, please."

Brexley gave Carlton a long list of items, including clothing, a new cell phone, and more. Carlton smiled reassuringly and told her he would handle it. He kissed her gently on the forehead and exited the room.

A few hours later, as Brexley slept in the hospital, Carlton arrived home with bags of items for her. He placed them in the guest room, assuming she would not want to sleep in the same room with him. Carlton hung the new clothes in the closet, taking a few items to the laundry room to wash. He wanted to clean them before bringing them to the hospital with him. Now that his house was for sale and he was leaving, how would Brexley handle the situation independently? Could he leave her alone right now? Probably not. He placed the clothes into the washer and headed to his office to read some emails.

Back at the hospital, Maddie and Devvyn walked into the room armed with two bouquets of flowers. Both were shocked to receive Carlton's phone call informing them of the tragic loss of Brexley's home and her hospitalization. As they entered the small private room, Brexley was still asleep. Devvyn approached the bed and sat down next to her, waiting for Brexley to wake up. After a few minutes, she gently touched her hand, causing Brexley to open her eyes.

"Devvyn, when did you get here?" Brexley asked with a hoarse-sounding voice. Her throat was still sore. She was happy to see her friend's face.

"A little while ago," replied Devvyn, with a worried look on her face.

"How are you feeling?" Maddie asked, concerned.

"I am okay. My throat feels raw, my hand aches, and my face feels hot. Do not worry. I will be okay."

"Where is Carlton?" asked Maddie, curious why he was not there with her. It upset Maddie to see Brexley all alone.

"I gave him a list of things I needed. Everything is gone, you guys! My house is a total loss. I cannot believe it. Why would someone do that to me?" Brexley began sobbing, feeling helpless. It was finally sinking in. Her life had changed drastically, for the worse. She felt lost and disheartened.

"I know. It is awful. I sure hope the police find out who did this. What can we do for you, Brexley?" asked Devvyn, gently squeezing Brexley's good hand. She felt sick to her stomach watching Brexley look so vulnerable. Devvyn stood up and brushed Brexley's hair from her face, wiping her friend's tears with a tissue from her purse. It was an awful moment.

"Nothing. I plan to stay with Carlton for now. Before the fire, he listed his house for sale and planned to move to Seattle. He is mad at me and wants to start over someplace far away. I feel terrible. I cannot believe he is leaving." Brexley cried, making her throat hurt worse.

"Yes, I know. Carlton told me about it. Brexley, you should have known. He was not going to wait for you forever. I am your friend, so I will be honest with you. It would help if you opened your eyes. He is a good man. Don't let him get away. You will regret it, trust me." Maddie said, staring at Brexley. Devvyn agreed with Maddie, observing Brexley and nodding her head.

Devvyn loathed the idea of Carlton leaving town. She knew it would destroy Brexley. The two were close and loved each other dearly. However, both were very stubborn at times. It was their stubbornness that seemed to cause a rift in their relationship. Devvyn knew neither would survive without the other. Destiny continued to draw them together.

The three friends conversed for a while longer, and when Maddie noticed Brexley was falling asleep, she nudged Devvyn, implying it was time to leave. They quietly exited the room, leaving Brexley to rest.

Carlton finished making the bed for Brexley. He pulled back the top sheet and placed the flowers on the nightstand. Brexley loved yellow roses with lots of baby's breath. He wanted everything to be perfect for her. Carlton stocked the bathroom with fresh towels, washcloths, and makeup on the counter. She now had everything she requested.

Lastly, he packed the big, black bag with clean clothes and other items. He slipped the new cell phone into his jacket pocket. As he walked out the garage door, he wondered if Brexley was happy to be coming home with him. He realized she could have stayed with Devvyn but agreed to stay with him. That was a great start. Maybe they would have the opportunity to discuss their relationship and figure out some things.

Brexley woke up in the hospital bed, feeling uncomfortable and tired. The doctor gave her a long list of instructions she needed to follow after her hospital release. She listened carefully, wondering where Carlton was and why he had not yet returned to the hospital. He called the previous night and informed her he would return in the morning, still getting things ready for her. She felt disappointed he chose not to come back to the hospital to spend some time with her. Brexley wanted to see him and discuss his plans for moving to Seattle.

Frustrated and ready to leave the hospital, Brexley waited impatiently for Carlton, listening to the morning news. She sat up straight in bed, hearing about the fire of her house on the news.

The reporter stood outside her destroyed home, talking with Fire Marshal Garrett. The reporter asked the Fire Marshal about the possible reason for the fire. She was curious why the house was engulfed so quickly in flames.

It was heartwrenching watching the news report. Brexley turned off the television, feeling queasy. It hit her hard. Her house was gone. She knew it was true, but it seemed so final now. Brexley's world was becoming a surreal nightmare. She wished she could wake up and find out everything was okay, but there was no chance of that happening. *'Why would someone do this to me?'* Brexley wondered.

Carlton entered the room, carrying a large tote filled to the top. Brexley greeted him with a smile, happy to see his familiar face. She loved him so much. It seemed strange to her to think he would soon be gone, living in Washington state, so far away. Instantly, she panicked, wondering how she could live without him.

"I see you are ready to get out of here," Carlton said as he handed her the heavy bag, placing it on the bed beside her.

"Definitely! Thank you for purchasing all the things. I promise I will pay you back."

"You do not owe me anything. I did this because I love you and care about you. I have everything ready at the house, too. Do you want me to help you get dressed?" Carlton offered as he saw her struggling to put on a sweatshirt.

"Yes, please. My hand still hurts."

Brexley held the signed discharge papers as she sat in the wheelchair, with the bag on her lap, heading to the hospital's main lobby.

Carlton was already downstairs, pulling the car up to the front of the hospital so she could expeditiously get into the vehicle.

Once in the car, Carlton drove toward his home while the rain came down hard. It was a cold, wet, and dreary fall day. Brexley wondered where she would be sleeping. Did Carlton put her in his room or a guest room? She hoped it was in his room. She did not want to sleep alone.

Brexley gazed at her phone, thankful she would be able to get her life back together soon. It was a good thing she still shared a phone carrier with Carlton. Though they each paid their portion of the bill, they remained on the same contract. It was one of the small things they still shared, keeping them connected to each other.

Carlton could purchase and activate a new phone for Brexley without any hassle. He restored her phone and had it up and running when he handed it to her. Carlton knew all her passwords and saved them on his computer.

Hoping to surprise Brexley, Carlton bought her a new laptop, which he placed next to the bed on the nightstand. He worried she would be upset when realizing the computer no longer existed.

Hopefully, she saved all the information to cloud storage. Brexley would have to start her life from scratch, which would not be easy.

Carlton pulled into the driveway less than thirty minutes later, and instantly, Brexley noticed the For-Sale sign was not on the lawn. She chose to remain silent about it. She assumed he removed it temporarily to allow quiet in the house while she recovered. It was so like Carlton to always think of her first. She almost cried, realizing how much she adored him.

Brexley waited for Carlton to help her out of the car. He led her to the guest room. Immediately, she felt offended. It was not his room. Her heart sank. 'WOW,' she thought. Brexley made it to the bed and noticed the laptop box on the nightstand.

"Thank you for everything, Carlton. Did you purchase a new laptop for me? Why?" she asked.

"Honey, everything in your house is gone. I wanted you to be able to start over. I know you conduct the majority of your business on your laptop. I hope it helps." He winked, opening up the closet doors.

"Here are some clothes. We can shop for more tomorrow if you need other items. I only bought a few things, unsure about what you wanted. I also placed undergarments and a pair of pajamas inside the dresser for you. Let me know if you feel that you require anything else. I am going to make lunch. How about some soup? Does that sound okay? I assume your throat is still bothering you." Carlton asked lovingly.

"Everything is perfect. You have done too much. I am eternally grateful. I want to take a shower, put on pajamas, and relax. Please be so kind as to let me know when the food is ready."

"Sure, take your time, Luv. I will be in the kitchen." Carlton closed the bedroom door, leaving her alone. He walked toward the kitchen, eager to start making food. He contemplated what he should do next after Brexley's home loss. He still needed to call Becker and tell him to hold off on the home sale temporarily. It would have to wait a few weeks, depending on how things progressed with

Brexley. She required a new home and car since the fire destroyed both. Maddie was handling all of the staging business, so that was one less thing to worry about at the moment. He stood in the kitchen, stirring the soup, wondering if he should leave San Antonio and move to Seattle.

Carlton also planned to call Devvyn to see if she could help out with things. Devvyn would be a great help to Brexley once he moved out of state. If he moved, he wanted Brexley to have all the support she needed. He realized it would be a challenge for her to start over. This time, he would not be there to help. The thought scared him, but he knew he had to do what was in his best interest for a change. No matter what!

The fire changed his plans. He hoped to speak with Brexley but felt right now was not the right time. She needed to heal, and it was almost Christmas. Maybe they could decorate the house together? That way, she would have something else to think about other than the fire. After all, Christmas was her favorite holiday. Maybe she would not be in the mood to celebrate the season.

Brexley showered and thought about the fire. She was scared to admit it, but she could not help but think that someone was still out there, ready to hurt her. She looked around the room, remembering the day she decorated it. Carlton was adamant they chose light and neutral colors for the room. Carlton ultimately agreed on blue-grey walls with white and Navy accents. Brexley had picked out matte gold accessories. She wanted to add some warmer-colored items to the color palette, but Carlton told her, *'Absolutely not!'*

Brexley loved the final color choices and felt the room was welcoming. Carlton had given her leeway in allowing her to change some things, but he remained firm in wanting a fabric headboard. As a tiny concession, he agreed to the wallpaper behind the bed, which he thought was unnecessary, though Brexley reassured him—wallpaper was back and big in the industry! So, reluctantly, he let her add the wall-Paper. Later, Carlton agreed. It looked great.

On the other end of town, the woman paced back and forth at a warehouse, violently angry. The rain was relentless. The noise from the pounding rain on the metal roof startled her.

"I told you NOT to burn down her house, you freaking idiot. I told you to burn down the warehouse if you were to do anything. I want her out of the way, not dead. You better pray she is not hurt," she screamed at him.

"You said you wanted her out of the way. My interpretation is that you wanted her gone. The notes all implied you wanted her dead. Now you want to back-pedal? No, I did the job you hired me to do. Now, you can take business away from her. She will be too scared to do anything for a while," he retorted adamantly.

"No, her warehouse is intact. She is still the biggest competition out there. She continues to destroy me in every way. Now, she even has Carlton back. I am so sick of her," the woman responded, pacing around nervously.

"Okay, so what do you want me to do?" he asked.

"I want you to make sure she stays away. I want her so scared that she shuts down her business and leaves town. I am tired of all of it. Make it happen, but keep her alive. I do not want her harmed. That is crossing the line, even for me." He nodded, pretending to care, heading to her warehouse.

On the other side of town, Carlton called Becker to discuss the current situation. Becker was gracious and understanding, agreeing to temporarily pull the house off the market through the holidays. This allowed Brexley and Carlton to get things in order before his departure to Seattle. Becker planned to relist the house on January 2nd after the new year.

Carlton placed a bowl of soup on the dining room table with some soft rolls and crackers. He did not know if Brexley wanted either or if she could eat them with her painful throat. He also made a cup of peppermint tea, her favorite. Brexley appeared in the dining room wearing pajamas. Her long hair was pulled back into a ponytail. She looked frail and tired. Her cheeks were still dark pink from the fire. She sat down and approvingly smiled at Carlton, grateful for all his help.

"So, I was thinking. Why don't we drive to the car dealership in the morning and look at a new car or SUV for you? What do you think?" Carlton suggested, eating his salad and sipping on red wine.

"A new SUV or car?" she asked, confused.

"Yes. You will need a new vehicle. You cannot walk all over the place," Carlton joked.

"Oh! Crap, I did not think about the fact my SUV was in the garage during the fire. That really stinks. I just bought it a year ago! It was basically still new. I suppose we need to call the insurance company too. Boy, there is so much to think about and do to rebuild my life," Brexley sighed. She pushed away the soup bowl. Carlton observed her actions. She seemed terrified and overwhelmed. Her bottom lip quivered, and she played with her hands nervously.

"One thing at a time, Brexley. Do not worry. I have already called the insurance company for you. I still have my power of attorney. So, I got the ball rolling on that for you. Mr. Easton said there was nothing to worry about with the claim. They have already been by the house and have requested documentation from the Fire Marshall's office on the fire. In the meantime, we should purchase you a new car. The new house can wait through the holidays if you prefer not to go house hunting. I thought we would decorate my house."

"Carlton, I thought you were selling this house and moving? Why would we decorate it?" She contemplated his offer but felt perplexed.

"I asked Becker to pull the house off the market until January 2nd of next year. After the new year, I will relist it. I talked with my new employer in Seattle and moved my start date to March 1st. They understand the circumstance, and there is no problem. Let's focus on you. We need to get you back on your feet. You are my priority. Nothing else matters. Maddie has everything under control at the warehouse. She is currently at the Willerton staging. She will call you later tonight with an update. Maddie does not want you to worry," Carlton explained, hoping to ease tension and nerves.

"Okay. I would like to return to bed. I am still exhausted and hurting. I hope that is okay. Can we talk later, Carlton?" Brexley asked, standing up.

"Sure. I will check on you in a little while." He watched as she wandered toward her room, her head down, still carrying the teacup in her right hand. She was distraught. He knew she felt overwhelmed. Carlton was glad he postponed his move. She would be okay, but it would take some time. Brexley was resilient. Hopefully, she would bounce back.

Maddie arrived at the warehouse and saw the truck parked off to the side with someone inside. She decided to head inside the building and ask one of the workers to find out who it was. After everything that had happened lately, she was reluctant to approach the truck on her own.

"Maddie, he drove off when I approached. It was a big guy in the truck. He looked tall. I did not get a chance to talk with him. The second he spotted me, he drove off in a hurry. I did not get a license plate number — there was no license plate! It is very suspicious. I gotta say," George added, rubbing his chin.

He was apprehensive and wondered what was happening. Two of his crew quit that morning, citing the job was not worth dying over. Everyone was fearful. The threats were now public, and no one felt comfortable.

George and six other men and two women still worked at the warehouse, but two others were on the verge of leaving from the pressure they received from their significant others.

Maddie reassured everyone that security guards were hired to work 24 hours a day at the warehouse. It was Carlton's idea, and he called numerous security firms interviewing them to ensure the proper security force was in place to protect the warehouse. He realized it was all Brexley had left. There was no way someone would take that from her too. Carlton would not allow it.

Brexley sat up in bed, with the new laptop next to her. Thirsty, she sipped the warm Peppermint tea, making her throat feel better. Her mind wandered, thinking about all that had occurred recently.

Brexley felt overcome by emotions and scooted down in the bed, pulling the sheet up to her chest. Staring at the ceiling, she became mesmerized by the moving ceiling fan. She wondered if Carlton would move despite all the new circumstances. Where would it leave them and their relationship? Maybe she should try to speak to him. Brexley knew he wasn't into sharing his emotions with her. He was also still hurt and upset with her.

She reminisced about the day Carlton planned to propose. She recalled the entire day, still feeling horrible for how it ended. Had she made a colossal mistake? *'Why can I not commit to Carlton? He is such a great man,'* Brexley thought. She rolled onto her side and stared out the window. It was still raining and dreary. The pain medication was making her tired, and she closed her eyes.

Carlton sat on a couch in the living room wearing his old grey sweatpants. He also had on thick socks and a sweatshirt. It was a chilly evening as he read emails on his cell phone. The fireplace was warm and cozy. His mind was not on the emails but instead on Brexley. Part of him wanted to join her in the bedroom and slip into bed, holding her. He loved her so much. Another part of him wanted to leave her alone to think about how much she hurt him.

He sighed, shaking his head. Confused about everything, he dropped the cell phone on the couch and headed to the guest room to see if Brexley was okay, assuming she was asleep.

Maddie finished working in her office and decided to head home for the day. Several warehouse workers were still around, pulling furniture to load in the morning. Maddie informed George she would head home, letting him secure the building. As she was about to get into her car, she noticed a flat front tire. Frustrated, she turned around to head back inside, asking George for help.

Suddenly, someone grabbed her from behind and covered her mouth. She felt something prick her, and then she passed out. The burly man dragged her body to his truck, hiding behind the row of dumpsters. He then drove off hurriedly, with Maddie in the front seat slumped over, passed out.

Thunder woke Brexley on the other side of town. She felt something on her back, quickly realizing it was Carlton. He crawled into bed with her, rubbing her back and playing with her hair. She felt warm and comfortable.

"Are you awake?" he asked, running his hands down her back and rubbing her butt. He loved her body.

"Yes, I am. When did you come into bed?" Brexley asked. She felt her heart racing, feeling his hand on her bottom. She moaned.

"I wanted to check on you. You look so beautiful in bed. I was cold and thought I would warm up," Carlton replied, chuckling.

"Mmmm, you did, huh?" She rolled over and faced him. He pulled her closer, kissing her. She surrendered to his touch. He held her tightly, passionately kissing her. She wanted him so badly but was weak and tired and chose to pull away.

"Is something wrong?" he asked, confused.

"No. I am exhausted and achy. Please, don't be mad," Brexley responded. She noticed the dejected look on his face. He appeared mad or frustrated with her. She wasn't sure which. She hoped he would understand.

"Of course. I get it. I did not come to make love to you if that is what you think. I just wanted to be near you. It just feels natural to hold and kiss you," Carlton said as he jumped out of bed. He stood before her. She saw the prominent, erect bulge in his sweats and felt herself getting hot all over again. She wanted him badly but forced herself to look away.

Carlton turned his back to her, now feeling awkward. He turned around briefly at the door, asking her, "Do you need anything? I am going to my room."

"No, thank you. I will be fine. Are we okay?" Brexley asked hesitantly, convinced she pissed him off.

"Yes, why not?"

"Okay, Carlton. I love you," Brexley replied.

Carlton left her alone without responding. He bit his bottom lip, wringing his hands. Frustrated, he shook his head as he walked toward his room. The mood was gone, and he felt indignant. 'Why does she always make everything so complicated?' Carlton wondered as he entered his bedroom and slammed the door.

Brexley closed her eyes and sniffed the cologne scent on her pillow. She loved the way Carlton smelled. Brexley jumped as she heard the loud slamming noise. Apparently, Carlton was peeved. She could not help but think about his kisses and how he touched her. He knew her body and was well aware of how she would respond to him. He still planned to move away from her, yet he chose to crawl into her bed, arousing her.

It was apparent he wanted to make love to her. There was no denying it. What kind of game was he playing? She rolled onto the other side of the bed, accidentally touching her hand. She winced in pain, rolling onto her back. *What is it about Carlton? It is nearly impossible for me to stay away from him.'* She contemplated. Brexley loved him dearly, yet why could she not commit to marriage? Marriage seemed like the logical next step. *'What is really keeping me from marriage?'* Her head was spinning. She closed her eyes, tired and irritated.

Carlton sat on the edge of the bed, speculating if Brexley would ever change. He was tired of the games and wanted to make love to her. She was beautiful, and he adored her. *'Is that wrong? Hell, no!'* He said aloud. Carlton contemplated returning to her room to speak with her.

Suddenly, he heard his cell phone ringing in the living room. He jumped off the bed and ran to the couch to pick it up, hoping it was not more bad news.

"Carlton, it is George. Listen, Maddie told me she was leaving forty-five minutes ago. I locked up the warehouse and sent the crew home. Her car is still in the back of the warehouse. One of the tires has been slashed and is flat. I cannot find Maddie. I tried calling her cell phone, but it went straight to voicemail. I think something is wrong!"

"That is strange. Listen, I am calling my friend. He's a cop. Will you please stay at the warehouse until I get there?" Carlton requested as he began looking for his keys and wallet.

"Sure, I will be here. Thanks, Carlton. Are you going to tell Brexley, or should I?" asked George.

"NO! Do not call her right now. I will handle

this. She is asleep and needs rest," demanded Carlton, heading to Brexley's room. Carlton entered the guest room and turned on the lights.

Brexley sat up in bed, confused. She rubbed her eyes, looking drowsy. "What is going on?" she asked, panicked.

"Something has happened. I need to leave for a bit. Will you be okay alone? I will lock up and turn on the alarm. Please do not worry."

"Sure, I will be okay. What happened?" Brexley asked, now feeling apprehensive.

"I will talk with you when I get back. Please keep your cell phone close in case I need to reach you." He bent down, gently kissing her forehead, squeezing her hand. "Don't worry. I will be back shortly. I promise." Carlton left her room and headed to the garage.

There was no way Brexley could sleep now that he was gone. She knew something was amiss, assuming it had everything to do with the notes. Frantically, she picked up the cell phone and called Maddie. It rang, eventually going to voicemail. Brexley frowned. *Why is she not picking up? That is not like her.'* She redialed Maddie's number. Same thing—voicemail.

Worrying about Maddie's welfare, Brexley left a voicemail. "Hey, can you call me ASAP? I need to speak with you. I hope everything is okay at the warehouse." She ended the call and decided to follow up with a text. Brexley impatiently stared at the phone, wondering why Maddie was not responding. She felt her hands become clammy. Brexley wanted to scream. Something was very wrong. *'My God, please let Maddie be okay. I hope nothing is wrong.'*

Within a few minutes, Carlton pulled up next to Maddie's car. He walked around the vehicle, inspecting it, noticing the deep gash in the tire. Carlton tried to open the car doors but unfortunately found them locked. He was about to head inside the warehouse when he saw a black SUV approaching. He remained standing by the car. Abruptly, the SUV stopped and backed up quickly. The SUV drove off in the same direction from where it had come.

Carlton watched, wondering what the heck was going on here. He looked around to see if anyone else was around. *'George must still be inside,'* he thought to himself. The big metal garage door to the warehouse opened, and George appeared, waving to Carlton. George was a tall and muscular man in his early forties. His hair was thick and black with a bit of grey. George was a hard worker and a fantastic leader, always smiling. Everyone at the warehouse adored him.

"Oh, thank goodness you made it. I heard a noise outside and figured it was you. What do you think about the slashed tire? Has anyone heard from Maddie? I gotta tell you...I am getting a bit worried. My staff is not happy either. I lost 50% of my team in the last three days. What are we going do, Carlton?" asked George, standing before him, wearing dark grey pants and a matching shirt. He had his arms crossed, looking scared, his eyebrows furrowed.

"Yes, I can only imagine. Listen, George. This is a difficult time for everyone. I understand your staff is frightened and apprehensive. However, the threats are against Brexley, not anyone else. It would help if you kept them calm. This situation will blow over in time." Carlton stood next to George, analyzing his facial expressions. George nodded, acknowledging what he had heard.

"So, do you want me to stay until your cop friend arrives?" George offered.

"No, you don't have to…I'll be okay," replied Carlton.

"Well, I would feel better waiting. Just in case," George reassured Carlton he would stay. The two sat on the loading dock with their legs dangling off the edge. Neither spoke.

Not far away, Brexley remained in bed, impatiently staring at her cell phone. She wondered why Carlton left abruptly. *Why is Maddie not answering her cell phone? Something horrible has happened. I know it!'*

Nervously, Brexley dialed Carlton's cell, but her call went directly to his voicemail too. She started to visualize horrific things in her head. *What if something has happened to Maddie and Carlton? What if someone is out to get revenge against me using my friends?'* Brexley felt her heart racing. She became scared, dialing Devvyn's number, hoping to speak with her.

Unfortunately, Devvyn failed to answer. Exasperated and scared, Brexley jumped out of bed, sprinting to the closet to find jeans to wear. She planned to head to the warehouse, eager to find out if anything was happening there. Where else would Carlton have gone? It seemed like the logical destination.

After what seemed like an eternity to Carlton, Detective Johnson arrived in a non-marked Ford Explorer. He jumped out of the vehicle and walked toward Carlton. The two nodded at each other, and Carlton made the introductions. George respectfully shook the detective's hand.

"Thanks for coming out, Shawn. I know you are a busy man. The situations with the fire and notes have me alarmed. Maddie is missing, and someone slashed the tire on her vehicle. I asked George if we could pull up a surveillance video of the parking lot. Hopefully, we can catch the perpetrator in action."

"Great. Shall we head inside to check it out?" asked Detective Shawn Johnson. The three men walked inside the warehouse, not noticing the black SUV down the road, with someone inside watching them through binoculars.

CHAPTER 4

Maddie heard noises. She felt drowsy, trying desperately to open her eyes. Slowly, she opened them, visually scanning the area. She was in what appeared to be a stock room in a warehouse. The lighting was dim, and it was cold. She shivered. Where exactly was she? Hopefully, she was still in Texas, though she honestly had no clue. She heard rain outside, making pinging noises on the metal roof. *'What time is it?'* Maddie wondered.

The room was getting darker by the minute. She heard a woman's voice, now getting louder.

"What are your plans with her? Why on earth would you bring her here? Are you out of your mind?" a woman screamed.

"You said for me to do something. I figured kidnapping the woman would give us negotiating power if need be...Brexley will do what we want to ensure her safety. You know it, and I know it. So, just say THANK YOU…and stop being so damn ungrateful," he yelled back. He was in her face, making sure she knew he was angry and tired of her micromanaging him. His sister was unappreciative, and he now regretted agreeing to help her.

The two continued to argue. Maddie listened, though she began feeling nauseous. 'Who kidnapped me? Why would anyone want to hurt Brexley?' Brexley was the most moral human being she knew. Maddie continued listening to the two people arguing. The woman's voice sounded a little familiar. Did she know her?

The room became dark, and Maddie wished for light. A tall man entered the room wearing a Halloween mask over his face. He turned on the overhead fluorescent light. It illuminated, making a buzzing sound. Maddie tried not to laugh, catching a glimpse of him. He looked ridiculous in his monster mask.

"You know it's not Halloween, right?" she asked him sarcastically.

"Aren't we the funny one?" he responded, approaching her, not amused.

"You know, you will not get away with this. Someone will find me, and you will end up in prison. I suggest you let me go. It will be your best option," Maddie replied sternly. She hoped to scare the kidnappers.

"Say what whatcha want. I am here to ask ya if you're hungry. Nothin' more. So, what's it gonna be? Do ya want food or not?" he barked at her, irritated. He held a bag in his hand. It contained a sandwich and a bottle of water.

Maddie remained silent, looking down at her lap, ignoring him. She was not hungry and did not care to answer. She no longer felt the need to be polite. Maddie wondered if Carlton and Brexley were looking for her. George would have alerted Carlton to tell him she was missing. He was detail-oriented and would have noticed her car with the slashed tire. Maddie wished Shawn would appear, rescuing her.

At the *Sinclaire Premier Staging* warehouse, Carlton and Shawn sat behind the large desk, reviewing the video surveillance footage with George. *'Half of it is blank, which is very odd! How can that be?'* Wondered Carlton, squirming in his seat.

Shawn was thinking the same thing. He

looked at Carlton, shaking his head, suggesting the two head to the police station. He wanted to put out an APB/BOLO—all points bulletin/be on (the) look-out—for Maddie.

Shawn realized that they had to find her quickly. The longer it took, the more likely she would not be found alive. He hated thinking about that and chose to keep his mouth closed. He did not want to upset Carlton further.

Also, Shawn thought it would be a good idea to chat with Brexley to determine what happened in the last few weeks. Something was missing. He was eager to find out what she knew.

Brexley sat on the couch inside Carlton's home, contemplating calling a ride-share or a taxi. She wanted to head to the warehouse. Part of her thought it was best to wait to hear from Carlton. *'Why has he not called yet? What is taking him so darn long?'* She picked up her cell phone and decided to call Carlton again.

Carlton saw the incoming call from Brexley. He hesitated. *'Should I answer?'* He did not want her to worry more since he lacked further information. *'So, why should I upset her more?'* Carlton did not answer the call and followed Shawn to the police station through the pouring rain and strong wind gusts.

Brexley stared at the phone. *'Why is Carlton not picking up? Is he okay?'* She panicked, feeling her heart pounding out of her chest, a nauseous suffocating sensation taking over. She stood up quickly, pacing around the room, struggling to gasp for air. *'Am I dying? Is it a panic attack?'* She dropped to her knees, trying to inhale, her lungs burning. She cried, curling up in a ball on the fluffy, dark-grey carpet in the living room, wishing Carlton was there with her.

Pulling up in front of the police station, Carlton jumped out of his car and locked it. Shawn drove to the parking garage located at the back of the building. Carlton was supposed to meet Shawn in the lobby.

Once inside, Carlton sat on the peeling black, faux leather chairs, waiting for Shawn. Carlton held his cell phone, contemplating reaching out to Brexley.

Shawn approached just as he was about to call her, holding a folder. "Hey, let's head upstairs to my office. We can talk there. Are you okay?" Shawn asked, noticing Carlton frowning, staring at his phone.

"Yes, I am fine. Sure, lead the way." Shawn walked toward the elevator, Carlton followed closely behind. He placed his cell phone on silent and slid it into his pant pocket, eager to formulate a plan to find Maddie.

The storm subsided, and the room was pitch dark. Maddie sat tied up in the chair, wishing she was home in front of the warm fireplace. She hated the darkness. It frightened her. Now, she was even more apprehensive, especially since she did not know where she was and if she would live to see another day.

Maddie's hands ached as she tried to loosen the rough ropes, cutting into her wrists. Unfortunately, she could not get them to come off, no matter what she tried. The building was quiet, making her wonder if anyone was around. 'Has everyone left the building? Am I alone in this dark room?' She shivered with fright.

Suddenly, Maddie felt the urgent need to pee, which made her even more un-uncomfortable. She squirmed in the seat with her bladder full, now in pain. "I have to pee!!!!" Maddie shouted. "Can someone please take me to the restroom? I am gonna pee in my pants, for God's sake." She waited—still complete silence in the building. Maddie began to panic. *'Will they come back?'* What was she supposed to do? The urge to urinate became painful. There was no holding it.

Maddie became angry, thinking she would be forced to pee in her pants. It was barbaric. Maddie cried. It became clear this was a serious situation. She prayed someone would find her quickly.

Lonely and scared, Maddie thought about Shawn, wishing he would magically appear, much like a superhero, coming to her rescue. Sadly, she realized that was unlikely. He probably was not even aware of her absence. The only hope Maddie felt was knowing George had probably telephoned Carlton. Hopefully, Carlton, in turn, called Shawn. Maddie could only pray, attempting to stay optimistic given her current circumstance. She shook her head, feeling drained.

At the police station downtown, Shawn turned on the computer and began typing quickly. He pecked away on the old keyboard, occasionally stopping to gather his thoughts. Carlton sat quietly in the chair by the desk, fidgeting with a pencil he found on the desk. He stared ahead at the posters on the wall, wondering how all this mess began.

Carlton noticed the MISSING PERSON posters, which immediately scared him to death. What if Maddie never returned? Would her face be plastered on a sign like the ones in this room? The thought was horrifying, and Carlton closed his eyes, praying she would be found. His mind wandered, and he wondered how he would break the news to Brexley.

Shawn continued typing. Every once in a while, he made a short phone call to a colleague. After he finished, Shawn informed Carlton that law enforcement would now be on the lookout for Maddie. He also told him that usually, law enforcement waited 24 hours after a disappearance before issuing an alert. However, Shawn knew Maddie, so he typed up the paperwork, expediting it. Thank goodness Carlton saved the picture of Maddie and Brexley on his phone from the Holiday party last year. He could crop it and text it to Shawn to use with the Texas Department of Public Safety Missing Persons Clearinghouse Report Form.

Shawn escorted Carlton back to the lobby on the main floor. He stood next to him, waiting for Carlton to speak. Carlton seemed in a daze, staring at the front door. Shawn finally spoke up.

"So, there isn't anything else we can do for now. I realize it is upsetting, but we have done everything we can. Do you want me to follow you back to the house to speak with Brexley, or should it wait until the morning? You know her better than I do. Please, tell me what you think."

"I will head back to the house and fill Brexley in on everything. Let's wait on that conversation with Brexley until the morning, if possible. She is already so stressed and anxious. Let's not make it worse. I am worried she could have a mental breakdown. May I call you in the morning to set something up?" Carlton replied, observing Shawn's face.

"Please realize I must conduct an interview with Brexley and take her statement. So, let's plan for 9 a.m. at your house, shall we? That way, I can get things on record and fill out the report completely. She can rest tonight. I am so sorry you and Brexley have to go through this. Maddie is a great person. I feel horrible that Maddie may have become a victim. Rest assured, we will find her. Please head home, take care of Brexley, and tell her I will do all I can, okay?" Shawn smiled awkwardly, patting Carlton on the back. He returned to his office, finishing up other paperwork.

Brexley crawled onto the couch. She still felt breathless but realized it was a panic attack. When was the last time she had one of those? She couldn't recall. It had been a very long time. *'Why is this happening,'* Brexley wondered. A few seconds later, she heard the front door lock clicking, and Carlton appeared. He punched in the alarm code to deactivate the alarm. He approached the couch, looking worried, noticing she was shaking.

"Well, tell me what is going on," she asked anxiously. She was furious with Carlton for not calling her earlier. Her imagination had run wild with horrific thoughts.

Carlton sat down next to her, eyebrows raised and his mouth puckered. He looked distressed. She felt nauseous all over again.

"What is it?" She begged. "Please, don't spare me. I need to know. I know something is wrong. I can see it by the look on your face. I know you! You have to tell me," she screamed while tears ran down her face.

"Honey, calm down. Let me tell you everything. First, though, you need to realize none of it is your fault," Carlton said, holding her hand carefully.

"What the hell does that mean?" she snapped, getting angry.

"There is no easy way to tell you. Maddie may have been kidnapped. George called me and informed me that Maddie had told him she was leaving to head home. He found her car with a tire slashed. George became worried and called me. We are unable to locate her. After calling Shawn to report the incident, he believes there is enough evidence to support her kidnapping. Though, we still do not know why."

Brexley slapped his hand away and jumped off the couch. It was the fastest he had seen her move in days. She cried, walking around, shaking her fists in anger. Carlton wanted to stop her and force her to sit down, but he knew she would resist. Instead, he decided to let Brexley release her emotions. She would sit when she was ready.

It seemed like an eternity before she finally plopped down, wringing her hands. Carlton watched her intently, remaining silent. Suddenly, Brexley scooted right next to him and grabbed his hand.

"Okay, tell me everything. I am calm. I need to know," Brexley said, trying to act stoic. Though inside, she felt like dying. She absolutely felt responsible for Maddie's kidnapping, and it was more than she could bear.

"Are you sure?" Carlton asked cautiously.

"Without a doubt. I need to know. Please!" Carlton spent a few minutes filling Brexley in on everything he knew. She listened and sat motionless the entire time. Her lack of reaction worried Carlton even more. It was not like her to sit so quietly. *'What is she thinking? Did she hear me?'* He wondered.

Brexley eventually nodded her head. It was the first sign she understood what he had told her. She stood up and strolled to the kitchen without saying a word.

Confused, Carlton followed her. Brexley opened the refrigerator and grabbed a bottle of water. She plopped on the barstool opposite the large kitchen island, sipping the water.

Carlton became nervous. *'Why is she not talking? What is going through her head? Is she okay?'* Carlton wondered.

Brexley placed the water bottle on the shiny counter. She closed her eyes, remaining silent. Finally, Carlton couldn't take it anymore. Something was wrong. He had to confront her.

"Brexley, did you hear me? Did you understand everything I told you in the living room? Honey, are you okay?" He watched her face, which looked blank. *'My God, did she have a stroke?'* He wondered, now panicking. Scared, he shook her lightly, attempting to gain a response. Brexley stared at him and yet said nothing. Carlton contemplated calling 911 to get EMS to check her out. Something was wrong with her.

"Brexley, you are starting to worry me. Please, Luv, say something, anything. Are you okay?" He begged one last time.

Finally, she blinked, sitting up straight on the barstool. "Yes, I heard every word. I get it. I am not stupid. Sorry, I have no clue what I should say right now. I feel fully responsible for Maddie's possible kidnapping. How can I not feel that way? It is because of me she is in this situation. What can I do about it? Does Shawn feel he can find her? Dammit, Carlton, it should never have been Maddie. It should have been MEEEEE!" Brexley shrieked. "Has anyone called Devvyn to make sure she is okay? What if she is next? She is my best friend, for God's sake! For all we know, she could be next!" Brexley looked pale as a ghost.

Carlton wanted to hug her and reassure her all would be okay. Except, he did not know if it would be. Carlton refused to give her false hope. He assumed Maddie would be found safe and sound, but then…maybe she wouldn't. Then what? It would drive Brexley insane. He worried about the repercussions of the kidnapping on her mental well-being in the long term. *'Will Brexley be okay?'* He silently questioned, observing her. Carlton also worried Devvyn could potentially become the next target. He planned to share that thought with Shawn in the morning.

Minutes later, Shawn pulled up in front of his home, feeling like shit. He should have told Carlton about Maddie. He had a right to know. However, Shawn wanted to act professionally, refusing to allow his personal feelings to get in the way of doing his job.

If Carlton knew about Shawn and Maddie, he might have insisted that Shawn turn the case over to someone else. That is why Shawn did not tell anyone about his relationship with Maddie. He felt it was better this way, though ethically, he realized that he would have to inform others and give the case to someone else in time.

In the morning, he planned to speak with Brian, his close friend, and his work partner. Brian could take over the investigation, and Shawn would still be privy to information about the case.

Shawn and Maddie met at last year's Christmas Holiday Party at Brexley's. It was an instant attraction for both. After dating for a month, they tried to keep it casual but quickly realized their relationship was much more complicated. Shawn told Maddie over dinner on their one-month anniversary of dating he loved her and wanted to go public with their relationship, tired of hiding.

However, Maddie asked Shawn to keep it on the down-low, not wanting Brexley to know. She and Carlton were having issues, and Maddie did not want to tell her about Shawn, fearing it would seem like she was boasting about her new relationship with Shawn. Plus, Maddie was an immensely private person.

So, Maddie and Shawn kept their relationship private, not displaying any kind of public affection. Shawn regretted his actions now and wished he had insisted they tell everyone.

Shawn was madly in love with Maddie and wanted to marry her. He felt helpless and scared now that her life was in danger. Shawn dropped his jacket on the floor and walked to the window. He looked out onto the street. It was still raining. In the distance, he saw flashes of lightning, hearing the rumblings of thunder. He was sleepy and wanted to take a nap. Shawn figured there was no way he could sleep under the current circumstances. He sank into his favorite chair, leaned back, and snuggled under a blanket. Finally, he closed his eyes, hoping for much-needed rest.

The loud thunder rattled the house, making creaking noises. Brexley looked around nervously, still on edge. She wondered if Carlton was aware of Maddie and Shawn's relationship. Brexley discovered the two were dating shortly after the holiday party. She noticed how Shawn looked at Maddie every time she walked into the room. He always acted like a gentleman around her, tending to her every need.

One day, Brexley asked Maddie about Shawn. Maddie vehemently denied any romantic feelings for him, stating, "We are good friends, that's all!" But, Brexley was not stupid, having picked up on the obvious signs. She wondered why the two kept denying their relationship to everyone. It seemed silly. They were perfect for each other. Brexley loved the idea of Shawn and Maddie getting married. She could see them together. They were an ideal match.

In the dimly lit room, Maddie finally decided she could not hold it anymore. Feeling humiliated, Maddie let go, feeling the warmth running down her legs. It was a disgusting sensation. *'How can they do this to me?'* Maddie thought, feeling mortified. She was also thirsty and felt weak. *'When was the last time I ate? It must have been breakfast. What time is it?'* After a few minutes, Maddie closed her eyes, falling asleep, still tied to the wooden chair, now soaked in urine.

Over an hour passed, and Shawn looked at his cell phone, waking up from a nap. He wanted to call Brian. It was late, almost midnight. Reluctantly, he dialed Brian's number, hoping he was still awake.

"Hey, Shawn. Are you okay?" asked Brian as he answered his phone, sounding like he had been sleeping. He realized something was amiss. Shawn would not call this late at night unless it were urgent. Nervously, Brian sat up in bed.

"No, man. I am not. I need to speak with you. It is an urgent matter. Can you come to my house? I know it is late. I wouldn't ask you if it wasn't important. Please?" Shawn begged.
"Of course. Will you be okay until I get there?" Brian asked, feeling concerned.

"Yes. I will. Thanks, Brian. I owe you."
Shawn hung up the cell phone. He placed his elbows on his knees, sitting in the recliner. Sorrowfully, he held his head in his hands, crying, worried about Maddie. He had no idea if he would ever see her again, which broke his heart.

In San Antonio, on the other side of the city, Brexley opened her eyes and immediately grabbed her cell phone off the nightstand. It was late. She had been tossing and turning most of the night, feeling restless. Her mind was too active, and she could not get it to stop. Before finally falling asleep earlier, she showered while her hand throbbed the entire time, making her miserable.

Once in bed, it seemed impossible for her to get comfortable. She wanted to scream but chose to whimper in silence.

Carlton never came to her room to say goodnight. She wondered what had happened to him and if he was slowly withdrawing from her. It would not be the first time.

Maybe he thought it was easier, especially once he moved. Either way, she was becoming increasingly annoyed. *'Why did he not check on me?'* She contemplated. His actions seemed very cold and heartless to her, very unlike Carlton. Hours passed as she tried to fall back asleep, unsuccessfully. Morning finally arrived, and she reluctantly decided to get up.

A few doors down, Carlton woke up with a painful erection. He pushed it down as he tried to get out of bed, irritated. Plopping back down on the bed naked, he stared at his erection. Carlton hoped to speak to Brexley last night, wishing to crawl into bed with her. He missed her. Earlier in the evening, he observed her in the kitchen, wearing her pajamas, as her boobs peeked out, seemingly teasing him. He wanted to make love to her badly. Carlton thought about kissing and enticing her. Unfortunately, Brexley would not have allowed it.

Feeling unsatisfied, Carlton touched his erection briefly and then changed his mind. With a naughty grin on his face, he laughed at himself. Seconds later, he jumped out of bed, wanting to shower, forgetting about his aching penis and Brexley. Maybe he could seduce her later. She probably wanted him just as badly as he needed her. Still feeling aroused, he jumped in the steamy shower. Carlton thought about Brexley and her luscious body. He lathered and caressed himself with soap, leaning against the tiled shower wall, moaning, feeling his legs become weak.

Brexley heard the shower and assumed Carlton was getting ready for the day. She dressed and pulled on a pair of black lace panties. Looking at herself in the full-length mirror, she was shocked at the reflection. She looked dreadfully thin.

Brexley carefully put on her bra, trying not to touch her hand, which seemed slightly better. Dressing in the only pair of jeans in her closet, she reached for a white blouse, putting it on as she headed to the bathroom. She heard music coming from Carlton's room, wondering what he was doing. *'He must be in a good mood,'* she thought, snickering to herself.

Brexley sat on the stool in front of the counter, pulling her hair into a messy bun. She decided to go make-up free, except for lipstick. She never went anywhere without lipstick. Brexley grabbed her wallet, the only thing she managed to save on her way out of the burning house. She was eager to go shopping with Carlton to buy other clothes and look at cars. She knew there wasn't much else she could do right now. Later, she also planned to call Shawn and talk with him about Maddie. Shawn would finally disclose everything.

CHAPTER 5

Earlier, during the night, Brian knocked on the dark-blue metal door. It only took a minute before Shawn opened it, looking rough. His hair was unkempt, and he smelled of alcohol. Shawn motioned for Brian to enter. He led him into the living room. Brian chose to sit down and patiently waited for Shawn to speak. However, it became apparent that Shawn was not ready, so Brian initiated the conversation.

"Hey, you don't look so great. Are you drunk?" Brian asked. It was apparent Shawn had been drinking. Brian noticed several empty beer cans on the table. He also spotted an opened bottle of whiskey and a half-full glass of liquor. A pack of cigarettes and an ashtray were on the floor by the fireplace. The fire was almost burned out, and only red coals were still glowing.

'Since when has Shawn smoked?' Brian wondered. He never knew Shawn to smoke or drink. There was something very wrong. His friend was in crisis. Instantly he frowned.

"Tell me, what is going on, friend? You have me scared. This is not like you," Brian exclaimed, pointing to the cans, bottle, and cigarettes. *'What is happening to Shawn?'* Brian contemplated.

Shawn bent down and picked up the cigarette pack. He lit a cigarette and took the ashtray with him, sitting in the recliner. Brian observed him, concerned. Shawn inhaled and then blew the smoke toward the fireplace, sighing. He flicked the cigarette ashes into the ashtray while tapping his right foot nervously.

"Okay. You are right. There is something wrong. First, thank you for your friendship and for coming over so quickly. I am in trouble, and I require your help. Let me tell you what has happened." Shawn spent some time explaining everything to Brian. He described how he met

Maddie, her working relationship with Brexley, how Carlton fit into the picture, Brexley's death threats, and more.

After the lengthy explanation, Shawn lit another cigarette. Jittery, he reached for the glass of whiskey and took a giant drink. He slammed the glass on the table, frustrated, still shaking. It was a slight relief to tell someone about his relationship with Maddie.

"Alright, Shawn. I get the picture. You didn't do anything wrong. You took the report and then called me. You did the right thing. I will take over the investigation, and you will not compromise it. Everything will be fine. Regarding Maddie, why didn't you tell me about your relationship with her before? It seems dumb to hide it from me. I am your friend and work partner." Brian felt hurt. It was not like Shawn to hide information from him, especially something so important.

"Maddie didn't want anyone to know yet. We discussed it and decided to wait. As it turns out, the proper time never happened. Now, I wish we had told everyone a long time ago. You are correct. It is stupid—downright dumb. Trust me. I am no longer hiding my feelings for Maddie. That is why I need you to take this case over right away. I have to distance myself. I don't want the Chief to think I was doing something unethical. I am supposed to make sergeant at the end of this month. I don't want him to lose faith in me. You understand, right?" Shawn asked, putting out the cigarette.

Brian reassured Shawn he understood his intent. He also reminded him he was human. It was a small mistake, and they would rectify it now.

Shawn agreed, feeling better. He offered Brian some whiskey, but he turned him down, citing having to drive home. Shawn felt grateful to Brian for his friendship and understanding. Brian walked to the door. He stopped to pat Shawn on the back, reassuring him everything would work out.

"See you later, buddy." Brian headed to the car, still confused why Shawn hid his relationship with Maddie from everyone for so long. Shawn closed and locked the door, turned around, and headed back to the chair to light another cigarette. He had not smoked in over ten years. It was a filthy habit, one he hated.

Unfortunately, on the way home from the police station the night before, he stopped at Bob's Quick Stop and purchased a six-pack of beer. When he stood in front of the counter, ready to pay, he stared at the cigarette case. He knew it was unwise, but he bought a pack, lit up in the car, inhaled, and instantly relaxed.

Now, it was early in the morning, and Shawn was exhausted. Before crashing, he put out the cigarette and headed to the bathroom to brush his teeth. All he wanted was to sleep and forget about Maddie's possible kidnapping. After all, no one knew for sure where she was and what had happened to her. Shawn needed rest and had to clear his head. The sun would be coming up soon enough.

The warehouse was dark and quiet. The woman entered the room and switched on the overhead lights, wearing a cat mask. She wanted to speak with Maddie and reassure her there was no intent to harm her. Her idiot brother should never have brought her to the building. It was a huge mistake, one she planned to rectify. Immediately, she heard snoring. Maddie was still asleep.

The woman gagged, smelling the pungent odor of urine. She felt terrible, realizing Maddie had sat in urine all night. 'So disgusting,' she thought.

Maddie woke up when the overhead light turned on. She squinted her eyes but jumped in her seat when she saw a cat face mask staring at her. Her heart raced.

"Good morning. I am here to let you know I plan to release you soon. You were never supposed to be here. I have breakfast in the other room. Are you hungry?" she asked Maddie cordially.

"Go to hell. I don't want your food. Let me go!" shouted Maddie, enraged.

"Calm down! I told you I would release you soon enough. First, there are a few things that must happen. So, in the meantime, you are my guest. As my guest, I want to remove the ropes. You have to promise me you won't do anything stupid. If you do, I will shoot you. I do not want to do that. Believe me." The woman moved closer to Maddie, a knife in her left hand.

The woman stepped behind Maddie and bent down, cutting the ropes off her wrists. The woman in the cat mask quickly made her way back to the door. She observed Maddie as she rubbed her aching wrists and hands.

"Do you have any clean clothes for me? I peed on myself because you could not be here to take me to the restroom. What kind of freaking nasty person are you?" Maddie whines. She stood up, her pants stained. It was embarrassing to reek like urine. She wanted to cry.

"Yes, I brought you a pair of pants and a T-shirt. There is also a sweater. I know it is cold here. I figured you wanted clean clothes, but now I realize you need some wipes or a washcloth. I will bring you the sanitary wipes from my office. You can wash up with those. There is no shower here, sorry. I will have someone bring you a cot to sleep on later. Stay here and remain silent. I will be back." The woman left to retrieve the food and clothing, locking the door on her way out.

Maddie sat back down on the cold wooden chair, wishing she could shower. *Where is*

Brexley? Is she aware of my kidnapping? Has Brexley called Shawn and reported me missing? Where is everyone?' She worried, praying for a speedy rescue.

Brexley entered the kitchen fully dressed, holding her cell phone in her right hand. Carlton poured a cup of coffee, handing it to Brexley. She looked refreshed. Her eyes sparkled for the first time in days. Her burned hand looked pink, not red. He was happy about that, noticing it was healing, though he wondered why she removed the gauze bandage.

"Good morning, beautiful. Here is your coffee," Carlton handed it to Brexley. "Do you want to head to town today to buy more clothes? Or do you have something else in mind?" he asked Brexley.

"Yes, I need other things to wear. A sweater or two would be great. I am freezing. The weather changed quickly. Fall is definitely here. I also need some more undergarments. I would also like to check out vehicles later if that is okay. I need to run by Michelle's office. I told her I would come by today. She wants to show me a list of homes for sale." Brexley smiled, hoping he would be okay running so many different errands with her in one day.

"Oh! I didn't realize you wanted to purchase a new home before the holidays. What is the rush?" He felt crushed. Carlton hoped to have

Brexley at his house for Christmas. He wanted to make the holiday festive for her, knowing she would love decorating the inside while he put up the lights and décor outside.

Thanksgiving was just around the corner, and he thought it would be nice to invite a few friends over, maybe even her father, Harrison. Carlton would cook since Brexley hated it, and she could bake. Together, they would make a fantastic meal, like before when they were a couple.

"I am exploring all my options. I know you are eager to get to Seattle. The sooner I move out, the quicker you can sell your home." She sipped her coffee while standing. She wanted him to know she wouldn't stand in his way if he wanted to move. She refused to beg him to stay. Brexley was done fighting.

"I told you — I am not ready to leave the area. I am not planning to move until after the new year. I am in no hurry. We can have a peaceful, relaxing holiday together first." He said it in a stern voice, sounding furious.

"Well, I still want to see what Michelle has found for me. I need my life back. The sooner, the better." She shouted back. Brexley placed the empty coffee mug in the sink. "Are you ready to head out?" she asked with impatience.

"No, not yet. Shawn still needs to speak with you. He will be here shortly. After the interview, we can leave. Okay?" Carlton replied, noticing she looked annoyed. At the same time, the doorbell rang. Carlton headed to the front door.

"Good morning, Carlton!" It was Brian. He stood by the door, his head partially covered by a black rain jacket.

"Hey Brian, I was expecting Shawn. Come on in, please. Are you alone?" asked Carlton. Carlton was familiar with Brian. However, he was confused about his presence. When he spoke with Shawn, he informed him he would be the one coming to talk to them, which made sense since they were friends.

Brian explained why he was alone and would be in charge of the investigation, keeping Shawn out of it as much as possible. The two entered the kitchen. Brexley was eating a bowl of cereal and checking her phone. She looked tired to Brian. He sat down next to Brexley and began the interrogation. After twenty minutes of her recounting previous events, Brian turned off his tablet.

"Well, that is all I need for now. Please call me if anything else happens. I will be in touch." Carlton escorted Brian to the door. The two talked for a few more minutes. Carlton closed and locked the door, heading back to the kitchen. When he returned, Brexley was gone. He assumed she was in her room. Wanting to head out and run errands, he knocked on her bedroom door. Brexley quickly appeared and opened it, saying, "Can we go? I need to get out of here. It has been a shitty day already."

"Sure. Let me grab my wallet. I'll meet you in the garage." He walked to the back door, locking it. Brexley headed to the garage to wait for him in his car.

Carlton set the alarm and opened the garage door. They pulled out of the driveway in his vehicle. Brexley looked at the sky. It looked dark and gloomy. *'Is it going to rain again? She wondered. Why is it so wet and rainy this year? It seems wetter than usual. Nasty. I am so ready for Spring!'*

Brexley hated the gloominess. She closed her eyes with her head resting on the back of the seat, listening to holiday music, making her feel sleepy. Carlton pulled up in front of the real estate office. Brexley jumped out of the car, running toward the door as it rained hard, causing her almost to slip and fall.

Carlton joined her inside the building. Michelle handed Brexley a printed list of addresses. On each address line was a picture of the front of a home with basic information such as bedrooms, bathrooms, square footage, etc. Brexley skimmed over the list and handed it to Carlton.

"Is it possible to see any of these today? Or do we have to make an appointment first? I'd like to see the first three. Two are in my old neighborhood, and one is in Carlton's." Brexley asked Michelle.

Michelle nodded and made phone calls, spending a few minutes on the computer. After making arrangements, she informed the couple that they could check out the three homes. She would be happy to show them the properties. Michelle agreed to ride with them in the car.

After spending two hours touring the houses, Carlton and Brexley dropped Michelle off at her office. Carlton walked Michelle inside, thanking her for her time. He swiftly returned to the car, joining Brexley, who acted indifferent. She stared out the window.

"Did you like any of the houses? You seemed disinterested. Are you hurting or just not in the mood to look at homes? I think the last place is perfect for you. It is in your old neighborhood, a one-story, spacious, and new. The price is excellent as well. How do you feel about that?" he asked her, attempting to sound upbeat. He knew she wanted a new home, but maybe she wasn't quite ready.

"Yes, the homes were all fine. I suppose I am not too eager to buy right now. You are right. I should probably hold off on purchasing a home until after Christmas. My mind is not on moving and having to decorate a new house right away." Brexley closed her eyes. She looked exhausted. She opened her wallet and took out a pill, popping it in her mouth. Her hand throbbed, and her head hurt. She wanted to rest. Shopping for clothing would have to wait. There was no way she had enough energy to do that.

Brexley told Carlton she didn't want to shop, preferring to return to his home. He understood and agreed to take her back to the house to rest. On the way home, he picked up Chinese food for dinner so they could have something to eat. Brexley loved the idea and was grateful for his thoughtfulness.

Sitting on the couch, eating the food directly from the carton with chopsticks, the two observed each other. It had been a long time since they both felt so comfortable. Brexley sat with her legs crossed, barefoot, eating. Carlton sat beside her, eating Chicken Lo-mein, enjoying the meal and company. Brexley cracked open a fortune cookie and laughed.

"What's so funny?" Carlton asked.

"My fortune says, '*After the disaster, you will find your rainbow!*' She shook her head, finding it quite humorous, given the current situation.

"Well, let's hope that is true. If so, your good fortune is just around the corner," Carlton announced. He shrugged his shoulders, glad to see Brexley acted amused at the fortune. Everything had been so awful for her lately. He wondered how much longer she could survive it all. She deserved some good news for once.

Unexpectedly, Carlton's phone rang. He looked at the screen, recognizing Shawn's number. Immediately, Carlton placed the carton of Chinese food on the table and sat back, answering the phone. He intently listened to Shawn. Brexley put her food down, wondering who Carlton was talking to on the phone.

"Yes, I understand. Thank you for the update. I will let Brexley know. No problem. Okay." Carlton hung up the phone and grabbed his glass of red wine. He chugged the glass of the Pinot Noir and placed the empty glass next to him on the side table.

"Well, here is the update. That was Shawn on the phone. He wants you to know that Brian will continue to conduct a thorough investigation. Since Shawn has been dating Maddie, it would be unethical for him to be involved in this case. Shawn and Maddie have dated since last December. They got together after your Holiday party. They did not wish to tell anyone because you and I had been having issues. Maddie thought it would be awkward. So, they agreed to keep quiet about their relationship. Shawn felt it was best to stay impartial and turn the potential kidnapping case over to Brian. That is why he was here today without Shawn taking your statement. Anyway, Shawn wanted me to relay the information. He seems to feel guilty, though he shouldn't. Shawn is a good person."

"I knew they were seeing each other. It was no secret. It was quite obvious. They are not fooling anyone," Brexley said, giggling.

Carlton thought it was great to see her laugh. She looked happy. "So, now what? Do they have any leads? What are we supposed to do? Has anyone been to Maddie's house to feed Willa? She must be starving?"

"Who is Willa?" asked Carlton, worried.

"Her cat. Please call Shawn and ask him to feed Willa. If not, we must feed her. If anything happens to Willa, Maddie will kill us. That is her baby."

Carlton agreed to call Shawn and relay the message. After a few minutes, Carlton threw the empty food cartons in the garbage. He returned to the living room. Brexley was passed out on the couch, curled up with her arm dangling down the side. He walked to the couch, placed her arm gently next to her body, and took a blanket off the black leather chair, covering her up. She looked peaceful, and he did not want to disturb her.

After he ensured she was okay, he walked to his office to log onto his computer to research SUV's for Brexley. He was not tired and figured he could use the distraction.

Back at the warehouse, George checked on Brexley's office before leaving for the day. He stood in front of the door. Believing he heard someone inside, he became curious. Not thinking, George opened the door. The startled, masked intruder shot George in the chest multiple times before running out of the building with files in hand.

The security guard, Dereck, heard the shots and ran toward the office. George bled profusely, sprawled out on the floor, his eyes rolled in the back of his head. Dereck called 911, dropping to the ground to check on George. He instantly realized it was too late—George was already dead. Dereck shook his head. He knew it was imperative to call Carlton right away. He would want to know what happened. He dialed Carlton's number apprehensively, worried about how he would take the horrific news.

The phone rang at 8:13 p.m. Carlton did not recognize the number and almost didn't answer it. He picked up the phone. "Hello?" he asked.

"Hi Carlton, I mean Mr. Chastain. It is Dereck, head of security at the warehouse. I wanted you to know I called 911. George has been shot. I am so sorry to inform you...he is dead."

"What? What the hell happened? Why did you not prevent this tragic event? I paid you to protect the workers at the warehouse." Carlton screamed, enraged.

"Sir, I made my rounds earlier, twenty minutes before. Ms. Sinclaire's office was locked. I ran toward the office as quickly as possible when I heard the shots. Once I arrived, I found the door wide open and George on the floor, dead, shot in the chest. There was nothing anyone could have done. Believe me. I have to hang up. The police are here. I will call you back," Dereck ended the call, leaving Carlton confused and angry. Carlton felt reluctant to share the news with Brexley.

Brexley woke up when she heard Carlton's loud voice. She quietly stood outside the office, eavesdropping. When Carlton shouted into the phone, she became alarmed and entered his office. "What happened?" She asked, concerned. In a way, she did not want to know. In her gut, she knew it was more bad news. By the look on Carlton's face, it was something disastrous!

"Brexley, I am not going to sugarcoat the situation. George has been shot and killed in your office! I do not have all the details. I am waiting to hear more." Carlton felt sick. He disliked having to inform her of such horrible news.

"Brexley, we should shut down the staging business for the holiday season early. With everything going on and now George's murder, it is the right thing to do for the other workers."

Brexley dropped to the ground, crying. "Not George," she screamed. Her head pounded, and she felt ill. She could not understand how someone else she cared about became a victim. She wondered when this madness would stop. However, Brexley knew Carlton was right. The business could not remain open. She refused to risk someone else getting hurt.

Bravely, she spoke up, "Will you make the calls for me? I can't right now. Tell the crew they will get paid from now until January 2nd of next year. I will give each of them a $2000 bonus. I want them to come back after the new year. I know they are scared. That is the only option I have to make it up to them. I can never replace George. I will have to live with his tragic murder for the rest of my life, knowing he died because of me."

It killed Carlton to see what was happening to her. He knelt next to her, holding her tightly. Instinctively, he began rocking her gently, allowing her to cry and vent. After a few minutes, she gazed at Carlton, her face soaking wet. He wiped away the tears, gently kissing her lips. She tried smiling, looking awkward, her eyes red and swollen.

"Brexley, let's go to bed. We will hear from law enforcement later, I am sure. For now, there is nothing we can do. You look bushed. Take a tranquilizer and try to get some sleep. I will stay with you. I promise I won't leave."

She nodded, and the two headed to his room. She quickly removed most of the clothes, only leaving on her bra and panties. Carlton left her alone briefly, walking to her room to retrieve the tranquilizers given to her by the doctor. Returning swiftly, he handed Brexley one of the pills with a glass of water. She took it and closed her eyes, praying for sleep. She wanted to forget about the day and the miserable news.

Carlton undressed and slid into bed. Brexley cuddled up next to him, wrapping her arm around his stomach. She rested her head on his chest. She fell asleep quickly, feeling secure. Carlton stared up at the ceiling, his arm protectively wrapped around her.

It was dark outside, and he wanted to go downstairs to secure the house and turn on the alarm, but he did not want to wake her. He felt warm and happy, drifting off to sleep, never hearing the back door opening downstairs.

At *Sinclaire Premier Staging*, Brian peered down at George's body. After being shot, George fell backward, landing awkwardly on the concrete flooring. His head tilted to the right side.

George's chest was covered in blood, running down the side of his body, pooling all around him. The forensic crime team—the Homicide Unit, was already there, taking pictures and securing the scene. Shawn arrived at the warehouse within a few minutes, hearing the call on the radio. He shook his head. He knew this would affect Brexley. George was like a brother to her. The two had been extremely close. Shawn could not imagine what she was going through right now. He recalled the story Brexley told him one night they were out bowling. She met George through a family friend. George was looking for work and had heard Brexley needed someone to run the warehouse.

Having worked as a foreman at a warehouse in Austin for many years, George was ready to try something new. He was tired of living in Austin and wanted to change his life. He applied at *Sinclaire Premier Staging*.

During the interview, he felt at home. Brexley was a kind and funny person. George liked her right away. The two clicked. Brexley hired him on the spot, never regretting the decision. The two became very close. Yes, George was like a big brother to Brexley, and she loved him dearly. His death would leave a giant void she could never fill.

Dereck stood outside Brexley's office while Brian took his statement. Two other workers had been in the building at the time of George's death. They, too, were interviewed and ordered to go home.

"Brian, what do you think?" Shawn asked.

"Looking at the body, George must have opened the door and surprised the perpetrator. The perp probably panicked and shot George. It's weird he would shoot him more than once, though! The bloody footprints over there are very small and narrow." He pointed to the bloody, smeared footprints leading down the hallway toward the exit. "I have to assume the perp briefly returned for some reason. How else would the perp have left a trail of bloody footprints? Also, how much time passed from when George was shot to when Dereck, the security guard, arrived? I will also need to speak with Brexley right away. Can you call Carlton and arrange it?" Brian demanded, taking notes on his phone.

"It is getting late. They are probably in bed. Can it wait?" pleaded Shawn, unhappy at the idea of giving more bad news to Brexley, especially at this hour of the day.

"No, it cannot. Do you want me to call? I know you are friends with them. I don't mind calling if it is uncomfortable for you," offered Brian, remaining firm. He could see Shawn's reluctance.

"No, I'll do it." Shawn dialed Carlton's cell phone, hoping he was still awake.

"Hello?" answered Carlton, sounding groggy.

"Hi, Carlton. It is Shawn. Brian and I need to come over and interview Brexley. Is she awake?"

"No, she isn't. Can you wait to speak with her in the morning?" asked Carlton, annoyed. He was reluctant to try and wake Brexley. She was finally asleep, resting.

"Brian insists on speaking with her tonight. Murder is considered an urgent matter. You get it, right?" Shawn sounded firm.

"Of course. I will attempt to rouse Brexley

out of her deep sleep. Give us thirty minutes, please. She took a pain pill and is out of it," responded Carlton, trying to wake Brexley.

"See you in thirty minutes," Shawn replied, hanging up the phone.

Brexley snored, deeply asleep, making odd muffling noises. Carlton watched her, hating the fact he had to wake her. The police would arrive soon. He pulled the sheets back and nudged her, hoping she would wake up.

Trying several more times without success, he realized it would take louder noises to wake Brexley. He bent down and said, "Brexley — get up! The police are on their way. We must get you dressed and head downstairs." She did not respond. Carlton frowned. *'Why is she not waking up? She only took one tranquilizer!'* Instantly, he worried. *'Did she take more pills or drink alcohol with them?'* He chose to shake her a little, forcing her to regain consciousness. That seemed to do the trick. She opened her eyes, staring at him.

Brexley sat up, looking groggy. "What the hell? I was sleeping soundly. What do you want?" she interrogated, annoyed. She pulled the bedsheet over her head.

"Brexley — the police will arrive any minute. You must get dressed. Here, put on some clothing. Can you do it, or do you need my help? I am heading downstairs to turn on the lights and make coffee."

Reluctantly, Brexley dressed in yoga pants and a shirt. She was irritated and not in the mood to talk with anyone. Carlton headed down the stairs to wait for the police.

He thought it was odd they refused to wait until later in the morning to interview Brexley. Carlton entered the kitchen. It was cold. He looked around and saw the backdoor was not closed all the way. *'What the heck?'* He thought. He quickly walked to the door and locked it, looking through the glass into the backyard. *'Was someone in the house? Darn it. Did I forget to turn on the alarm? Oh, right, we fell asleep. Shit!'* Carlton surveyed the room, determining if anything was missing or out of place.

After a few minutes, Brexley appeared, still looking tired and out of it. She swayed back and forth, almost falling over. She managed to sit on the couch.

Feeling exhausted, she was tempted to curl up on the sofa but knew that would cause her to fall back asleep. Brexley decided to sit up, forcing herself to stay awake.

Carlton entered the living room, holding a cup of coffee. He handed it to Brexley. "Please drink it, Luv. It will help you stay alert."

Brexley held the cup with shaky hands. Her eyes were closed. She did not want to drink coffee.

"Honey, you need to stay awake. I am sorry, but you must." Carlton sat next to her, urging her to drink. He saw headlights in the driveway, assuming it was Brian and Shawn. "They are here. Let me answer the door. Please try to stay conscious," he urged, leaving her alone to open the front door.

Brexley watched him walk toward the entryway. She was tired, but the warm coffee felt great going down her sore throat. She saw the front door open, and Shawn and someone else entered. They followed Carlton into the living room.

Shawn sat down next to Brexley. He smiled but felt shitty that she had to be interviewed again, given how late it was. Protectively, Carlton sat on the other side of Brexley, placing his hand on her thigh. They waited for Brian to start the interview. Shawn stood next to the fireplace, watching the three on the sofa.

"Thank you for allowing me to come by to speak with you, Brexley. I realize it is a considerable inconvenience. Sorry, but I need information. Are you ready?" Brian asked, now the tablet in his lap, holding the stylus with his right hand.

"Sure. What else do you need from me? We already talked this morning. I have not been in the warehouse for days. Not sure what I can tell you that will help?" Brexley felt it was ridiculous she had to answer questions in the middle of the night.

"We need to know where you were tonight

between 8 and 9 p.m.?" Brian asked, looking directly at Brexley. She looked tired, her eyes fluttering, and she nodded off here and there.

"I was here, with Carlton, sleeping. I took a pain pill, and I am tired as hell. So, what else do you need, Brian?" she replied, feeling frustrated.

"Carlton, can you corroborate her timeline? Was she here with you between 8 and 9 p.m.?"

"What is going on, Brian? You don't seriously believe Brexley had anything to do with George's death, do you? For crap's sake! She was in bed upstairs with me. You know this because you called, waking us!" yelled Carlton, tired of his line of questioning. "Should I call Dennis McGarther, our attorney?"

"Calm down, Carlton. These are standard questions. Brexley, do you know why someone would want to break into your office?"

"Someone broke into my office?" Brexley asked, perplexed.

"Yes, we believe someone broke into your office. George probably heard something and entered the office to investigate. He may have startled the intruder, getting shot. What is inside your office that someone would want to steal? Anything valuable?"

"Anything of value is in the wall safe. You know that. Was it opened?" Brexley responded.

"We did not see a wall safe. Is it hidden?" asked Shawn, listening to the conversation.

Brian became curious about the wall safe. The only thing noticeable in her office was the messy filing cabinet. Also, files were strewn all over.

Carlton explained the wall safe's location behind the large modern blue, white, and grey painting behind the glass desk. Only three people had the combination and access to the wall safe—Carlton, Maddie, and Brexley.

Brian nodded, saving the information on the tablet. "Could one of you check on the wall safe to find out if anything is missing? I need to know," Brian added.

"So, we only noticed the mess of files on the floor. I am not sure if anything is missing. You will be able to return to the office later. I can meet you there. You cannot enter the building by yourself. It is still a crime scene. I have one more question for you, Brexley. Do you know of anyone that would want to harm you? Is there something you are not disclosing?" Brian squinted his eyes, looking directly at Brexley.

"There is the matter of the continued threats and notes. But I thought you already knew all about them?" Brexley declared.

"Yes, Carlton told me. There is nothing else? Do you have any idea why someone would kidnap Maddie?" Brian continued to stare at Brexley, making her uncomfortable.

"NO! Why would I? I have no idea why any of this is happening. Do you think I like this?

My house is destroyed. I have lost my car, my friend is missing, and now…another dear friend has been murdered." Brexley cried, covering her face with her hands. Carlton stood up.

"Gentlemen, I think that is enough. If you need anything else, please call me. Ms. Sinclaire needs to rest. It has been a tragic time, and she is beyond exhausted. I hope you understand. Please, let me show you out," Carlton stood up, directing them toward the door.

Brian turned around and saw Brexley still crying on the couch. He felt horrible. It was not his intention to make her feel worse. He realized she was probably innocent, but he had to interrogate her. The murder was committed in her office at the warehouse she owned.

Brian was thorough and wanted to ensure his file was complete. He graciously allowed Shawn to accompany him to speak with Brexley because they were friends. He could have forced Brexley to appear at the police station, but because he respected Brexley, he conducted his interview with her at Carlton's home, keeping it semi-casual.

Shawn and Brian left quickly, leaving Carlton and Brexley alone. She stood up, now looking angry. She walked toward Carlton and yelled, "When is this shit going to stop? This situation is out of control. I need to move out of your home. My presence is putting your life in danger as well. I cannot and will not be responsible for anything happening to you. I plan to call Michelle tomorrow and look at the houses again. My staying here is too much of a risk. I hope you agree." Brexley turned and walked up the stairs to compose an email to Michelle, her realtor.

Brexley was frightened to live on her own right now, but putting Carlton's life in jeopardy was even worse. She would rather be dead than have something happen to him.

Carlton knew there was no arguing with Brexley. Once her mind was made up, she usually followed through. Feeling powerless, Carlton remained on the recliner, wondering what he could say or do to keep Brexley from moving out. He worried for her safety. She would not be okay living alone with a murderer on the loose.

Brexley decided to email Michelle once she woke up. She was too tired and irritated to compose an email at the moment. Her head pounded, and she required sleep. Weary, she crawled into bed, praying for rest.

Carlton sat in his office, composing an email to the employees working for Brexley. He wanted them to stay away from the warehouse until the following year — January 2nd. Carlton informed them of the generous bonus of $2000 per employee that Brexley would distribute in the next few days and pay them until January 2nd their full salary. It was a small token of appreciation for all they had endured.

Carlton closed his laptop, interlaced his fingers, and placed them behind his head, leaning back in his leather chair. He looked outside, noticing the sun coming up. *'How did the morning arrive so quickly?'* He questioned. For some reason, he thought it was only 4 or 5 a.m. *'Well, I should get some sleep. Brexley is probably deep asleep.'*

Tired, he dragged himself up the stairs to his bedroom, eager to snuggle with Brexley. Entering the room, he noticed the empty bed and realized she had chosen to sleep in the guest room. His heart sank. *'Why would she do that? I cannot worry about that now,'* he said to himself. Carlton jumped into bed, quickly closing his eyes.

Dereck approached the warehouse wearing a black tracksuit. The black ski mask was pulled over his head to hide his face. He snuck around the backside of the large building to enter through the double metal doors, hoping the surveillance camera was still disabled. Once inside the building, he headed to Brexley's office to find the missing file. There was no way he would leave without it.

CHAPTER 6

Maddie was starving. She could hear her stomach rumbling, making her feel queasy. Her head hurt, too. She was dehydrated and hungry. The woman had promised her freedom. When would she be set free? *'Is the woman coming back today?'* Maddie was annoyed, thinking about how much she missed her warm, comfortable bed. She saw sunlight coming through the small window above her head. She squinted her eyes, the sunlight making her head ache more. *'What time is it?'* She wondered. *'How long have I been here?'*

Outside the stock room, the mysterious woman held a plate with food. She had made food she hoped Maddie would eat, though she had no clue what Maddie liked. The woman tucked a water bottle tightly under her arm. She hoped to release Maddie today, but first, she needed to ensure the items she wanted were found at the warehouse. She refused to release Maddie until she had what she wanted.

Maddie fidgeted with the thin, grey, raggedy foul-smelling blanket. However, she was freezing, and the nasty blanket was better than nothing. She pulled it up to her neck, attempting to stay warm. The cold air blasted down on her, causing her to shiver. The room was like an icebox. "Damn air conditioner," she cursed, rolling her eyes with displeasure.

Suddenly, Maddie heard something outside the door. It sounded like someone was approaching. She listened as the voices became louder, recognizing one of the voices as that of the woman. Maddie dropped the blanket and sat upright, waiting for the door to open. She hoped for food. Maddie was starving and willing to eat just about anything.

In the police station office downtown, Brian sat behind the work computer, completing his report. Shawn sat across from him, also on a computer. Neither spoke, busy typing. The only noise in the small room was the buzzing sound from the broken fluorescent light overhead. It flicked on and off every few minutes, driving Shawn crazy. Annoyed, he briefly looked at the ceiling light, shaking his head. He continued entering information into the computer program, hoping to finish his report before leaving the office. His mind was on Maddie. As if Brian had read his mind, he spoke up.

"You know, we will find her," Brian announced as he forced a smile on his face. He hoped to make Shawn feel better. It did not seem to work. Shawn frowned, chewing on his bottom lip, drawing blood. Tasting the blood, he wiped it away swiftly with his right hand. He felt sick to his stomach. The idea of never seeing Maddie again evoked strong emotions. He longed to hold her. Shawn stood up and looked at Brian, informing him he was heading home. Shawn wanted to regroup and read his notes to determine what to do next.

Brian stood up and left the office to find SGT. Kevin Hunter of the Homicide Unit to discuss the murder of George Hernández. Though the case appeared clear—he was an unfortunate victim of a burglary interrupted. However, Brian wondered what had been taken. He planned to meet Brexley in the afternoon so she could look through her office to potentially identify missing items. Brian suspected she knew more than she was willing to divulge. If she continued to play games with him, withholding information, he would become forceful, suggesting she retain an attorney. He would not allow her to suppress information, thus impeding his investigation.

One way or the other, she would tell the truth. He hated to think she was lying, but it was the only plausible explanation. Brian could also not allow his friendship with Shawn to get in the way of this investigation. Dragging himself down the hallway, Brian wondered why Brexley had received the threatening notes in the first place. *' Maybe she is embarrassed by the reason behind the threats? Perhaps it involves some shady business dealings.'* He honestly had no clue and very little to go on. He was determined to unravel the truth and expose Mr. Hernández's murderer.

The woman wearing the cat mask entered the room with food, wipes, and a water bottle. Maddie glared at her angrily, wishing to shower. She took a water bottle from the woman's left hand, noticing her gold ring. It was etched with floral designs. *'Very interesting,'* she thought to herself. *'A clue.'* Something she could relay to law enforcement later.

"Here, take the wipes. I should know later today if I can release you. I promise I am trying to get you out of here. I never meant for you to be here. It should have been Brexley Sinclaire! How can you work for her? She is such a witch!" stated the woman.

"First off, Ms. Sinclaire, Brexley, is not a witch. She is the most altruistic person I know. She is kind and ethical. I am not sure what your beef is with her, but get over it. You will not get away with whatever you are trying to do. As I said before, you will be caught. Count on it!"

Maddie removed all her clothing without care. She cleaned her body with the wipes and dressed in laundered clothes. The woman did not leave. Instead, she creepily watched her.

"Did you enjoy watching me get naked or what?" added Maddie, feeling self-conscious.

"No. I am shocked you have no issue getting naked before a stranger. I suppose you are like Brexley. A slut."

"A slut? Ouch...what is your problem? I am not a slut, and neither is Brexley."

"Sure...you keep telling yourself that, sweetie," the woman insisted, leaving the room.

Maddie watched her and wondered why she was so rude. *'Why does she hate Brexley so much? Is she one of her competitors? Did Brexley hurt her somehow?'*

The woman's words were chosen wisely, aimed at making a point. Cat-Face held a grudge against Brexley. Maddie questioned what that could be. The woman locked the door and headed to her office. She heard the van pull up, assuming it was Dereck, feeling optimistic he was able to retrieve the files. Her careless brother grabbed the wrong ones. He shot an innocent man in his haste and recklessness. According to the news, he died.

It was never her intention to get anyone killed. All she wanted was what belonged to her. Brexley took so much from her. Ms. Sinclaire would pay!

SGT Kevin Hunter reviewed the crime scene's digital photographs in an office on the second floor of the police station. Intrigued, he paid closer attention to the last few pictures of the bloody shoe prints. Reading the measurements next to the prints, Kevin agreed with Shawn's earlier assessment of the imprint size. It wasn't a large shoe. It was a smaller size, 7 or 8. It was also a very narrow shoe print with a zigzag sole pattern. He planned on running the shoe print's sole pattern through a database, hoping to find the shoe's brand name—perhaps providing him with a way to connect the shoe to its owner.

Brian knocked on the glass door. Kevin looked up from the desk and saw Brian. He stood up, walking toward the door.

"Hey, Brian! Come in. Are you here to see SGT Green or me?"

"No, I am here for you. I wanted to follow up on the investigation of the murder at

Sinclaire Premier Staging. I was wondering if you had any new leads?" asked Brian, looking serious.

Kevin led Brian to the back of the room and offered him a chair. The two talked for several minutes. "You know, I am still curious why someone was rummaging through the office in the first place. I concur. The victim was an innocent bystander in the scenario. Have you been able to lift any fingerprints? Did anything unusual come up? I plan to meet Ms. Sinclaire in a few hours at the warehouse. I hope she can shed some light on what may be missing, if anything." Brian explained.

"I am happy to hear that. We need more answers and fewer questions. Ms. Brexley Sinclaire does not seem to know very much, which seems odd, considering she is the warehouse owner. How well do you know her? Do you believe she is hiding something or protecting someone?" Kevin asked bluntly.

"It had occurred to me. I am just not sure. She seems forthright. I have not caught her in a lie, so I must assume, for now, that she is telling the truth. Her boyfriend, Carlton Chastain, is very protective. He never allows her to be alone. So, it isn't easy to get a good read of her. He spoke for her, and I had to ask him to leave the room before, which he refused. If we do not get any answers today, I will insist she appear at the station for a formal, in-depth statement.

She may not like it, but oh well."

Kevin agreed with Brian. It was best to wait and see what they would discover at the warehouse with Ms. Sinclaire present. Brian knew what he was doing and handled the investigation according to protocol. Kevin would do his part. Together, they would solve the crime. Kevin was stunned to hear someone had also been kidnapped, though they did not know for sure as no one had called Ms. Sinclaire asking for a ransom. Maybe the woman, Maddie, was missing but not kidnapped? The video surveillance tape did not show the woman's abduction. The tape was partially erased. Yes, that seemed very suspicious, but it did not prove a kidnapping. Kevin reminded Brian not to jump to conclusions regarding the woman's absence.

"The thing to remember, Kevin," Brian began, "there is the matter of Maddie's slashed tire. That alone is very suspicious."

"True! I did forget that part. Why has no one called for a ransom? Why else kidnap someone unless you want something in return? That makes no sense. We both know that to be true. So, why would someone want to kidnap Maddie? Did Maddie do something, or is it revenge aimed at Brexley Sinclaire? We should assume it involves Ms. Sinclaire and not Maddie since Brexley received threatening notes." The two men contemplated a variety of scenarios.

After another hour of talking, Brian thanked Kevin for his time, deciding to head to his office to call Carlton. He was eager to find out when Brexley would be at the warehouse. He wanted to get the meeting over with and determine if other suspects could be tied to the kidnapping, murder, and mysterious notes.

Brian managed to contact Carlton. They agreed to meet at 2 p.m. at the warehouse. Supposedly, Brexley had a follow-up doctor's appointment for injuries sustained during the house fire, and they would be in the area to meet Brian afterward.

Brexley was happy to hear her wounds were healing properly. The doctor was pleased with the minimal scarring. He informed her to return for a final follow-up with him in six weeks to ensure everything was healed. Brexley told the doctor she still had pain and wondered if it was okay to continue taking her pain medication. He felt it was fine, given that her burns extended from her hand to arm, with some slight burns on her cheeks and forehead.

Fortunately, the facial burns were minimal and were not even noticeable anymore. Initially, Brexley's face looked red and flushed, but there was zero blistering. Brexley had been extremely lucky.

After the appointment, Brexley and Carlton drove to the warehouse to meet with Brian. Though Carlton was getting sick of all the questions, he realized it was best to cooperate with law enforcement. He briefly spoke with his attorney, Dennis McGarther, asking for guidance.

Carlton worried the interrogations would drag on for a while, and he refused to allow Brexley to be subjected to constant calls, emails, and visits from the investigators.

Mr. McGarther reassured Carlton the inquisitions would stop in time. Since they were investigating a possible kidnapping and a murder, law enforcement had the right to ask as many questions as necessary. Mr. McGarther also suggested that Carlton and Brexley act cordially. Anything less could be considered uncooperative, leading to trouble for Brexley. So, Mr. McGarther firmly emphasized cooperation and open communication to show goodwill toward the investigation. Carlton was grateful for his insight and happy he had called him for advice.

Arriving at the warehouse, Brexley and Carlton waited in the vehicle for Brian. He pulled into the parking spot next to them within a few minutes. He escorted them to the building, where a police officer stood, guarding the structure with his partner. They allowed the three to enter the warehouse.

Once in Brexley's office, she faced the mess before her. She grimaced, horrified at the scene. The office looked nothing like before. The bloodstains remained on the concrete floor, making her nauseous, though now, they had turned a dark brown color. Carlton noticed she flinched when she walked toward her chair, walking around the crime scene area to get to the desk. He also saw her hands shaking.

Carlton wondered why the bloodstains had not been cleaned up. He assumed there was some kind of crime scene clean-up crew to complete that task. He planned to ask Brian about it later. Carlton did not want Brexley's office to look like this for much longer. It was an awful and disgusting sight.

"Ms. Sinclaire, please take your time. If you notice anything missing, please let me know. Also, could one of you please open the wall safe? I want to ensure that it is secure," requested Brian.

Carlton removed the artwork from the wall behind the desk and exposed the wall safe, leaning the large art piece against the wall. He punched in the code and swiped his finger over the small, round surface, opening it. Once the door popped open, he stepped back, allowing Brexley to look inside.

Brexley pulled out several files and a box. She opened the box, rifling through it. "Everything seems to be here. I do not see anything missing," Brexley announced, placing the items back into the wall safe. Brian took photographs of the wall safe and allowed her to close and secure it.

Brexley returned to her desk, pulling open the drawer. She opened the bottom tray, which required a key to unlock. She slid the key from her keychain into the box, unlocking it. Brexley lifted several file folders out of the box. She placed them on the desk, opening the top file. She glanced down, ensuring the documents were still in the file. After she felt satisfied knowing everything was there, she replaced the items and locked the box.

"Ms. Sinclaire, I am curious…why do you have so many places with lockboxes? I thought you were a design business. That seems excessive, given the type of business you run. Can you explain what you have secured in these boxes?" Brian asked, feeling suspicious.

"Brian, every business has legal documents. I also keep my employee files here. The documents in the wall safe are mostly personal, with a few legal documents pertaining to my business, such as the LLC paperwork and more. As far as the lockbox in the desk, it contains our banking files and checkbooks. So, you see, we are ensuring the safety and security of our business, nothing more or less."

Brexley felt offended that Brian thought she was doing something illegal or unethical, which was not the case, far from it. Brexley was a savvy businessperson. She knew it was imperative to secure all legal documents.

Now, more than ever, she was happy she insisted on installing a wall safe, though initially, she had a safety deposit box at a local bank. It felt wrong to have her legal documents so far away. Thus, in time, she hired a contractor to install a wall safe.

Brian contemplated her response and chose to nod without a verbal response. He observed Brexley and Carlton as they continued to take inventory of items. After a while, Brian asked if they were ready to leave. The three headed back to the parking lot to discuss the next step in the investigation.

Carlton stood next to his vehicle, listening to Brian. Brexley acted uninterested and distracted. He wondered what she was thinking. She stared at the warehouse, tilting her head awkwardly to the left. Carlton stood next to her. Brian finished speaking and left Carlton and Brexley in the parking lot.

"Come on, Luv. We should get out of here. The warehouse will be okay. I hired a new security firm. They have our contact information if they need to reach us. Shall we pick up some food on the way home?" Carlton observed Brexley as they finally sat in the car.

Brexley played with a strand of her hair, staring at the warehouse ahead. After a few minutes, Carlton realized she was not paying attention or listening to him.

"Brexley, did you hear me?" he asked.

Brexley continued to gaze ahead in silence. Irritated, he grabbed Brexley's arm, pulling her toward him. She snapped out of it and looked at him, a tear running down her face.

"Are you okay?" Carlton noticed she looked distraught.

"No, I am not. I was thinking about George. I was also wondering about Maddie's whereabouts and praying she was okay. I have not heard from Devvyn, though I have left her several messages. I suppose I feel like everything is swirling out of control, and I cannot stop it. Having to close the warehouse until after the new year is not something I wish to do. I will lose clients. Yes, I understand it is necessary, but I am stressed out!" She ripped her arm away from Carlton and turned her body, peering out the passenger window.

Carlton turned on the car and headed back toward town. He craved pizza and was determined to pick one up on the way home for dinner. Carlton assumed Brexley did not want to cook, and neither did he. He thought that Brexley might be in a better mood once she ate.

Brexley remained silent, playing with her hair and staring out the window. It started raining again. She sighed, closing her eyes as Carlton drove toward the pizza restaurant.

Frustrated as hell, Maddie stomped her foot. She was tired and cold. Her patience was non-existent. She wanted to escape the frigid building. The mysterious woman had not returned, and neither did the rude man. Maddie wondered what was happening on the outside. No rescue team had arrived, leaving her to wonder if she would ever be released. Maddie wanted to cry. *'How did I get into this mess?'* She pondered.

Undoubtedly, it had something to do with the scary notes sent to Brexley. Her kidnapping was not a coincidence. *'How will they return me?'* The thought scared Maddie. She did not want to see them. Seeing them meant she was a witness, and everyone knew what happens to witnesses—they were silenced! Maddie could hear her blood pressure in her ears thumping loudly.

Horrified, she shook in the chair, wishing for a warm and comfortable bed. She began thinking about Willa. *'Is someone feeding her?'* If anything happened to Willa, she would be devastated!

At the same time, Shawn entered Maddie's apartment, and Willa, the hungry cat, greeted him. The black cat with vibrant yellow eyes wrapped herself around his legs, purring. Shawn bent down, petting her, gently moving her aside so he could walk to the kitchen to feed her.

"Willa, let me get to the kitchen, silly," he said, getting frustrated. The cat would not let him move. "Come on, girl. I know you are hungry." Irritated, he pushed her away, rushing to the pantry to retrieve the cat's food. Willa jumped up on the counter to watch Shawn intently while he mixed canned food with dry food, swiftly placing it on the floor for Willa. He bent down to pick up the pink water bowl to fill it with cold, fresh water.

After ensuring Willa had been fed and given fresh water, he hurried to the laundry room to clean the cat box. Once he completed the disgusting task, he decided to head out for the day, briefly stopping by the front door.

Maddie's favorite white sweater, embroidered with small bees, hung on a hook. Shawn walked to it and pulled it off the hanger. He gently brought the garment up to his nose, inhaling the scent of the sweater. It smelled like Maddie. The floral perfume scent on the article made him smile, but he also missed her terribly. He felt tears running down his face. Feeling overwhelmingly sad, he reached the chair near the door and sank into it. He cried, holding her sweater, missing Maddie more than he ever imagined.

As if Willa knew Shawn was miserable, she jumped up on the chair's armrest, meowing at him. He dropped the sweater, letting it fall into his lap. Smiling at the cat, he petted her, listening to the loud purr. Willa kneaded her paws on the sweater, finally curling up on his lap and falling asleep.

Shawn closed his eyes, letting Willa sleep while he thought about Maddie. His heart ached, and he missed her dearly.

Carlton handed Brexley a plate with two slices of pizza. She took it and balanced it on her lap. He placed his plate on the table and took off to the kitchen to retrieve drinks. Carlton needed a drink and poured himself a glass of Pinot Noir. He took a bottle of sparkling water for Brexley. She was still taking painkillers, and he did not want her to drink alcohol, though she begged him twice for a glass of Chardonnay.

"I don't want water, Carlton. I need something stronger. How about I agree not to take painkillers, and you give me a glass of wine?" Brexley negotiated.

Reluctantly, Carlton agreed, returning to the kitchen to pour Brexley a glass of wine. He did not want her to drink and take drugs, even prescription drugs. He knew it could lead to a potentially life-threatening situation. So, he decided to watch Brexley, ensuring she did not surrender to the temptation and take the pills for the pain.

After eating the pizza and drinking her glass of Chardonnay, Brexley excused herself, stating she wanted to take a shower. Carlton followed her, hoping she was okay. Brexley took off her clothes and stumbled toward the bathroom. Carlton watched her.

Once she was inside the bathroom, and he heard the water running, he grabbed the pain medication bottle and took it to his room.

Brexley was not okay. George's death pushed her over the edge. Earlier, Carlton overheard Brexley's conversation with Marlah, George's wife. Brexley had been crying, talking to her on speakerphone.

Carlton listened as Brexley promised Marlah she would pay for the funeral. It was the least she felt she could do. She also offered to help Marlah with money for the next two months to help her recover after losing her husband. Marlah refused her help, asking her to stay away. Those words destroyed Brexley. Clearly, Marlah blamed Brexley for her husband's murder.

Carlton returned to the guest room and saw Brexley in bed. He assumed she was naked, noticing the pajamas draped across the bottom of the bed. Carlton sat down next to her. She looked drunk. Brexley scooted down deep into the bed, pulling the sheet up to her neck. He watched her, wondering if she was going to say anything. She finally spoke, sounding groggy.

"I have to confess… I took a pain pill before we ate dinner. I don't feel so good. I think the alcohol made it worse," she slurred her words.

"What the hell, Brexley? Are you trying to kill yourself? Dying will NOT bring George back to life. It will also not miraculously bring

Maddie home. You know that. Let's take you to the hospital, just to ensure you are okay," Carlton insisted.

"NO. I am not going anywhere. I am okay. I will sleep it off. If you are worried, call my father. He will tell you I am okay. After all, he is a doctor. Now, leave. I want to sleep alone!" She rolled onto her right side, ignoring him.

Reluctantly, he left the room, turning off the light and closing the door. He knew there was no reason to argue with Brexley. He planned to check on her later to ensure she was alive.

Carlton headed to his office, planning to call Dr. Harrison Sinclaire to fill him in on the multiple situations in Brexley's life. He also planned to seek guidance from Harrison on how to proceed with his relationship with Brexley. Carlton had a solid relationship with Harrison. The two golfed and had dinner a few times a year. Harrison recently divorced his wife of 35 years after discovering she had an affair with a much younger man. Brexley was still furious with her mother, refusing to see her even though it had been over a year since her parent's turbulent divorce.

Harrison answered the phone right away, happy to hear Carlton's voice. Carlton spoke with him for almost an hour. Dr. Harrison Sinclaire was easy to talk to, always giving sound advice, and a great listener. Harrison was furious with Carlton for not calling sooner and informing him of the tragic events. He was devastated to hear about George's death, Maddie's missing status, and Brexley's home loss. He offered to help, but Carlton reassured him he had it handled. Carlton promised Harrison an update as soon as he knew more.

After their conversation, Carlton climbed the stairs to the second floor to check on Brexley. Quietly entering her room, he walked toward the bed. Carlton could hear her making a slight sound. Feeling reassured she was alive and breathing, he returned to his room. It was now dark outside, and he felt worn out. He took off his clothes, letting them drop onto the floor, too lazy to put them in the laundry basket. Fatigued, he crawled into bed, not caring about a thing.

CHAPTER 7

Maddie stared at her dinner in disgust. She hated fish more than anything. The smell alone made her want to vomit. The vegetables were overcooked and mushy. *'Why would anyone cook carrots for so long?'* Maddie wondered. She played with her food, finally putting the plate on the floor. The woman with the cat mask watched her the entire time.

"Are you done eating? Why are you not hungry? Come on. You need to eat something!"

"Listen, Kitty. Why don't you eat the fish? You probably would like that, right?" Maddie replied sarcastically, trying to hide her smirk.

"Very funny. You should be a stand-up comedian. But hey, if you don't want to eat, no skin off my back. I really don't care. Here, have another bottle of water." Cat-face handed her another bottle. She stood in front of her, hands on her hips.

Maddie looked up at her, trying to take in all the clues. The woman wore flats that were scuffed but expensive designer shoes. She recognized the brand.

Cat-Face wore a knee-length skirt, exposing her firm and athletic legs, which were tan. Her hands were long and thin.

The floral ring from before was still on her hand. Maddie noticed a tiny tattoo on the inside of her wrist she had not seen before. It was a dragonfly tattoo. The Cat-Faced woman stared at her, wondering why she was not speaking. Frustrated, she leaned against the wall, watching Maddie.

"Are you ready to get out of here?" Cat-Face asked her.

"Duh, of course. I have been quite ready. When will that happen? Do I get to head home today or tomorrow?" Maddie asked, feeling hopeful.

"In the morning. I have made all of the arrangements. We will drop you off in town. You will not be harmed. As I said before, you were never supposed to be here. I am very sorry about that." Cat-Face approached.

"I understand. I want to get home, shower, and forget this ever happened," replied Maddie, hoping they would release her.

Cat-Face flinched. Maddie heard the noise, too. There was someone else in the building making a noise. Cat-Face turned around and left the room, securing the door on the way out. Maddie sat alone in the cold room. *Are they going to let me go so easily?* She wondered. She shivered, missing Shawn and Willa.

Cat-Face removed her mask on the other side of the door and held it in her left hand, walking toward the office. She figured it was either her idiot brother or Dereck, her brother's boyfriend. Either way, she wanted them out of the building. They were screwing up, and she did not need the complications.

She noticed the office door stood ajar. Dereck leaned against Ashton, her brother. They discussed something in a whisper. The second Ashton saw her, he rolled his eyes.

"What are you two doing here? I told you not to return until the morning. I fed her, and she remains locked up. While you are here, we might as well discuss how you plan to return her tomorrow."

"Return her? Why the hell would we do that? I thought you wanted to keep her locked up until you received everything you wanted. Did you look through the box of things I left over there?" Ashton pointed to a plastic crate filled with files and envelopes.

"No, not yet. I am not worried about that right now. I want Maddie out of the building. I do not want to be attached to the kidnapping! I told you — get her out of here in the morning. Blindfold her and drop her off near the warehouse where you took her. I do not need this kind of trouble. This has gone too far. Ashton, I cannot believe you shot a man. Holy hell!" she yelled, infuriated.

After talking for a while, the two men left, promising to return early in the morning while still dark to remove Maddie from the building. In the meantime, Cat-Face made her way to the fluffy and comfortable couch in her office. She covered up with a blue and white striped comforter, happy the day was almost over.

On the other side of the building, Maddie inspected the metal cot the man had brought into the barren room. The new blanket was warmer than the one she had before. Now, she even had two pillows. It was a vast improvement over what she had been dealing with for the last few days. She finally sat on the cot, looking out the small window near the ceiling, noticing the full moon and clear sky.

Maddie reminisced about Willa and wished her cat was curled up next to her. She felt utterly alone and afraid.

As dark clouds covered the moon hours later, Shawn woke up having horrible nightmares in the middle of the night. He dreamt about finding Maddie dead, her corpse cut up and bloody. He felt the dampness of his sweat and was shaking. Shawn sat up in bed crying, freaking out at the thought something awful had happened to Maddie. Unable to return to sleep because his mind was playing out one scenario after another, none of them good, he jumped out of bed and walked to the living room.

Flopping down on the recliner, he lit a cigarette. It pissed him off, realizing how much he enjoyed smoking again. Right now, he needed to smoke. It was the only way he would make it through the day. It was either that or staying drunk. Shawn had to keep his head clear. He knew that.

Brian was still awake, reading the notes and comparing stories. It was 2 a.m. Something was not right. Either Ms. Sinclaire was a saint or super talented at hiding the truth. Brian concluded it was time to ask her to come to the police station for an official interview, a recorded and taped session. She could bring her attorney, but Mr. Chastain was not welcome. Maybe she would tell him the truth once Brian had her confined alone in an interrogation room. Brexley Sinclaire was hiding more than she was willing to divulge. His instincts told him so. He could push her to see how she acted under pressure. It would give him a better read on her.

Hours later, Maddie woke up, having to pee, realizing it was still dark outside. She wondered what time it was and if Cat-Face was still in the building. Swinging her legs off the side of the cot, she felt sore. Her back felt stiff, and her head ached.

Maddie yearned for her comfortable home, wishing to crawl into her warm, fluffy bed after a long, hot shower. After she urinated into the bucket, which was primitive, she walked back to the cot to sit down and wait for someone to appear. It did not take long.

Cat-Face emerged with two others. One individual wore a monster mask. The other entered the room wearing a horse head mask. Maddie tried desperately not to laugh. The three looked ridiculous.

"Good morning, sunshine," Cat-Face announced, handing her new, clean clothes. Maddie looked at the black T-shirt, black pants, and black socks.

"Oh boy, are we going to rob someplace this morning? I am so lucky, my very own all-black outfit." Maddie replied sarcastically. She knew Cat-Face would not appreciate her comments.

"Umm, no. Just get dressed if you want to get out of here. I am tired of your smart mouth." Cat-Face turned and walked out of the room with the other two. Maddie changed into the new outfit quickly. She was eager to leave this hell hole. Nothing in the world would make her happier. She contemplated how they planned to return her. Would they take her back to the warehouse? The sun was not up yet, so it would be easy to return her without witnesses. Most people were probably still asleep. She overheard Cat-Face telling the other two it was a little after 3 a.m.

So, the sun would not be up for hours. Maybe that was why they chose this timeframe. Maddie sat back on the cot, waiting for Cat-Face to reappear. She smiled, thinking about her imminent release!

Shawn could not fall back asleep. He was still thinking about his missing girlfriend. His nightmare and the continual intrusive thoughts made him scared for her well-being. He wanted to call Brian but figured it was too early in the morning. Finally, after an hour of sitting in his living room, chain-smoking, Shawn dressed and headed to Maddie's apartment to feed and revisit Willa. He felt the need to be near Maddie's things. It would make him feel better, or so he believed.

Brexley woke up feeling nauseous. She ran to the bathroom, throwing up. Her legs felt weak, and the world was spinning all around her. She brushed her teeth and cleaned her face with a cold, wet washcloth. She wondered if the combination of the alcohol and pain pill made her feel so dreadful.

Brexley heard rain pelting the roof and saw a few stray flashes of lightning. Feeling sickly and displeased about the weather, she contemplated sneaking into Carlton's room and snuggling up to him in bed. She craved security. Looking in the mirror, she did not like what she saw.

Her hair looked messy, and she had dark circles under her eyes. *'Maybe I should put on some makeup? No! It is too early in the morning for that,'* she thought. She picked up the hairbrush from the counter and brushed her unruly hair, deciding to go to Carlton's room. Brexley yearned to be near him. He would understand. She opened his bedroom door and heard him snoring. Quietly, she disrobed and crawled into his bed, curling up against him. She placed her head on his chest, hearing his heartbeat, which soothed her. Was it weird that it made her feel so content? Carlton moved slightly, pulling her closer to his body. Happily, he drifted back off to sleep.

The rain was relentless, pouring out of the sky. The two men looked outside. Cat-Face approached, handing them a big burlap bag.

"Here, put this over her head. Take her to the

warehouse and drop her off. Be careful! There cameras. Make sure the van does not have any plates on it. I want her out of my warehouse. NEVER bring her back here. DO YOU HEAR ME?" she screamed. "You two better get your shit together. I am tired of your screw-ups."

Cat-Face entered the storage room to speak to Maddie before her release. She also had to figure out what to do next about Brexley.

Her brother and his boyfriend had royally messed up everything. Nothing had gone as planned. They had gone rogue, doing what they wanted. It pissed her off even more. She would have to develop a new plan to get Brexley out of the way without hurting anyone else. Cat-Face never intended for anyone to get harmed, not even Brexley.

All Cat-Face wanted was for Brexley to shut down her staging business so she could take business away from her. Brexley owed her. It made her sick how Brexley continued to become more and more successful while her business slowed down. She even heard gossip that Brexley and Carlton were back together. *'Why is Brexley so damn fortunate? What makes her so freaking special?'* Cat-Face thought it was disgusting that Brexley seemed untouchable. Everything always worked out for her perfectly. Maddie sat up with her hands folded when Cat-Face entered the room, followed by Ashton and Dereck. She approached Maddie and

159

informed her it was time to leave.

"Maddie, I want you to know I am not an evil person. I realize you think I am…but I am not. I had a plan, and somehow, it all went awry. I am sorry we kept you here. I hope you will be okay."

Cat-Face walked out of the room, leaving Maddie perplexed. *'Why is she so apologetic? Why does she care what I think?'* Maddie pondered. Ashton approached.

"I gotta put this on your head. Don't be scared. We will remove it when we get to where we will drop you off." He proceeded to place the dark burlap bag over her head. "Give me your hands," he demanded. Maddie put her hands straight out in front of her. He grabbed her wrists and wrapped the rough rope around them tightly. Maddie winced in pain as the cord cut into her flesh.

"Oh, stop and relax." The two guided her down the hallway toward the van. Just as they were about to open the back door, Ashton stopped. He saw headlights outside and quickly turned around and pointed to the lights. Dereck nodded, giving Ashton affirmation he understood. He grabbed Maddie's arms and led her back to the room. *Ashton looked at his watch. It was 4:20 a.m. 'Who comes to a warehouse at this hour?'* He wondered. Curious, he opened the door, heading out to confront the visitor.

The weather was dreadful, and the rain was

relentless. Shawn pulled into the apartment complex. Minutes later, he entered Maddie's apartment and was promptly greeted by Willa, encircling his legs and purring loudly. He smiled, looking at the fluffy black cat, bending down to pet her head.

Willa ran off toward the kitchen, probably trying to direct him toward her empty food container.

"Where are you going, Willa? Are you hungry again? Hold on! I am here to feed you." Shawn filled her dish with fresh food and refilled her water bowl. He looked around the kitchen, wondering when Maddie would be back. The thought caused him to tear up again. Not sure where to search for clues, he headed to her bedroom. Maddie's laptop was still open.

Shawn managed to log into it and looked around. Her email was open, and there were over 100 unread emails. Shawn skimmed through them, looking for anything unusual. After hours of not finding anything valuable, he looked outside to see the sun coming up. It was almost 7 a.m. Shawn slammed down the top of the laptop and walked to the front room to find Willa.

The cat was curled up in the bright yellow chair by the French doors leading out to the balcony. It was Maddie's favorite chair. She enjoyed reading in it with her feet up on the poufy ottoman. The tan faux fur blanket remained draped over the chair's back. Shawn noticed her reading glasses on top of a book she was reading, placed on the glass table. He picked up the book and placed it up against his chest, hugging it. It was an odd gesture.

Feeling defeated, he moved Willa and sat on the yellow chair, clutching the book like a precious object. Willa scurried toward Maddie's bedroom to find a dark place to hide and sleep. Shawn fell asleep in the chair, holding the book.

It was way too early, and Maddie became increasingly irritated. Someone forced her onto a chair. Immediately, she realized they had not yet left the building. Her hands were still bound, and she could hear Cat-Face talking with someone.

"What do you mean? I thought you were taking her back. NO! She is not staying here. I told you. Maddie has to go. Get her out of here, now!" she screamed.

"I have told you. There is someone here. Ashton is checking it out. In the meantime, keep her quiet. I will be back when I know more." He walked out, furiously slamming the door.

Cat-Face approached Maddie and pulled off the burlap sack bag. "Listen, we cannot take you back yet. There has been a small, unusual development. Once I know, I will let you know. In the meantime, please stay seated. I will be back," Cat-Face informed Maddie as she exited the room, once again securing the door on the way out.

Maddie wondered what kind of unusual development. Was it the police? Was it Shawn? She could only hope.

Outside, it was dark as Ashton approached the vehicle. The person inside the car rolled down the window.

"Good morning. I am sorry. I think I am lost. I am looking for a lumber yard. Do you know where I might find it? My GPS said it was here. I am confused. I am also late for my first day of work," the tall man asked, looking around.

"No, there is no lumber yard here. This is a warehouse. You are definitely lost. I suggest you find your way back to the main road." Ashton turned to walk back toward the warehouse's back door.

"Umm, no need to be so damn rude, man. I am lost. You could direct me." The man in the car turned off his car engine.

Ashton turned around and walked toward the man's vehicle. "Listen, you are trespassing. I understand you are lost. Now, I suggest you turn on your GPS, enter the address you are looking for, and head out. I cannot help you." Ashton became annoyed and wanted to pull his gun out. This moron obviously did not understand his kindness. Maybe he had to do something drastic to get him to leave. But then, he did not want to raise any suspicion or, worse, have him return with the police. So, he would be kind and try to help this lost soul and get him out of the area as quickly as possible. After a minute of feeling uneasy, the man in the car left as instructed.

Cat-Face and Dereck stood outside by the door, talking. Maddie overheard their conversation. They were not quietly speaking. Instead, they were shouting. Maddie could hear Cat-Face complaining about the sun coming up, stating Maddie would have to remain their guest another night. There was no way it was safe to move her now. The man agreed and suggested removing the ropes, getting Maddie something to eat, and making her comfortable for the extended stay.

Cat-Face agreed reluctantly, ordering him to do so immediately. She hated keeping the girl but knew it had to be.

Maddie was furious. *'Another day in this hell hole.'* She had her hopes up, believing she would be home, safe and sound, with her precious Willa by her side. Now, she understood that was not about to happen. Maddie began crying, feeling utterly defeated and frustrated. She felt little to no hope.

The man entered the room and approached, still wearing his monster mask. "Give me your hands," he ordered. Maddie pushed them out in front of her. He took the ropes off quickly. She saw her wrists were raw and red from the rough rope. They also ached. Immediately, she began rubbing them. He noticed, feeling awful.

"I will get you a healing ointment to put on that. Sorry. I did not realize the ropes were so rough. I will also bring you some food." He departed, and she heard the familiar sound of the door locking.

Grudgingly, Maddie lounged on the cot, giving in to the situation, unable to change it. Perhaps taking a nap would make her feel better. She stared at the ceiling, daydreaming about Shawn.

Cat-Face, Ashton, and Dereck sat around the table in the break area of the warehouse. The man in the car finally left. It was odd, but he took off without making a stink. Ashton stuffed his face with a chocolate-glazed doughnut, sipping hot black coffee. Dereck was quietly scrolling through his phone, leaning back in the chair. Cat-Face looked out the window, suddenly spotting a vehicle pulling into the parking lot.

Instantly, she jumped up. "We have more company. Go check on our girl. Make sure she stays quiet. I will find out what they want," Cat-Face ordered as she sprang from her chair, hoping to head off the visitors. The two officers approached the main doors.

Cat-Face opened one of the doors with a smile on her face. Even if it was a fake smile, she planned to appear friendly. "Good morning, gentlemen. How may I help you? Come on in." She directed them toward the set of navy velvet club chairs by the entry. "Would you care to take a seat?"She offered politely.

"Umm, no. I'd rather stand. I am Detective Sterling," he quickly flashed his badge for identification and looked around. "I assume you are the owner of this business? We are investigating numerous threats against someone in your industry. I believe you know her—Brexley Sinclaire?" Brian looked around while Cameron McIntyre, his partner, glared at her to read her reaction.

"Oh? Yes, of course, I know Brexley. We are acquaintances. We work in the same industry of staging and interior design. Yes, I am the owner of this business—Better By Design 4U. Please tell me what has happened to Brexley. Is she okay?" It took everything out of Cat-Face to act normally. She began to panic. Hopefully, they did not notice.

"Well, we are not sure yet. There have been several developments we are investigating. Have you had any threats against you or your business?" Brian asked.

"No. Not at all. Business has been normal. I did not realize there was a problem with Brexley. Goodness! I will need to call her and offer help. How dreadful! Can you tell me what has happened?" Cat-Face inquired, hoping to find out what they knew.

"No, ma'am. We are not allowed to discuss an ongoing investigation. So, nothing unusual has happened here at this warehouse? Have you noticed any strangers around your warehouse? Nothing out of the ordinary at all?" Brian pressed on.

"No…As I stated. Business as usual. Well, if there is nothing else. I have a meeting in a little while I must prepare for…may I walk you out?" Cat-Face offered, hoping they would leave."

"Just a minute more, please. Humor us. Please tell me, when was the last time you saw Ms. Sinclaire? Also, can you recall the last time you may have been to her warehouse?" Brian asked, hoping she would divulge something.

Detective McIntryre continued inspecting the pictures on the wall and peeking down the hallways while Brian interrogated her.

"No, I cannot recall either. Sorry. As I said, Brexley and I are acquaintances. We are not close friends. It has been quite a while since we spoke."

"Well, that may be true, but you both have a few things in common, don't you?" asked Brian, standing directly in front of her, making her uncomfortable. She clasped her hands, trying to keep calm.

"Like what, Detective?"

"Well, for starters, you both dated Carlton Chastain. I believe you dated up until last year. I also believe Ms. Sinclaire and Mr. Chastain are currently back in a relationship. Are you aware of that?"

"It is true. I dated Mr. Chastain for a few months on and off. And, no, I don't keep track of Carlton and his relationships with other women. I simply do not have time for that, nor do I care to know." She tried to sound reassuring, though her heart raced, making her feel breathless.

"Aha. Well, I thought, for some reason, there was more. How serious was your relationship with Mr. Chastain?" Brian continued to grill her. He felt she was hiding something.

"What does that have to do with anything, Detective?" she asked, sounding snippy. Now, she felt attacked.

"Just trying to connect all the dots, that's all. So, you dated for a few months? What caused the breakup? Do you remember?" He glared at her, making her feel even more uncomfortable than before. He figured she was attempting to concoct a lie.

"If you must know, Carlton said we were not compatible. He wanted to end our relationship. That is what happened. Are we done? I really do have a meeting in five minutes. I must go."

"Sure. We are done for now. Here, take my card. Call me if you can think of anything that you believe might be important. Any time of the day or night!" Brian handed her the card and waited for a reaction. She looked away.

Brian and Cameron exited the building and returned to the undercover police vehicle. Brian smiled.

"Well, what do you think?" he asked Cameron, starting the car and backing out of the parking stall.

"She is lying. It was all over her face. She was restless, with no eye contact, fidgeting with her hands, and squirming while standing. She knows something! Plus, she acted very defensive and irritable when you asked about Carlton Chastain." replied Cameron.

"I cannot believe it only took talking to two other staging businesses to find someone suspicious!"

"No shit! So, I guess we have a suspect!" The two drove toward town to find Shawn to provide him with an update.

Nervously, Cat-Face closed and locked the front doors, turning on the neon CLOSED sign. She pulled down the blinds, too. Ashton and Dereck were chatting on the couch in the break room, sipping drinks, when Cat-Face appeared.

"Well, what did they want? Who was it?" asked Ashton, dying to find out.

"It was the cops. That's who. They asked me questions about Brexley. They wanted to know about my relationship with her. When I saw her last and if I had received any threats against me or my business. I told them no. I hope to God they are not suspicious. I tried my best to act as normal as possible but was nervous. One of the cops snooped around while the other one talked to me. I wonder if they suspect me?"

"Why would they? There is no way they could figure it all out," retorted Ashton.

"WRONG! They knew about Carlton and me. The one cop also told me that Brexley and Carlton were back together. I am not sure if he was looking for a reaction or what. Anyway, I don't like them showing up. I think they may know something. Now, what do we do? I can tell you one thing. We have to remove Maddie from this building ASAP! Can you imagine if they return with a search warrant or something? Damn! We would be royally screwed."

Dereck and Ashton agreed. They would move Maddie during nightfall. They could not afford to keep her locked up in the warehouse. It was too risky. Now that two cops were sniffing around, that signaled a huge potential problem for all of them.

CHAPTER 8

Brexley woke up feeling aroused. Carlton ran his hand up and down between her legs, making her tingly. He kissed her passionately as he continued to tease her with his hand. She moaned and arched her back, ready to explode. It felt glorious. She had forgotten how much she loved his touch. He knew how to caress her, making her body quiver with delight.

A few minutes later, he gently thrust himself inside of her. She looked up at him, hot, sweaty, and beautiful. At that exact moment, Carlton knew he had to marry Brexley. She was his dream woman, and he could never imagine a life without her!

"That was a nice way to wake up," Brexley teased, her head resting on his chest a few minutes later. Her body was halfway on him. Though he felt hot from their lovemaking, he did not move her.

"Mmm, yes. Your body loves me," Carlton teased back, kissing her. She ran her hand down his belly. "Stop that. I am too tired for more."

"Sure, you know you want more." She jumped up and straddled him. He looked up at her with a mischievous smile.

"Okay, I give in," he teased. "Have your way with me. I am all yours," he joked as Brexley took control and made love to him this time, watching his face, eyes closed, appearing content.

The sky was still fairly dark as Shawn woke up feeling lousy. His back was sore from sleeping awkwardly. He opened his eyes and realized he had fallen asleep on the yellow chair in Maddie's apartment. Willa was curled up on his lap, sleeping. He moved the cat and strolled to the bathroom. While peeing, he stared out the small oval window, wondering about Maddie's return.

After washing his hands, he returned to the living room to find his phone. He picked it up and saw he had 11 missed calls. Eager to see who called, he quickly scrolled through the missed call log. There were seven calls from Brian and two from his mother. Then there were two unknown numbers listed as missed calls. He dialed Brian's number.

"Hey, where have you been? I need to speak with you. Where are you?" Brian asked, driving.

"I am at Maddie's house. I fell asleep taking care of her cat. What's up?" he asked, eager to find out the news.

"I'll be there in five minutes. Cameron will be with me. What is the apartment number again? We need to talk."

"It is 14. The code for the gate is 2364. See you soon." Shawn hung up the phone, walking to the kitchen. He required coffee to function fully. Shawn was curious about why Brian wanted to speak with him in person. *'Why is Cameron with him?'* Shawn wondered. *'It has to be important. God, please don't let it be bad news!!'* Shawn headed to the living room with his mug of hot coffee, waiting for Brian and Cameron to show up. His stomach was feeling odd. The anticipation was killing him.

The doorbell chimed a few minutes later, and Shawn pushed the button, allowing them into the secured building. Anxiously, he paced back and forth by the front door. There was a loud knock. Shawn immediately opened the door.

"Hey, Brian and Cameron! Nice to see you. Let's talk in the living room." Shawn showed them into the spacious room. Brian sat down on the sofa, and Cameron sat next to him. Shawn decided to sit down in the yellow chair, allowing him to look directly at the two.

"Well, what is it? Is it bad news? Be honest! I can handle it," Shawn announced, setting his coffee mug on the table next to him. He folded his hands and placed them on his lap, fiddling with his two thumbs.

"Shawn, we don't have any bad news. In fact, we keep hitting dead ends. Some things are just not adding up. What do you know about Brexley and Carlton? Can you tell us more about Brexley's business and Maddie? There is some kind of connection we are missing. I know it," replied Brian. The tablet was on, and he was ready to take notes.

"That is why you are here? Come on. Why are you really here? What did you find?" Shawn asked. He knew Brian well. He found something!

"Well, we did interview the owner of Better By Design 4U. She definitely has something to hide. Cameron and I both agree. We are not sure what. It might be nothing. We do not have enough to get a search warrant at this time. We need more. I have sent Officer Timmothy Henderson back to watch the warehouse. He was there earlier checking on the building. He will let us know if there is any usual activity," Brian confessed.

Shawn moved to the balcony door and opened it. He left the door open, smoking. He wanted to scream. *'Why is this so screwed up? Where is Maddie?'* He put the cigarette on the concrete balcony floor and returned inside.

Cameron and Brian stayed in the apartment, discussing the case with Shawn for a while. Shawn did not feel any better. In fact, he worried that things were not progressing as quickly as he had hoped. Once Brian and Cameron left, Shawn closed the door, returning to the balcony.

Frustrated, he lit another cigarette. He looked at the empty pack. "Time to head back to the store to get more," he told Willa as he closed the French doors. Willa curled up on the yellow chair, uninterested. Shawn planned to visit Brexley. He wanted to speak with her. If she were hiding something, he would make it clear he would not allow it to continue. Shawn was tired of the lies and deceit.

Cat-Face packed her bag and sat on the couch in her office while waiting for Ashton to show up. She called him, eager to move Maddie now. After the run-in with the cops, she knew it was best to get her out of the building as soon as possible. She did not want to wait until dark. Instead, it seemed wiser to move Maddie using a moving van in the daytime. It would look less suspicious. No one would suspect a thing. They would place Maddie in the vehicle they planned to use for a furniture pick-up at the airport. Some furnishings had arrived at the freight terminal. Cat-Face thought it would be a clever way to remove Maddie from the warehouse.

Ashton showed up at noon with Dereck. Both wore their usual uniforms—navy blue cargo pants, navy short-sleeved shirts, black boots, and a dark blue baseball cap embroidered in white lettering: Better By Design 4U.

Cat-Face approached the room, placing the cat mask on her head. She unlocked the door. Maddie was sitting on the cot, dressed. "Time to leave, sunshine." The woman announced. She was glad to finally get rid of Maddie.

"Well, it is about time. Thank God," Maddie responded. With the burlap sack on her head, Maddie waddled down the hallway. Ashton grabbed her wrists and helped her walk toward the back door.

"Hold on. I don't think we should move her with the thing on Maddie's head. What if someone sees her? They will know something weird is going on. I have a better idea," Cat-Face said, handing them a pair of dark glasses.

"What the hell? She will be able to see with those. She will identify the location and will able to tell the cops later," complained Ashton.

"Wrong! Put them on. They are black on the inside too. I personally spray-painted them last night on the inside. They wrap around so she cannot see out the sides. It is much less suspicious than the burlap bag on her head!"

The plan was in place. They would leave the building with Maddie, pretending she was part of the crew, quickly getting into the moving van. Yes, it would look strange since it was cloudy outside with her wearing sunglasses. However, it was still less obvious than the burlap bag on her head.

Maddie allowed them to remove the burlap bag from her head. They instructed her to close her eyes. Ashton placed the glasses on her face.

"Okay, you two do what we discussed. See you when you get back." Cat-Face walked back to her office, leaving Ashton and Dereck to return Maddie back to her world.

They opened the door, Aston leading the way to the van parked by the back door. Maddie was in the middle. Dereck guided her from behind so she would not fall over. Once in the van, they sped off toward Brexley's warehouse on the other end of town.

Timmothy Henderson took pictures of the three people getting into the van. The van sped off quickly, so he decided to stay behind to continue his undercover surveillance of the warehouse. He planned to follow the owner as soon as she exited the building. Timmothy picked up his cell phone, calling Brian to update him.

The van drove up the long driveway. Ashton looked around, worried someone would see them. Dereck stopped halfway to the building. "What do you want to do? Should we pull over and escort her to the building? There is a side entrance behind the fence," Ashton pointed in that direction.

"Yeah, there are no cameras over there. I made sure," agreed Dereck. The van pulled up behind a row of thick oak trees. Ashton opened the door and exited with Maddie. The two men guided her toward the building. Ashton stopped and pointed to the van, winking at Dereck. They ran back to the van without saying anything to Maddie. She remained standing, probably wondering what was happening. She heard the noise of the van peeling out of the driveway. That is when she knew they had left her alone.

Cautiously, she pulled the glasses off her face. The light stung her eyes. She looked around, rubbing her aching eyes. *'Oh, my God! I am back at the warehouse! Thank you, Lord!'* She declared, crying, feeling grateful she was okay. Shaking, she almost fell to the ground.

The two men headed back to the warehouse to update their boss. Neither was happy. They were promised a lot of money, but how would they get it now? There was no one left to hold for ransom. Ashton was pissed off, and he wanted revenge!

Maddie approached the warehouse. She punched in the code on the side entry panel by the loading dock. The metal garage doors opened. She ran into the building, rushing to her office to make a call, feeling unsteady and scared. She wondered if anyone else was in the warehouse. However, she did not see or hear anyone.

The clouds dissipated, and the morning turned out to be glorious. The sun was out for once, and it looked like a warm day. Feeling hungry, Brexley walked toward the kitchen to make some food. She finally felt better and craved eggs, bacon, and toast. She poured a tall glass of orange juice while she happily made the food. Carlton was in the shower. She could hear it.

Brexley wondered if they could start decorating the house for the holidays. She wanted to make this season one to remember. If Carlton planned to move soon, she wanted this Christmas to be the best one they ever had as a couple. 'WOAH,' did she just think of them as a couple? Brexley placed the glass of juice on the counter. She allowed herself to fall onto the tall, modern, stainless steel and leather stool. "I love Carlton," Brexley said out loud. "Oh my goodness, I really do!!" she smiled. Reaching for the glass, she took a giant gulp of the juice, thinking of replacing some of it with Prosecco. A Mimosa sounded delicious. Feeling happy for the first time in weeks, she finished making breakfast, eager to speak with Carlton.

Carlton dressed in jeans, a polo shirt, and designer loafers. He did not want to look too overdressed and planned to escort Brexley to the car dealership to find a new vehicle today. If nothing else, she would finally have a new car and regain a little of what she had lost.

Hopefully, shopping would help keep her mind preoccupied and off Maddie, George, and everything else. He also wanted to speak with her about making the house more festive. Carlton remained optimistic she would agree. It would help put her back in a good mood.

As he brushed his hair and spritzed on cologne, he smelled something delicious. If Brexley was cooking, that was a true sign she was on the road to recovery, which made him grateful and excited. Carlton could not wait to kiss her, telling Brexley he was ready to spend the rest of his life with her.

In the kitchen, Brexley arranged eggs, bacon, and toast on plates. She made herself a Mimosa and made one for Carlton, too, hoping she had something to celebrate with him in the near future. Carlton entered the kitchen, dressed, and appeared to be in a good mood.

"Hello, beautiful. That smells so good. I am starving." Carlton sat on one of the barstools in the kitchen and admired the meal. Then he noticed her half-empty plate. *'She must be hungry,'* he thought, laughing to himself.

"I hope you like it. I was starving. Can you tell?" Brexley joked, picking up another piece of bacon and taking a bite.

"Good Lord, girl...I am not sure I have seen you so ravenous. I guess I am not feeding you enough?" Carlton teased. The two teased each other, ate, and discussed the day. Brexley agreed with Carlton. She wanted to find a new vehicle, missing the freedom to drive herself. "I was also thinking about something else," Brexley began.

"Oh, what is that, Luv?" Carlton asked, finishing his eggs. He moved around the bacon on his plate.

"I would like to take you up on your offer. I want to decorate the house for Christmas, if your offer stands. I think it would be nice. Could we get started in the next few days? What do you think?" Brexley asked, optimistic he would agree.

"Absolutely. I think that would be a fantastic idea. In the meantime, let's get ready to head out for the day. We can plan the rest later. What do you say?" He stood up and kissed her on the cheek. "I will be back, Luv. Going to get my wallet so we can leave."

Brexley cleaned the kitchen, feeling energized and excited. She headed to her room to change into clean clothes.

Not far away, the big warehouse was quiet as Maddie sat behind her desk. She began to cry, not because she was hurting or scared. No, she was elated. It seemed like a dream to her that she was safe and sound. She picked up the phone and dialed the phone number of the only person she wanted to see. Her heart began racing as the phone rang.

Shawn sat in his car outside his house. He rolled down the window and lit a cigarette, resting his head on the back of the car seat. Closing his eyes, he thought about Maddie. His phone rang, causing him to look down at the phone on the passenger seat. He recognized the number but stared at the phone, confused. Why would someone from *Sinclaire Premier Staging* call him? He let it ring several times, and it finally reached his voicemail. Shawn dropped the cigarette into a half-empty soda can, extinguishing it. The phone rang again. Irritated, he picked it up.

"This is Shawn. Who is this?" He sounded gruff.

"Baby, I need you. Can you come to the warehouse," Maddie said in a low tone.

Shawn sat up quickly in his seat. "Oh my God, is that really you, Maddie?"

"Yes, hun. It is. Can you please come to Brexley's warehouse and get me? I am so scared, babe. I have just survived a horrible nightmare."

"I will be there in 10 minutes. Please do not do anything until I get there," Shawn declared and zoomed off toward the warehouse, still not believing she was there. He wanted to tell Brian about the call but decided against it, speeding down the road, eager to see the woman he loved more than life itself.

Brexley looked at the SUV. It was identical to the one she had purchased before. It felt right to her. She closed her eyes and took a deep breath, loving the new car and the leather smell. She started the vehicle and turned on the air conditioner, allowing the cool air to hit her face. "I will take it," she boldly informed the sales associate.

"Are you sure?" asked Carlton. "We can look at others. I thought you liked the smaller version of this vehicle too?"

"No. This is perfect for me. It is what I had before. I feel comfortable in it and want this one," Brexley replied adamantly. "It has plenty of room for all my things. It will make my job easier to have this large vehicle. I loved the one I had before. There is no reason for me to downsize."

"Okay, let's head inside the building to wrap up the paperwork," the sales associate said with a gleeful look on her face. She was about to make a great commission off this expensive, luxury SUV.

An hour and thirty minutes later, Brexley sat in the front seat of her new SUV. She started the vehicle, feeling whole. Finally, she regained a small piece of her life. She followed Carlton back to the house, worn out and ready for dinner.

Twenty minutes after receiving Maddie's call, Shawn arrived at the warehouse. He pulled into the parking stall, exited the vehicle, and ran toward the front doors of the building. Just as he was about to open the door, it swung open, and she stood facing him. She looked rough. Her hair was messy, she had bags under her eyes, and she wore cheap black clothing. Shawn assumed the kidnappers had given her those clothes.

Maddie looked dirty, as if she had not showered in a while. He saw her wrists, which looked red and raw. Instantly, he realized those were rope burns. He felt angry and upset.

Shawn pulled Maddie into his arms, not worried about how awful she smelled. He only cared that she was safe in his arms. She cried as she held him tightly. Shawn could barely breathe, but it did not matter. Maddie was alive. After a few minutes, he pulled away to get a better look at her.

"I am glad you are fine, Maddie. I was frightened. I had the worst thoughts and nightmares. We must call Brian, and you have to give him your statement. Are you ready to do that?" he asked, holding her hand.

"No. Please, first, I want to go home, shower, put on clean clothes, and see Willa. After I eat and relax for a while, we can call him. Would that be okay?" she asked apprehensively. Though Maddie was keenly aware law enforcement had to be notified of her return, she wanted to rest first.

All she wanted now was to head home with Shawn. Shawn agreed with one small concession. "We have to tell Brexley and Carlton. We can wait to call Brian. But they have to know, Maddie. They have been sick, frantically worried about your kidnapping. I believe Brexley feels responsible for what has happened to you. I want you to call and tell her you are okay, please!"

Maddie reluctantly agreed. She felt compelled to call Brexley, but in a way, she was angry. Part of her thought that Brexley was indirectly responsible for her kidnapping. Maddie wanted a little time to think before calling Brexley and Carlton. She also wanted a hot shower and clean clothes.

Shawn and Maddie left the warehouse, heading toward her apartment. Shawn drove, holding Maddie's hand, secretly vowing never to let her go. He counted his blessings, grateful for Maddie's return. Shawn looked down at the pack of cigarettes in the door pocket of his car. He smiled to himself, realizing he no longer craved them. It was a great feeling.

The drive to Maddie's apartment was quick. She caught a view of her apartment, staring at the building. Instant relief hit her. She smiled as Shawn helped her out of the vehicle.

Maddie noticed her legs felt rubbery. She lacked energy and stamina. They strolled, hand in hand, to the apartment. Shawn unlocked the door. Willa approached, meowing happily to see Maddie, who bent down to pick her up. The cat purred as she rubbed her face against Maddie's. The smile on Maddie's face was all Shawn needed. He headed to the kitchen to find food to prepare for Maddie while she relaxed on the couch with Willa in her lap.

Brexley and Carlton enjoyed an early dinner while discussing trimming the house for the season, including putting up a tree. She felt alive and well, thrilled about her new vehicle. Brexley also planned to call her real estate agent, requesting to find her a new home.

It could take time to find the right house, and she wanted to ensure she found one before Carlton left for Seattle. Brexley questioned if he would consider staying in San Antonio. She doubted he would but contemplated asking him in the future, though now was not the time. Things were going well, and she did not want to upset him.

"I have decorations in the attic and garage. I will start rummaging through them this weekend. Do you want to help me?" Carlton asked. "I know there are things you used to decorate my house last year. Maybe we could purchase a few new items as well? What do you think?"

Carlton wanted to involve Brexley as much as possible. It would make her forget about the tragic loss of her home and belongings, including precious Christmas decorations.

"Well, I have holiday décor at the warehouse too. Mostly outdoor items, but we can figure out if we want to use any of those?"

Brexley and Carlton stayed in the dining room discussing decorating when Carlton's cell phone rang. He switched the ringer off, irritated by the interruption.

Minutes later, he felt the phone's vibration on the table as it rang. Brexley pointed to the phone. Reluctantly, Carlton picked up the phone and answered it.

"This is Carlton."

"Carlton, it is Shawn. I have some news for you and Brexley. Is she there with you?" Shawn asked, eager to tell them about Maddie.

"She is. We are just finishing dinner. Let me put you on speakerphone. Go ahead. We are both here," announced Carlton, pushing the phone into the middle of the table.

"I have exciting news! Here, she will tell you," Shawn teased.

"Hello, you two. I am okay! I am home,"

Maddie yelled out in excitement.

"Oh my goodness! Maddie!!" Brexley shouted, thrilled to hear the familiar voice. Immediately, Brexley began crying from relief.

" I am alright, but tired and worn out. Shawn picked me up from the warehouse, where the kidnappers dropped me off. We will call the detective in charge of my case in a few minutes. I wanted to go home, shower, and relax before calling anyone. I cannot tell you how delighted I am to be home. Shawn is acting crazy. He won't let me go to the bathroom without standing by the door, haha. But...seriously, I just wanted to let you know I am safe."

The four talked for a while longer until Brexley noticed Maddie sounded exhausted. She ended the call, allowing her time to relax before calling Brian.

The evening turned out better than anyone could have imagined. Brexley was regaining her life, Maddie was returned unharmed, and the holidays were just around the corner. Brexley could not imagine life getting any better.

Unfortunately, Ashton and Dereck were not happy about the broken promise from Cat-Face. As they sat in their living room pouting, Ashton finally stood up and walked to the kitchen. He sounded angry as he made dinner, slamming dishes. Dereck knew something was wrong but felt compelled to stay away from him. After twenty minutes, Dereck knew Ashton would not stop yelling and complaining.

"What do you want to do, Ashton? She is your sister. Maybe you should talk to her and make her realize we are unhappy about the broken promises. We lost a lot of money, too!"

"No. She will not make it up to us. We will have to take matters into our own hands. As I see it, if we want that money promised to us, we must find a way to get it. I have an idea. Sit down and listen." Ashton insisted, with an evil grin on his face.

The evening was not a bust for Maddie and Shawn. After eating, showering, and dressing in clean clothes, Maddie sat happily on her couch, sipping hot tea. Willa curled up next to her, sleeping. Shawn sat in the yellow chair, watching Maddie's every move, acting overprotective. It was almost 7 p.m. when Shawn decided to call Brian.

He figured Maddie would not want to call, so he took it upon himself to initiate it. He would fill him in on what he already knew about the kidnapping. This would allow Maddie more downtime. Shawn looked at Maddie with an awkward smile as he dialed Brian's cell. It only took two rings for him to pick up.

"Hey, Shawn. How are you doing? Hanging in there? Let me tell you right off the bat—I do not have any news on Maddie. I am sorry. Is there something else you need?"

"Well, that is why I am calling you Brian. I have news! Are you sitting down?" he teased.

"Umm, yeah, why? You are scaring me! Are you okay?"Brian asked, sitting on the edge of the seat.

"Maddie is home. She is safe and alive. The kidnappers dropped her off at the warehouse. We would like you to come by the apartment to take her statement. I saved her clothes, too. I secured them in a big black bag, just in case. You can pick them up as evidence when you get here. Maddie has showered and is ready to talk. When will you be here?"

"That is fantastic news! I cannot believe it. I have so many questions. But...okay, let me head out. I should be there within twenty minutes. Thanks, man. I am so happy for you! Glad it all worked out."

Brian hung up the phone. Cameron sat next to him, giving him a strange look. Brian knew why. The two stood up and headed to the garage. It was time to get answers from Maddie.

Dinner was delicious. The rib-eye steaks and the sweet baked potato were exactly what Brexley had been craving. Carlton enjoyed his glass of Pinot Noir while she sipped on Chardonnay. He placed two candles on the dining room table and a small bouquet of roses in the center. Carlton was a romantic and wanted nothing more than for Brexley to love the atmosphere he tried to create.

After the meal, Brexley leaned back in the dining room chair, satiated, looking around the house. This house felt like home to her. Maybe it was because of Carlton? Perhaps it was because it was familiar? It did not matter. She planned to stay as long as he would have her.

Carlton cleaned the dishes and walked to the front door to lock up while Brexley lounged on the couch in the living room. As usual, he opened the front door to look outside before locking up. Carlton was about to close the door when he saw it. It stopped him instantly in his tracks. Nervously, he removed the note taped to the side of the front door.

It looked like all the previous ones with a tiny difference. This envelope did not have anyone's name on it. He stepped outside and closed the door. Cautiously, he ripped the envelope open and pulled out the notecard. It was typewritten. The words read, *"It is not over. You are not safe!"*

Carlton folded the note and envelope and slid them into the back pocket of his jeans. His hands felt clammy, and his stomach flip-flopped. *'How can this happen again? Maddie is home. We were safe! What the hell is going on?'* He said to himself in a whisper. Carlton drew in a deep breath and exhaled. He planned to hide this from Brexley for now. Everything was going too well, and he refused to let this new threat interfere with her happiness. Brexley's life was finally back on track, and this message would cause more turmoil. She did not need that, nope, not one bit.

Carlton opened the door, heading inside. Feeling apprehensive, he enabled the house alarm. Hopefully, she would understand when he told her the next part of his plan.

It started raining again as Brian and Cameron drove toward Maddie's apartment. Neither spoke. Brian kept shaking his head, mumbling to himself. Cameron left him alone. He knew he was upset, most likely thinking the same thing. Maddie's kidnapping was strange. *'Why would someone return her without a ransom request? Why bother kidnapping Maddie in the first place?'* The facts did not add up. Something was fishy, and Cameron felt convinced he had to lead this investigation. Brian was too close to Shawn and Maddie. He would mention it and see how he reacted.

As they pulled up in front of Maddie's apartment, Cameron spoke up reluctantly. "Hey, hold on one minute. I need to talk to you before we head inside. I believe you are too close to Maddie and Shawn. Why don't you allow me to interview her? I do not want you to feel awkward. Would that be okay?"

"Yes, you are right. I agree with you. I cannot act impartial in this matter. It could compromise the investigation. I will remain silent and let you do the talking unless you need something from me. Agreed?" Brian stated, feeling relieved Cameron would be the one asking the difficult questions. The two exited the vehicle, running to the large double doors as the rain pelted them.

Brian pushed the number 14 button on the panel by the door's right side. The door made a buzzing sound and clicked, opening. They entered, heading to the elevator, dripping water onto the shiny tile floor. Cameron ran his hands through his wet hair, pushing the UP button and waiting for the elevator doors to open.

Brian let out a sigh, feeling anxious about the interview. He would observe Shawn and keep him from talking. They needed Maddie to tell her story without interruption. If Shawn interfered, they would have to insist they finish the interview at the station. This would make the entire process complicated. Brian hoped it would not come to that.

Maddie was shaky and felt nervous about the interview. She knew it was a casual interview, but it still bothered her. It was an interview with a police officer. Shawn reassured her Brian was a professional and a friend. He would not be too pushy. Still, she hated the idea of them interrogating her about the events.

Shawn opened the door and greeted Brian and Cameron, leading them into the apartment. Maddie stood up and approached them, shaking their hands. Politely, she offered them something to drink, but they both declined. Shawn directed them toward the sofa. He allowed Maddie to sit in the yellow chair while he sat on the fluffy rug next to her.

"Thank you for calling us, Maddie. For the record, may I please have your full name?" asked Cameron, taking notes on the tablet on his lap.

"Of course. It is Maddison Suzane Thorton. My friends call me Maddie, as you know." She replied.

"Great. May I also have your birthdate, please?" Cameron asked.

"Yes, it is August 24th, 1992. I was born in San Antonio if you also need that information." Maddie elaborated, hoping to move things along.

"Thank you. So, why don't you start by telling us what happened and how it happened? To your best knowledge, of course. Please take your time. We are not in a hurry." Cameron smiled, waiting.

Maddie nodded and began talking. She explained how she left the warehouse to head home for the day, discovering her front tire slashed. Hoping George could assist her with the flat tire, Maddie was about to walk back to the warehouse to speak with him when someone grabbed her from behind. She recalled feeling a prick in her neck, instantly feeling woozy, passing out. The next thing Maddie remembered was sitting tied up in a chair, in a room that looked like a storage room similar to the one in Brexley's warehouse, though it was dirty and darker.

She elaborated more about the lady she called Cat-Face and the two other men, presumably her accomplices. Both had their faces covered in strange animal masks. After thirty minutes of talking, Maddie stopped. She looked at the cops, wondering if they believed her. In a way, she did not care. She spoke the truth, and that is all that mattered.

"Well, and then I was left at Brexley's business, still wearing the dark glasses. I took them off, discovered I was at the warehouse, and decided to enter the building to call Shawn. I could enter using an entry code on the side of the loading dock doors panel. I walked inside my office and called Shawn. He came to retrieve me. After I finished eating, showering, and relaxing, he called you. Now you are here, taking my statement." Maddie folded her hands. She felt cold, shivers running up and down her spine.

"I see. That is all? Can you recall anything else about the people or the building? Please, think! We must get as much information as possible," Brian chimed in.

"Two things. First, I noticed a gold ring on her left hand. It was etched with an intricate floral design—very unusual and pretty. Second, there was the tattoo on her wrist. It was a small dragonfly. It had unusual colors. Purple and yellow, I believe."

"Okay! That is great. Do you remember which wrist the tattoo was on? Please think. It may help us identify her later."

"I think it was on her left wrist. She used that hand the most. I tried to observe as much as possible without looking too suspicious." Maddie announced, confident in her answer.

"AHA! So, she is probably left-handed. If it were her dominant hand, that would make sense. Good information, Maddie," Cameron said.

"So, my final question for you is this—why do you believe you were kidnapped and returned without a ransom? Did you hear them discussing your release?" Brian asked.

"Cat-Face yelled a lot. I believe one of the men was her brother. I could have sworn I heard her calling him her *'idiot brother'*...Cat-Face told me numerous times she was very sorry. I was not supposed to be kidnapped. She also said she did not want anyone hurt, declaring she was not an evil person. Rather, she just wanted to make Brexley pay. She owed her."

"Owed her? Like what? Did she elaborate?" Brian questioned her.

"No. She never said. I do not believe my

kidnapping was her doing, though. I think her brother and the other guy are responsible. She seemed pretty mad when they brought me to the building where I was kept. During the last couple of days of my confinement, I overheard her insisting they remove me from the building and take me back. She was nervous that someone would find me in the building."

"That is interesting. So, Cat-Face had regrets? Wonder why? Did she say anything else to you?" Brian looked at Maddie, noticing she did not look well. She was nodding off, falling asleep.

"No. I am sorry, gentlemen. I do not. I have a massive headache, and I am so tired. Are we done?" Maddie asked, hoping they would wrap up the interview. She wanted to sleep.

Brian stood up. "Yes, I think we have all we need for now. Why don't you rest? We will be in touch in the event we require more information. Shawn, thanks for calling. I will be in touch with you tomorrow. Have a great night. Come on, Cameron. Let's go."

Brian and Cameron left quickly, allowing Maddie to head to her bedroom. She wanted to sleep in a plush, comfortable bed with Shawn.
In the police cruiser downtown, Brian glanced at Cameron.

"Well, what do you think?" he asked eagerly.

"I am convinced Maddie told us everything

she remembers. We need to focus on people who hold a grudge against Brexley. It is time to pay her another visit."

"You are right, Cameron. It is high time Brexley Sinclaire tells us everything. I think she is leaving out some vital information. I will call her in the morning to make an appointment to meet with her. Hopefully, Carlton Chastain will not be there," Brian added.

"Yes, Mr. Chastain seems to get in the way. He needs to shut his mouth and let Ms. Sinclaire do the talking. If he cannot do that, we must insist she comes into the station. We cannot take NO for an answer this time. Agreed?" Cameron insisted, looking at Brian.

It would be uncomfortable for Shawn, but they would try to keep him out of the interview, if possible, since Shawn was close to Carlton because of Brexley. Cameron would take the lead and be the bad guy if need be. It did not bother him. In fact, he preferred it this way!

CHAPTER 9

Brexley knew something was wrong. His statement was vague, but he obviously had something he felt he needed to share, which she assumed made him nervous. Carlton was fidgety, playing with some paperwork.

"Listen, why don't you tell me what is going on? Something is bothering you. Spill it." Brexley watched his face. Carlton looked up.

"Nothing is wrong. Don't worry about it," Carlton replied. He shuffled around papers on the counter and continued to stare at his phone.

"Yeah, right. I know you better than that. So, why don't you just tell me? I will find out eventually, anyway. At this point, you are just pissing me off. So, what is going on?" Brexley replied in a huff.

Carlton looked around the kitchen, avoiding eye contact. He knew it was best he told her before someone else did.

"Okay. I did not want to tell you this. I found another note. I knew you were happy that Maddie was back unharmed. I did not feel it was the right time to bring it up. I took a picture of the note and texted it to Brian and Shawn." He sat on the stool next to her and tried to grab her hand. Before he could, she stood up quickly, backing away from him.

"Are you freaking serious? What did it say? Show me! Dammit. Why would you try to hide this from me?" Brexley adamantly demanded. Her stern look made Carlton realize how angry she was at him.

"Luv, listen. I did not want to upset you. This whole situation has been a surreal nightmare. You have been through more than most, and I did not feel I had to add more garbage onto your load. I figured I would send it to Shawn and Brian and hear what they had to say about it." Carlton stood up and approached Brexley, hoping to reassure her all would be okay.

Brexley stood next to the kitchen sink, drinking a glass of water. Her hands shook, and she did not appear well. She spun around to face him, still holding the water glass in her unsteady right hand.

"Carlton, I thought you did not lie to me. So, why hide this? I think I am more upset that you did not tell me. I can handle it. I am not some fragile flower you need to protect." She slammed the glass on the counter, almost breaking it. Frustrated, she walked back to the stool and sat down. Carlton remained by the sink, facing her.

Suddenly, his phone rang. They both looked at the ringing and vibrating phone. Carlton picked it up off the kitchen island, answering it. He listened intently, occasionally replying, "Okay, yeah, got it."

Brexley watched him closely, wishing he would hurry up and end the call so she could find out who it was and what was happening. After a few minutes, Carlton hung up the phone and placed it back on the counter. He looked at Brexley with furrowed eyebrows. She knew it was bad news and tried to brace herself for what he was about to say.

Rather than speak immediately, he walked to the refrigerator, withdrawing a beer. However, it was early in the morning. Brexley knew this was not good. She calmly remained in her seat, trying to keep her composure.

Carlton approached with the beer in his hand. He opened the bottle and took a big swig, placing the glass bottle on the countertop. He walked up to Brexley and grabbed her hands, now with a fake smile.

"Brexley, that was Shawn. He wanted me to tell you that we were not the only ones who received a note during the night. Supposedly, Shawn found one taped to his car outside Maddie's apartment. Also, there was a fire at the warehouse. I am sorry. Fortunately, since it is primarily a concrete and metal structure, not much burned, but there is smoke damage inside. Shawn stated that Brian talked with the Fire Marshall and confirmed it was not an accident." Carlton felt her pulling away. He released her hand. He knew this was it—the last straw. She would probably not survive this.

'How could this be happening?' Brexley wondered. Her head spun, making her feel nauseous. Carlton walked to the refrigerator, withdrawing a bottle of water. She sat on the cold kitchen tile flooring, leaning against the cabinets, speechless. There was nothing to say. Her life was now basically destroyed. Nothing was left. How could she rebuild? Did she want to rebuild? Her heart raced. She gasped, horrified, attempting to breathe and stay calm. Carlton rushed to her side, bending down to look at her. Her lips turned blue as if she had stopped breathing.

Carlton gently shook her, yelling, "Brexley, breathe, babe. Come on. You can do it." After what seemed like an eternity, she took a giant breath and collapsed on the tile floor. She curled up in a fetal position, holding her knees, pulling them up against her body. Carlton shook his head, feeling like crap. He knew this would push her over the edge. Immediately, Carlton had an idea. He wanted to make a quick phone call.

"Babe, stay here. I will be right back. Hang on." Carlton stated as he jumped up, rushing to the living room to speak with him. Hopefully, he could help.

Brexley closed her eyes, wishing she was dead. She could not recall ever feeling this defeated. She was a strong woman, but this was more than she could bear. Her heart hurt. Everything had been taken from her, well, except Carlton. For now, he was still around.

Carlton spent almost half an hour on the phone. He remained in the living room on one of the couches, explaining the entire situation. Brexley was not safe in San Antonio. It was in her best interest to leave town. Brexley's safety was his priority, and Carlton assumed her dad was the best person to protect her. After thirty minutes of planning, he felt relieved the arrangements were complete.

Carlton found Brexley where he had left her, except she was now sitting upright, drinking water. She stared ahead as if in a trance. He bent down and tried to assist her in getting off the floor. She was like dead weight. Carlton lifted her up, aiding her in walking to the living room. A minute later, Carlton sat beside her on the couch, praying she would speak.

"Brexley, we need to talk. I have a plan, and I hope you will agree."

"No. The answer is no. I do not want to hear it. You want me to leave San Antonio. You don't feel I am safe here anymore, right?"

"How did you know? Did you overhear my conversation with Harrison?

"No. I know you, Carlton. I figured that would be the plan. I am not leaving. You and I—that is all I have left in my life. I am not scurrying away. They, whoever they are, can just go to hell. I am staying. I am planning to fight for my life. There is no way I am running away like a coward."

"Luv, listen. I know you want to be brave. I applaud you for that. However, staying at this point is too risky. Your dad agrees with me. He wants you to come home. It is not far away, but it is a distance from here. I thought about sending you to my parents or my sister's in North Carolina, but I knew you would refuse to leave Texas. So, stop acting so stubbornly. Your dad's house is safe. I will accompany you.

Please, think about it." Carlton begged. He could see it on Brexley's face. Her mind was made up. She planned to stay. Carlton shook his head, realizing he had lost. She would not budge.

Shawn met with Brian and Cameron at the police station. The three men sat around a brown, oval conference table on the second floor of the building. Brian opened three files, and Cameron removed a pile of photos, spreading them out on the table.

"Did you see the text from Carlton?" Shawn asked the two men. Both nodded.

"Yeah. What about the warning message you received, Shawn? What did it say? You have not added that to this file," responded Cameron.

"No, it was identical to the one Brexley and Carlton received. I have not informed Maddie yet. I did not want to burden her with more awful news. She is blissfully unaware of what is happening. I don't want to upset her. She is just beginning to feel safe at home again. If I show her the note, she will freak out."

Shawn looked at the whiteboard mounted on the wall. Cameron taped several pictures onto it, writing with a black dry-erase marker underneath each image.

"I get it. The situation is horrible. What do we know about the fire at Brexley's warehouse last night? Has it been confirmed as arson?"

asked Brian, shaking his head.

Shawn replied, explaining the report was still pending, but the assumption was arson due to the location and other matters not yet fully disclosed.

Cameron sat quietly in the seat, leaning back and staring at the ceiling. It would be to be a long day. The three men realized the case was not over, and the danger for Brexley and Maddie still existed. Someone was still out there, hoping to harm them. The question remained—why? Cameron turned his head, observing Shawn, and spoke up.

"Well, I suppose we can hold off on our chat with Brexley? Obviously, she is the victim. I was wrong. I thought she was hiding something. We need to look closely at other associates in the staging industry. There is no other reason someone would want her out of the way unless she were competition. So, let's focus on that for now, agreed?" The three men nodded, ready to formulate a new plan.

On the other end of San Antonio, Maddie lounged in her pajamas, petting Willa on her lap. She sipped coffee and enjoyed the moment of peace. She contemplated when Shawn would return. He reassured her he would not be gone for long, having to meet with Cameron and Brian to discuss the case. Maddie assumed it was to wrap up loose ends.

Nothing else was happening, or so she

believed. Feeling relieved and happy, Maddie removed Willa and walked to the bedroom, planning to shower and dress for the day. She was eager to head to the market and buy groceries to surprise Shawn with a delicious and romantic meal. Life was fantastic, and she intended to enjoy each second of it.

The day was not turning out as planned for everyone, especially for Brexley. She left Carlton in the living room, running to the guest room to change. Brexley wanted to leave the house and meet with Maddie. She texted her and hoped Maddie would respond quickly.

Later, Brexley hoped to visit Michelle and discuss the two houses she liked the most from the recent list of available homes for sale. Michelle emailed them to her the previous night. Brexley remained hopeful she could purchase a new home soon, allowing her some sanity. She was eager to reassemble her life, one small piece at a time. Maybe she would visit her dad once this horrific situation ended. Brexley missed him dearly and knew he worried about her. She had always been close to her dad, Harrison Sinclaire. He was a loving and doting father.

Harrison was a handsome man with a full head of grey hair and sparkly blue eyes. He loved to play golf and was an avid runner. Brexley treasured the time hanging out with her dad, especially when they played golf together in the summer. There was nothing she cherished more than quality time with her father.

In a way, Brexley was furious with Carlton for informing her father of what had recently occurred. She disliked upsetting him. Harrison was not entirely over his painful divorce and lately experienced a few health scares. His blood pressure was sky-high, and the medication did not help much.

Brexley was concerned Harrison would have a stroke or heart attack. Sharing this disturbing news could exacerbate his health-related issues. Brexley picked up her wallet, car keys, and sunglasses. She was eager to get downtown, needing space away from Carlton and this house. She felt like she was choking, yearning for some "me time." She strutted into the kitchen and found Carlton making sandwiches. Carlton smiled when he noticed her until he saw the keys in her hand. She wore designer sunglasses and dressed casually in jeans, a white blouse, and tennis shoes.

"Hello, Luv. What are you doing?" he asked, wondering where she was headed. Carlton knew she was getting cabin fever, constantly stuck in the house. But he also realized staying in the house was in her best interest. Leaving could potentially put her at risk. What if someone wanted to kidnap her next? Or worse—harm or kill her? The thought crossed his mind more than he could count, and the ideas became more graphic and violent each time. He hated that he thought that way, but Carlton was scared. It was his job to protect her and ensure her safety. He could not do that if she planned to leave the house alone.

Brexley removed the sunglasses, placed the keys on the counter, and glared at him. "I cannot remain in this house 24 hours a day. It is becoming my personal prison. You are constantly with me, no matter where I go. I need to do some things that do not involve you. Now, I know you love me, but please...understand. I am heading out for a few hours. I will be fine. Stop worrying," Brexley demanded.

Carlton shook his head. *'NOOOOOOO,'* he wanted to scream. He said it in his head numerous times, watching her. His heart raced. *'She is so stubborn. Why is she so insistent on leaving alone? Does she not realize how dangerous it is? She knows about the new threat and notes. Why is she not taking this seriously?'* Carlton was beyond frustrated with her and her nonchalant attitude toward the situation. He roughly grabbed her arm and pulled her toward him.

"Knock it off, Brexley. You are acting like a spoiled child. You cannot always get your way, Brexley. You also cannot leave the house without someone else. It is way too dangerous. I will not allow it."

"You will not allow it? Excuse me! Who do you think you are? You do NOT own me. I make my own decisions. I appreciate what you have done for me and know how much you love me, but you do NOT decide what I will and will not do. So, deal with it." She yelled into his face, now inches away. Her face flushed with anger.

"Calm down, Luv. You know exactly what I meant. I am scared. I love you. I am always here to protect you. Please, I beg you. Don't do this. Let me tag along. I will stay behind you. Watching. Just enough to make sure you are okay."

"I do not want nor need your personal security. I am grateful you worry about me, but I am leaving alone. I need this for me. Please understand." She picked up her keys, slid the sunglasses on, and walked toward the garage. She was determined to depart quickly without him. Brexley was done negotiating.

Reluctantly, Carlton did not stop her. He had a feeling it was a moot point. She had her mind set on doing her own thing, and he was wasting his breath trying to convince her otherwise. Brexley would not budge. It infuriated him greatly that she was so stubborn. He hoped and prayed all would be okay, realizing he had to let her do what she wanted. She was right about one thing…he did not own her. They were technically not even a couple anymore. Carlton decided to stay at home and await her return.

Brexley pulled out of the driveway and closed the garage. She sped off toward town, heading toward Maddie's apartment, feeling free.

Maddie had not yet returned her text, so she planned to surprise her. Along the way, Brexley intended to pick up a bouquet of flowers to bring with her. Brexley felt alive. It was exhilarating to drive her new vehicle, going where she wanted without someone tagging along. Finally, things turned around again. She had some independence, and it felt amazing!

The sun was out, and it was balmy 75 degrees. It turned out to be a fabulous day. Brexley turned on the radio and listened to Nat King Cole singing one of her favorite holiday songs, unaware of the dark blue car following closely behind.

Carlton paced back and forth in his office at home. He felt restless, worried about Brexley. He could not sit still, though he tried to do so numerous times. Eventually, he sat down in the desk chair and picked up his cell phone from his desk, dialing Shawn's number.

Shawn answered on the second ring, surprised to hear Carlton's voice. "Hey, what's up? I am surprised to hear from you." He said, answering the call. Carlton did not know how he wanted to begin the conversation. He felt compelled to inform Shawn about Brexley's speedy, unaccompanied exit.

"What do you mean she left alone? You and I both know that is a bad idea. With the new threat, I wish Brexley would have remained home," complained Shawn, highly irritated.

"I know. I am upset, too. Brexley refused to divulge her plans with me. She adamantly insisted that I did not accompany her. I am worried. What if something happens? What are you doing to keep Maddie safe?" Carlton asked. Shawn explained that Maddie did not know about the other note. He felt it was best to keep it under wraps for now. Also, he assumed Maddie would stay home since she was still exhausted from her ordeal.

Something in the back of Shawn's mind made him wonder, though. Maddie was not someone who stayed home for too long. She liked to be out and about.

"Hey, let me call you back, Carlton. I have a call I need to make," Shawn said, now concerned Maddie would leave the house too. The phone several times. Maddie did not answer. She was not at home.

Maddie pushed the grocery cart down the aisle and headed to the meat department to buy rib-eye steaks for dinner. She planned to make a fabulous meal, including Crème Brulee, his favorite dessert. Shawn would be pleasantly surprised. Someone accidentally bumped into her cart as she stood in front of the glass counter at the butcher's, attempting to pick out two smaller rib-eye steaks.

"Oh my gosh, I am so sorry, Miss. Please, forgive me," the man said, gently touching her arm.

Maddie flinched and moved to the other side of the cart. "Oh, no problem. Have a great day." She replied nervously.

"Hey, allow me to make it up to you." The man insisted. He was tall, blonde, and wearing aviator sunglasses with a San Antonio Spurs cap on his head. His jeans had numerous holes in the knees. He wore an obnoxiously bright white T-shirt and grinned at her. The man was handsome and cleanly shaven. Maddie noticed his well-manicured nails, too.

"Nothing to make up. It happens. Yes, Sir, I will take the two smaller rib-eyes on the bottom there," Maddie pointed to the meat case, and the man behind the counter smiled, weighing the items, wrapping them up in brown butcher paper, plastering on the price sticker, then handing it to her.

"Will there be anything else?" the man behind the counter asked, noticing the gentleman beside her staring.

"No, sir. Thank you. Have a great day." Maddie took the packet of steaks and placed them in her cart, quickly walking away, hoping the mysterious man would leave her alone. Unfortunately, the man followed.

"Come on. Don't be like that. I said I was

sorry. Please allow me to buy you a cup of coffee or something. I feel horrible."

Maddie spun around and faced the man. "Okay, hear me...I have a boyfriend. I am not interested in being picked up by you. I am okay. No harm was done. It was an accident. My foot is fine. You ran it over with your cart. No biggie. Now, I have things I must do, so...have a great day." Feeling irritated, she sped off with her cart to head to the register. The man followed again!

At the cash register, she turned around, noticing the creepy stranger standing behind her, holding a bag of tortilla chips with a jar of salsa.

Maddie waited for the young man to finish ringing up her purchases. She quickly headed for the exit, taking her two bags, desperately yearning for her car's security. The stranger made her feel uncomfortable.

Panicked, Maddie quickly unlocked the car and turned around to see if the man was still there. He wasn't. She sighed, feeling a tiny bit of relief. Turning on the vehicle, she zoomed off toward her apartment, hoping he was gone once and for all.

As she listened to holiday music on the radio, something in her mind clicked. She pulled the car to the side of the road. It hit her hard. *'Oh my God, I recognized his voice. Is he one of the kidnappers? There's no way,'* she said to herself, now shaking. She maneuvered the car back on the road and sped away, heading for the apartment complex. Her hands were shaky, and she felt ill.

Brexley pulled up in front of Maddie's apartment building. Maddie still did not answer the phone. She was about to call her again when she noticed Maddie's car approaching with her driving.

Brexley jumped out of the SUV and locked her vehicle, heading to intercept Maddie. The two met by the gate leading up to the elevator.

"What are you doing here?" asked Maddie, surprised to see Brexley. Brexley handed her a humongous bouquet with a smile.

"I am here to see you, silly. How are you?" She hugged Maddie, grabbing a bag from her hand. "Here, let me help."

"Sure," responded Maddie, acting cordial. Maddie wondered why Brexley was at her apartment complex. She hardly ever came to her home. It seemed like a strange gesture to Maddie.

"I see you had your tire replaced. Thank goodness for that," noted Brexley.

"Yes, Shawn had it done. He is always so thoughtful!" Maddie replied.

The two approached the apartment, and Maddie unlocked the door, turning off the alarm system. They were greeted by Willa, meowing. The two women walked toward the kitchen to drop off the grocery bags and flowers.

Maddie pulled a vase off the top shelf in the laundry room, arranging the gorgeous flowers in it. "Thank you for the pretty bouquet. What an unexpected and wonderful surprise." She felt it was odd that Brexley visited her.

Maddie quickly put away the groceries so she could talk with Brexley. "So, what brings you here, really? You have only been to my apartment a few times."

"Well, I wanted to check on you. Are you feeling okay? What can I do for you? I still feel terrible about what happened. I hope you believe that." Brexley nervously played with the car keys in her hands.

Maddie knew Brexley felt guilty about what transpired but felt it was not her fault. "I am fine. I told Shawn the same thing. Stop worrying about me. I had to leave the house for a bit. I decided to make Shawn a nice dinner. I don't want to go out to eat, not yet. So, I drove to the store."

"Gotcha. Yeah. That is why I am here, too. I had to leave the house. Carlton is overly protective. I cannot fart in peace," Brexley laughed, trying to lighten the conversation.

"Haha, nice. That's such a ladylike comment!" Maddie said, joking. The two sat around the kitchen island, sipping sweet tea. Maddie brought out some chocolate chip cookies for them to share. After an hour of conversing, Brexley felt it was best to head home. Maddie kept looking at the clock on the kitchen wall over the sink, wishing Brexley would finally leave.

"Well, if you need anything, please let me know. I will pay you until January 2nd. You should receive your bonus too. Again, I am very sorry for what has happened to you and pray they find out who did this to you. Also, there is no rush for you to return to work. Take your time. We can discuss your return later, after the new year."

"Yes, I am hopeful they will find the kidnappers, too. Thanks, Brexley. Have a great day, friend," Maddie said as she escorted her to the front door. She gave her a quick hug and closed and locked the door.

Brexley stood in the hallway, still feeling miserable about the current situation. She strolled toward the elevator when a handsome man exited the elevator in front of her. He smiled and said, "Good afternoon, ma'am," and walked off in the direction from which Brexley had just come. She reciprocated the smile, getting into the elevator.

The man reached the door. He leaned against it, placing his ear on the cold surface. He listened for noises inside the apartment. Music played in the background. She was in the apartment. He figured so. He withdrew the envelope from his jeans jacket, taped it to the door wearing gloves, and then quickly headed back to the elevator to exit the building. In the elevator, he whistled, grinning. "Wait until she finds the note," he laughed aloud. "She will die! Haha." The man pulled his cell phone out of his pant pocket and dialed a number, eager to share the news with him.

Cat-Face stared at the computer screen. She saw the vehicle twice in two days, parked down the road. She knew it was an undercover cop car. It made her anxious. Were they onto her? Did they know what she did? Were they just fishing, hoping to catch her doing something, giving them a cause to get a search warrant? Either way, she hoped Dereck would be back soon.

Ashton was working in the warehouse, preparing the crew for a staging later in the week. She currently had very few staging contracts. It angered her greatly. She wondered what was happening with Brexley's business. Ashton entered her office with an odd smirk on his face. Instantly, she knew he had done something awful.

"What did you do?" Cat-Face screamed.

"I did what I had to…did you see it on the news? Sorry, I guess it was not a total loss. The damn building is all metal and concrete. Only the inside got some smoke damage."

"What are you saying, Ashton?"

"Dereck and I torched her warehouse. Well, technically, I did. He watched. Unfortunately, the security team called the fire department, and they controlled it. I don't think we can try again. It was our one shot at destroying it. Sorry, Sis." Ashton plopped down on the chair in front of her desk.

"You are an asshole! Will you stop already? I told you enough. This is over. No more! The cops are sniffing around, and I do not want to get caught. Stop your shit already. Get your boyfriend under control. Where is Dereck, anyway?"

"Umm, he went to pay someone a visit. Why?"

"It better not have anything to do with all of this. I am warning you! Knock it off, Ashton."

"Whatever you say, Sis. You forgot something very important, though! You promised us a lot of money. We didn't get a dime. So, if we have to take things into our own hands, we will. So, you can kiss my big butt."

Ashton stood up and flipped her off as he left the building. He was tired of her bossy attitude. He wanted his money, and he would get it. If he had to kidnap that little girl all over again, he would. Maybe this time, they would send pieces of her to her boyfriend …yeah, that would do it. Or, perhaps, they would threaten to kill her. That would get someone's attention, for sure.

Ashton was ready to do what had to be done. He was not afraid to get his hands dirty. If he had to hurt the girl, he would do it. Dereck loved that about him. Aston was a doer, unlike his whiny sister. All she did was complain. She was also extremely ungrateful, never compensating them for all their hard work in kidnapping the girl in the first place.

No, they would be in charge and get the job done this time. Alexandria, his sister, would be kept out of it. Ashton was determined to get the money he felt they were owed and move to a non-extradition country, preferably someplace tropical, living out his life with Dereck by his side.

CHAPTER 10

The sun hid behind clouds rolling in as the sky turned dark and gloomy once again. Brexley drove home, feeling exhausted. Her hand throbbed, which added to her frustration. She had a new list of available properties for sale in the area. Earlier, Michelle handed it to Brexley, offering to take her to see the homes. Unfortunately, Brexley was too tired to do anything else. It had been a long day. She thanked Michelle and left quickly, heading to the grocery store to pick up wine and snacks. Her cell phone rang as she pulled out of the grocery store parking lot.

"This is Brexley. How may I help you?" She answered politely, not recognizing the number displayed on the screen.

"Well, you can start by dying or, better yet, dropping off da planet. How 'bout that?" the raspy voice on the other line said with a heavy Texas drawl.

"Excuse me?" is all she managed to reply.

"Bitch, you heard me. I said, how 'bout you die and do us a favor? Jist git it through your head. Or maybe we hurt someone else ya love? Ya are dumber than a box of rocks."

"Who the hell is this?" Brexley screamed into the phone.

"I reckon you're gettin' a bit nervous, huh? Well, sista, you should be. I'm tired of dis shit. So, you better be ready cause the shit is 'bout to hit da fan. I am fixin' to show ya." He hung up before she could respond or ask any other questions.

Brexley shook her head in disbelief. *'What is transpiring? Who is the crude man on the other line? What the hell???'Nervously*, she raced home to fill Carlton in on the call and show him the phone number. Maybe Shawn, Cameron, or Brian could run a trace and find the owner of the number.

Carlton heard the garage door opening and breathed a massive sigh of relief. She was back. "Thank God," he said under his breath as he walked toward the garage to intercept her. He heard the garage door closing, and Brexley flew through the door, almost knocking him over. She looked wild-eyed, almost hysterical. She dropped the bags, grabbed him, and started talking rather quickly to the point where he could not understand her.

"What are you saying? What about a man? A phone call? Slow down, Brexley, please. Here, let's sit down in the kitchen." He led her to one of the stools and gently pushed her into the seat. She obliged, staring at him.

"He said I should die, drop off the planet. He also said if I didn't, maybe someone else I loved would be hurt."

"Who? Who said this, and when?" Carlton asked apprehensively.

"The man on the phone. The one that just called me. I have no idea who he is. He had a heavy southern drawl and was very rude." Brexley calmed down and managed to catch her breath. Carlton looked downright scared.

"Honey, where is your phone? May I see it?" Brexley handed it to him. He looked at the call log and looked at the phone number. It was not a number he recognized. "Okay, I am calling Shawn. I will ask him to come over immediately. It would help if you relayed everything that happened while it is still fresh in your mind. Are you okay with that?"

"Yes, I am. Please, call him now," Brexley added eagerly. She was beside herself with worry, scared for her life as well as Carlton's. It seemed as if this nightmare situation would never end.

Shawn, Brian, and Cameron arrived at Carlton's house less than twenty minutes later. Shawn arrived first. He had been on his way home to see Maddie when Brian called him. Carlton led the three men into the living room. Brexley sat cross-legged in a chair, wearing leggings and a sweatshirt. She held a cup of coffee and took a sip when Shawn approached.

"Hello, friend. How are you? I understand you had quite a scare today. Are you ready to fill us in?" Shawn asked, noticing she fidgeted with her coffee cup. She also looked nervous.

"Of course. Thank you for coming over so quickly. I appreciate it very much. Let me know when you are ready." Cameron opened his tablet and nodded, implying he was ready to take notes.

Brexley recounted the information she previously told Carlton, with one small exception. She added that she came from Maddie's apartment. The four men listened intently. Carlton wondered why she did not mention her visit with Maddie. It seemed strange. *'Maybe she just forgot?'* He pondered.

Brexley ended the story recap by handing Shawn her cell phone and showing him the number that called her. Her hands trembled, and she was on the verge of crying again. Shawn immediately wrote it down and asked Cameron to run a trace to see if they could find the phone number's owner.

"You know, it is probably a burner phone. I doubt the man was stupid enough to use his personal cell," added Brian.

"A what kind of phone?" asked Brexley, unfamiliar with the term.

"A burner phone. A phone bought with cash, without a contract — pre-paid phone, and is pretty much untraceable," explained Brian. "People use them for whatever purpose, often for illegal activity, and then trash them when they are done."

"Yeah, still, we should attempt to trace the number," replied Shawn, knowing there was a slim chance the phone number would connect anyone.

"Why were you at Maddie's apartment? Did she call you? Is everything okay?" Shawn asked, concerned.

"I wanted to bring her flowers and talk to her. I still feel awful about everything. She has not picked up her phone or answered my texts. I just wanted to confirm she was not mad at me. I need her to know I am here to help with anything she requires." Brexley explained.

"Oh, okay. How was Maddie today? Did she seem alright to you?" Shawn asked, hoping to gain some insight from someone else. She seemed distant to him, and he wanted to know how Brexley interpreted her actions and responses.

"She seemed preoccupied and not that happy to see me. She was...cordial. That is the best way I can explain her interaction with me today. I hope she will be okay."

Shawn frowned. That was not what he hoped to hear. Brexley and Maddie had always been very close friends. It worried him Maddie seemed to be so dismissive of Brexley. Maybe Maddie held a grudge against Brexley because of the kidnapping? *'Time will tell.'* In the meantime, he wanted to hurry and return to the apartment and spend time with her. His job here was done. He stood up and chose to speak with Brian before heading out. Brian nodded. Shawn excused himself and left, eager to see Maddie.

Brian and Cameron stuck around briefly, finishing notes and questioning Brexley. Finally, after what seemed like an eternity to Brexley, they left. She wanted to make dinner and relax. It had been a dreadful day.

Carlton wrung his hands, worrying. He asked Cameron if they could have a police cruiser come by every few hours for security. Cameron told him he would see what he could do — no promises given.

Brexley breaded three chicken breasts in the kitchen and fried them up in a deep pan. She was hungry. Breaded chicken, fettuccine alfredo, and green garlic beans sounded excellent, plus it was one of the only meals she was good at making. She was a superb baker but not that great of a cook. That was Carlton's specialty. However, tonight, she wanted to cook. It helped keep her mind off the current situation.

Carlton smelled the food, causing his stomach to growl. He was delightfully surprised to see Brexley cooking. She acted as if she was feeling better. He walked to the dining room table and decided to set it for dinner. Carlton also placed numerous candles on the table. She loved candles, and seeing them would make her smile. Lastly, Carlton hurried to the garage and opened the wine cooler to remove a bottle of Chardonnay. That was when Carlton heard the noise by the side door. He quickly placed the bottle of wine back into the wine cooler.

Cautiously, he opened the door to peek outside. It was drizzling rain, and it was getting dark. He flicked on the outside porch light. That was when he saw the gruesome mess. It made his stomach turn. It was a gigantic dead rat, cut up and bloody, with a laminated note wrapped around its tiny neck. The message was legible. It read, "*Your next.*" '*Great, the idiots cannot spell either,*' he thought, walking back into the garage, grabbing a black plastic bag. Carlton carefully lifted the dead rodent off the ground using the bag. He hurled it into the trash can in the garage. Carlton knew he could not keep it in the garage long. It would smell, but he wanted the evidence. He was surprised at how much blood came from such a tiny being — staring at the rodent. He planned to text Brian after dinner when he was back inside the house.

Carlton refused to ruin the evening with Brexley, as her day had been shitty. On his way back into the house, he clutched the bottle of Chardonnay and attempted to act normally, not to draw attention to what had just happened. The food smelled delicious. Brexley sat in the dining room, admiring the plates overflowing with food. Obviously, she was starving. Brexley smiled, holding out her wine glass, ready to drink.

"What took you so long in the garage? Did you get lost?" Brexley joked as he opened the bottle, pouring her a glass.

"No, Luv. I was taking inventory. Making sure I did not have to run to the store tomorrow to get more wine."

"Oh, okay, that makes sense. Well, I am hungry. Can you tell?" She pointed to the plates and took a sip of wine. Carlton sat down, placing the cloth napkin on his lap. He took a giant swig of wine, pushing the thought of texting Brian out of his mind for now. The two enjoyed their dinner by candlelight. Brexley jumped as thunder boomed overhead, causing rattling noises.

"WOW, that was loud," she said, looking nervously out the window. Rain poured out of the sky. The wind howled, snapping branches on trees. They heard a loud crackling noise, and then the house became dark.

Nervously, she stared at Carlton. He stood up and grabbed a candle walking to the living room. "Hey, I am going to start a fire. I will be right back, Luv." Brexley cleared the dishes and placed them into the sink. She headed toward the living room to join Carlton. The fire roared. It was warm and inviting.

Carlton, however, wasn't in the room. Confused, she walked back to the dining room and picked up her glass of wine, topping it off before heading back to the living room. Feeling relaxed and comfortable, she sat back on the couch, pulling up the blanket and draping it over her feet.

"Carlton, where are you?" Brexley called out. No answer. "Hey, babe. What are you doing? Do you need my help?" she offered — still, no reply. Brexley shrugged. She assumed he was in the bedroom changing or looking at the breaker in the garage.

Carlton entered his office to make a call. He wished to be discrete, not wanting Brexley to overhear the conversation. Now that the electricity had gone out, he had an excuse to leave the room, pretending to be fixing something.

"Hey, Brian. I need to tell you something. I found a dead rat by the back door a few minutes ago."

"So, that shit happens, man," Brian responded, laughing.

"No, you don't get it. It was cut up and bloody and had a laminated note attached. It read: *Your next*!"

"Oh, crap. That changes things for sure. So, what did you do with the rat and note? I hope you kept them?" Brian asked.

"Of course. It is in a plastic bag in the garage. I cannot leave it there forever, as it will start to stink. So, when can you come by to get it?"

"Well, not right this moment. Half the city is without electricity. There are accidents all over, powerlines down. It will be a while. If it is sealed well, you could leave it by the door outside, and I can send someone over there later to get it. Okay?"

"Okay, thanks. Stay safe. It sounds like it will be a hell of a night." Carlton hung up the phone, heading to the garage to remove the bag he had not yet secured.

Walking toward the garage, he saw her

staring at the garbage can. She was crying. Brexley saw the bag dangling out of the garbage can. Something dripped onto the concrete floor.

"When were you going to tell me? When did you find it?"

"Brexley, I never wanted you to see it."

"Yeah, well, I was dumping the garbage from the kitchen and saw this bag was not tied completely, hanging out. And what is that?" Brexley pointed to the ground.

"Is that blood? Oh my lord, I cannot believe this." Disgusted, she slammed the lid on the garbage can and walked back into the house. Carlton withdrew the rat with the note and tied up the bag. He placed it outside the side door for the cops to pick up later.

Before reaching the living room, Carton walked to the bathroom and washed his hands. Entering the living room, he saw Brexley sipping wine, rocking back and forth on the chair. She looked frightened.

"Babe, it's okay. I called Brian. They are sending someone to get it. I planned to toss it, but Brian suggested we keep it. They are going to take pictures and log the note as evidence. I have no idea how it got there, but it could not have been that long ago. When I was retrieving the wine from the cooler in the garage, I heard someone outside." Carlton hoped he could make her feel more secure, but looking at her — he quickly realized that was not happening.

Brexley looked distraught. The wind became noticeably louder. Leaves and branches smacked into the window, startling Brexley. She flinched.

Carlton walked toward her and knelt by the chair, looking up at her. "Honey, what can I do? Do you want to go to bed? We could watch a movie on my tablet. It has cellular service. What do you want?"

"Want? I want this dreadful situation to be over. I want my life back. I want to forget this ever happened. I want no one to get hurt." Brexley yelled, crying, almost spilling her glass of wine.

Carlton removed it from her hand, placing it on the fireplace hearth. He gently took her hands into his, holding her. "Luv, I know. I meant now. What can I do now to make things a little better?"

"Babe, there is nothing anyone can do until the miserable human beings that are doing this are caught and locked up. Until then, we suffer." She pulled her hands away, bent down, and snatched her glass of wine off the hearth, chugging the entire glass at once. She handed the empty glass to Carlton as she stood up and walked toward the bathroom. Carlton watched her, shaking his head, feeling helpless.

Brexley peed in the dark hall bathroom. She sat on the toilet, crying. She was tired and drunk. It was not like her to drink several glasses of wine at once. Brexley was a light drinker, enjoying a glass or two here and there. Lately, she drank a lot more alcohol and enjoyed it immensely. She washed her hands and left the bathroom, heading to the guest room, eager to slip into her pajamas. She used her cellphone's flashlight feature to illuminate the way.

Once changed into her comfortable pajamas, with fuzzy slippers on her feet, she slowly shuffled down the hallway to head back to the living room to discuss things with Carlton.

Brexley felt awful about how she acted toward him. He tried to be helpful and kind, and she lost her shit, yelling at him. Carlton was a gentleman, always protective and kind. She realized he did not deserve her wrath. Perhaps she could make it up to him. Maybe she could seduce him by the fire's light in front of the fireplace. He would love that. Brexley entered the living room to find him curled up on the couch—a blanket draped over his body. *'He must have fallen asleep,'* she figured.

Disappointed there would be no sex tonight because he was asleep, she pouted. She was horny as hell. Maybe the wine was making her feel amorous. She wanted to ravage his sexy body and jump onto his lap, riding him until he moaned loudly with her on top. "Not happening tonight," she said aloud. Upset, she walked to the other couch to rest, leaving him alone. Minutes later, she drifted off to sleep.

Carlton was not asleep. Brexley did not know this, of course. While Brexley used the restroom and changed into her pajamas, a hooded figure appeared from behind the couch and knocked him unconscious. The man positioned Carlton's body on the sofa to look like he was sleeping, then covered him with a blanket.

He placed Carlton's middle finger on the gummy surface, making a copy of his fingerprint, hoping to use it to open the wall safe successfully. He knew this method might not work, but he wanted to try it. He had conducted research and found that some had successfully lifted fingerprints this way. It was the last chance to attempt to unlock the wall safe.

The intruder heard Brexley coming down the hallway. Panicking, the prowler swiftly ran to the kitchen to hide. She held a loud conversation with herself, and he remained out of sight, observing her. She looked at Carlton but did not touch him nor speak with him. Instead, she seemed mad and stormed off toward the other couch, talking to herself about 'not happening tonight' and other comments.

Minutes later, he heard her making huffing noises, and then she was snoring, fast asleep. The man decided he had what he needed, leaving without harming her, exiting through the side garage door.

Hours later, Carlton woke up with a giant headache. He rubbed the back of his head, feeling the big, round knot. 'What happened?' He tried to recall. His eyesight was blurry.

Last he remembered, he was waiting for Brexley. She had gone to her room to change after using the restroom. He recalled hearing something and assumed it was her coming down the hallway. The next thing to happen was Carlton feeling a sharp pain in the back of his head. Later, he woke up on the couch.

Carlton looked around the area. The fire was dead, and it was chilly in the room. Brexley was snoring on the other couch, covered with a blanket, her foot sticking out. The electricity was still out. He had left the kitchen light on just in case, so they would know when it returned. He walked to the kitchen to get a water bottle from the fridge. It was still cold. Feeling woozy, he walked to the sofa to wake Brexley.

"Babe, wake up," he said as he shook her shoulders gently. She immediately sat up, drool on her face from sleeping deeply. She felt it and wiped it away, feeling embarrassed.

"What is it?"

"Hey, will you look at my head? I am hurting. I think someone was in the house last night and knocked me out." Carlton did not want to alarm her, but he worried about the size of the lump on his head.

"What? Oh my God, let me see," she insisted. She gently parted his hair to look at the lump. She held her phone's flashlight near the bump to get a better look.

"It is okay, no blood. It is pretty good-sized, though. Should we drive you to the hospital? Maybe you have a concussion?" She asked apprehensively.

"No. I am fine. I would like to know how someone entered the house. Why were they here, and what did they take? Did you hear anything? You weren't suspicious when you returned and saw me on the sofa passed out?" Carlton asked, feeling angry.

"Babe, we had a lot of wine. I thought you crashed from being tipsy. Don't be like that. I was horny and wanted you, but you were sleeping, so…I fell asleep."

"Fell asleep, huh?" he teased.

"Knock it off. I am not in the mood. Did you not turn on the alarm?"

"No, I was going to do that when we went to bed, plus the electricity was out, so it was a moot point unless the battery backup kicked in. I never checked the status of the alarm!"

"Should we call the police? We have to report this," Brexley added. She wanted law enforcement to look around to see if they could find any new clues.

"Of course. We have to call. I need to take

something for my headache first. Okay?" Carlton stood up and walked toward his bedroom, swaying as he felt dizzy. Everything was spinning.

It was dark and rainy, but the lovebirds, Shawn and Maddie, slept in the queen-sized bed in Maddie's apartment, their bodies intertwined. Hours before, they shared a fabulous dinner she had prepared to surprise him. After dinner, Shawn seduced Maddie and made love to her twice. The lovers slept soundly. The note found earlier was not discussed. Shawn's phone rang at 2:46 a.m.

Under most circumstances, he would have let it roll over to voicemail. However, given the current events and all the craziness, he picked up his cell off the nightstand.

"This is Shawn," he answered the phone, sounding disoriented.

"Hey, sorry to wake you. I need to tell you what happened." Shawn listened for a few minutes while Carlton filled him in on the two events of the night—the rat and note and the whacking him on the head incident.

Maddie was awake, watching Shawn's facial expressions. She heard his responses, figuring out Carlton was on the phone, providing more bad news. Maddie wondered if the constant emergencies would stop. Irritated, she jumped out of bed to make coffee. She knew Shawn would be heading out, needing some coffee to go. Fuming, Maddie made noises as she slammed down the utensils and other items. She began crying out of frustration.

Shawn entered the kitchen and wrapped his arms around her, whispering into her ear. "It is okay, baby. I will be back. Go back to sleep."

"NO, nothing is okay. I am tired of all this shit. You have no idea. What are y'all doing to solve this case? I cannot stand this anymore. I am at my wit's end, seriously, Shawn." She pushed him away, feeling irritated.

Shawn rolled his eyes. He knew she was not well. She experienced nightmares every night since her return, screaming and thrashing around in the bed, sometimes whimpering as she cried in her sleep. It killed him to see her like that.

"I have to run to Carlton's house and take a report. A lot has transpired tonight. Please try to go back to sleep. Take one of the tranquilizers the doctor gave you. I will return as soon as I can, I promise." He took the keys off the kitchen counter, grabbed the coffee cup, kissed her cheek, and walked out the door.

After his departure, Maddie locked the front door and returned to the bedroom, hoping she could sleep.

It was pure darkness driving up the hill to Carlton's house. Shawn inquired about when the electricity would be restored to the city by calling the local utility company. Their response was less than helpful, stating within a few hours. The majority of San Antonio was still without power from the horrible weather. A new squall of storms was expected later in the morning. Hopefully, the technicians could restore power to the city before the new storms hit. The turbulent weather conditions were rare this time of year for the area.

A little after 3:30 in the morning, Shawn arrived at Carlton's house. Brian's police cruiser was in the driveway. Shawn did not realize that Carlton had phoned Brian as well.

Carlton opened the front door, looking disheveled. His hair was messy, which was unusual for him, and he looked pissy.

Shawn entered the house lit with candlelight since the electricity was still out. Brian was seated by the fireplace when Shawn entered the room. Brexley sat on a couch, covered up, looking cold and exhausted. Brian took notes, looking up when he heard Shawn.

"So, Carlton, I have the pictures of the injury. Are you sure you don't want to see a doctor? I agree with Brexley. You should have it checked out to ensure it is not serious. You could have internal injuries. Please, let me call an ambulance or take you to the downtown trauma center," Brian insisted.

"No, I don't even have a headache. It is just a little achy, that is all. Don't worry. If anything changes, I promise to drive to the hospital for a check-up," Carlton added, struggling to sound chipper.

Truth be told, his head did hurt, though not severely. It throbbed and ached. His eyes felt strange, too. There was pressure in the back of his eye, with some sensitivity. He did not want to upset Brexley more and make a big deal out of nothing.

"You were knocked out. Why? What did they take? Why not harm Brexley? It doesn't add up. Something is fishy," added Brian.

"Hey, I have no idea. That is your job to figure out. I am just here relaying the information about what occurred," Carlton said in a huff, feeling attacked.

"All I am saying is...it seems strange. Someone snuck into your house, knocked you out, which is not easy to do, did not harm Brexley, and left? Something has to be missing from the home. No one just comes to knock someone out. They were here for a reason. Can either of you think of something that they would want or need? Is there something you have not told us? Please, think about it," insisted Brian.

Shawn remained silent. He wondered the same thing. *'Why would someone risk getting caught in a house they had just broken into unless they were looking for something vital?'* Shawn scratched his head. He stared at Brexley. She seemed to have a clue, her eyes were wide, and she turned away when she noticed Shawn looking at her.

"Brexley, what is it?" Shawn demanded. He was not going to let her get away with remaining silent. She knew something.

"I was just thinking. Nothing is missing, as far as we can tell. The intruder specifically targeted Carlton. What does Carlton have that nobody else has? Well, only Carlton, Maddie, and I have the code to the wall safe. Also, Carlton and I are the only two capable of unlocking the wall safe with our fingerprints. Maybe they needed that?"

"Are you talking about the wall safe at the warehouse? I thought you said there was nothing in there of value. What are you not telling us, Brexley? You think they came into the house to make an imprint of Carlton's fingerprint. I hope you know that does not work well. In the movies, yes, in real life, not often." Shawn inched closer to her, getting angry. He began to question her honesty. She seemed aggravated and jittery.

Brexley looked down at her lap. Carlton stared at her. *'My goodness, she is hiding something! What the hell?'* Carlton approached Brexley. "Babe, is there something you have to tell us? What is in the wall safe? Please, you have to say something," insisted Carlton.

Shawn and Brian gave each other the *'I told you so'* look. They suspected something was amiss with the whole situation.

"There is nothing unusual in the wall safe. You know this, Carlton. You have access to it." Brexley was tired of the inquisition and accusations flung at her.

"Who else has access to the wall safe? Who knows about it?" asked Shawn.

"We have already told you. Three of us have access—Maddie, Carlton, and me. George knew about it but did not have the code. He knew where it was, nothing more," elaborated Brexley, arms crossed, squinting at the men, fuming.

"Okay, so why would they need someone's fingerprint? Can it be unlocked with just a fingerprint, or is it a combination of fingerprint and code?" Brian wanted clarification. It mattered.

"You need both," Carlton stated, sitting beside Brexley.

"So, how would they have gotten the code? It doesn't seem very helpful to have the fingerprint to open the box if they don't have the code. Why go through so much hassle to attain it if there is nothing of value within the wall safe? Something is still not right about any of this," declared Shawn.

The group remained silent, preoccupied with formulating a plausible explanation for why someone would want to hurt Carlton or potentially attempt to lift his fingerprint. What else could be the reason why they would have hit him over the head? The intruder also did not steal anything from the house, which seemed odd. The main point of interest was they did not harm Brexley, even though she was the main target from the get-go, and they left her unharmed in the house. Why?

Shawn and Brian stood by the kitchen sink, deep in a discussion. Brexley and Carlton remained on the couch. Carlton held an ice pack on the back of his head. It was now a little after 5 a.m. Brexley yawned, wanting to return to sleep.

"So, we are going to head out. You two, try to get some rest. Also, Carlton, I wish you would see someone about your head injury later today. Please!" Shawn said, giving Carlton a stern look.

"I will think about it. Thanks for coming out so quickly. I appreciate it. Brexley and I are very sorry about all the drama happening lately. I know it affects you both."

"Hey, it is our job. You are totally fine. Please do not hesitate to call if anything else happens or if you think of something you want us to know," added Brian.

Carlton stopped Brian. "About the rat. Do you still want that? I left it by the back door in a bag."

"Sure, I will take it, but I am more interested in the note." The two men left.

Brexley followed them to the front door, securing it after their departure. She was hesitant to leave the door unlocked, quickly punching in the alarm code for good measure now that electricity had been restored. It was early morning, and Brexley was ready to sleep a little longer.

Carlton looked exhausted. The two walked to his bedroom and crawled into bed without conversing. Brexley gently snuggled up against his back, avoiding his hurting head. He smiled, falling asleep and feeling her warm, naked body up against his.

Maddie stayed awake, reading, after Shawn's departure. Willa was curled up by the fireplace, staying warm. At six in the morning, she heard the noise of the keys jingling, and then the front door opened. Shawn entered, looking beat.

After a few minutes of conversing, Shawn suggested they try to sleep. Maddie remained wide awake and told him she planned to read her new book in the living room. For once, Shawn didn't argue. Instead, he made his way to the bathroom to shower.

Brexley heard birds chirping and saw the bright sunlight coming into the room. She left the blinds open the night before. It looked like a gorgeous day. Not a cloud in the sky. She stretched, jumped out of bed, and reached for her pants and T-shirt, which were still on the floor. She took them into the bathroom with her to shower and dress later. Hearing her stomach growl, Brexley headed to the kitchen, eager to make breakfast. She thought about making Eggs Benedict, Carlton's favorite breakfast. Brexley knew how to make it and decided it was the dish she would serve. It took almost thirty minutes to make the eggs and hollandaise sauce and set the table.

The coffee brewed, and its aroma made her smile. Brexley looked outside, noticing the beautiful trees displaying gold, orange, and brown colors. Brexley was eager to start decorating the house. She was finally in a festive mood. Fall in Texas was spectacular. She picked up her cell phone and read emails when Carlton appeared wearing a black tracksuit and sneakers. He looked freshly showered, his hair combed but damp.

He approached and kissed her on the lips. "Hello, gorgeous," he said, grabbing her butt playfully.

"I see. Someone is feeling better," Brexley joked back.

"What's on our agenda for the day?"

"Well, we will start with Eggs Benedict, coffee, and orange juice. Then, I thought, we could drag out the holiday décor and start decorating unless your head is still not well," Brexley said, handing him a cup of strong black coffee.

He smelled it approvingly and then took a drink. "Sounds like a plan to me. I see breakfast is ready. Wow, I am astonished you made an elaborate dish like Eggs Benedict! I did not know you had it in you." He kiddingly announced as he sat down to eat.

"Stop your sassiness, Sir. I am capable. I don't enjoy cooking as much as baking. You know this," she said, laughing. The two ate their delicious breakfast, happy and content.

Earlier in the morning, the warehouse was dark and quiet. Cat-Face, Alexandria, sat silently in a desk chair, alone in the office. She wondered if Dereck and Ashton would show up soon. She texted Ashton, asking him to come to the workplace to discuss a few things. He never responded. When she called, he declined the call. Alexandria fumed.

Alexandria saw the warehouse fire and investigation report on the local news. She planned to distance herself from the entire situation. Their plot to destroy Brexley Sinclaire had failed.

In the beginning, she had a well-thought-out strategy, tasking Dereck and Ashton to remove Brexley's business from the area by burning down her warehouse.

Now, unfortunately, the warehouse only sustained minor damage. It seemed as if the two morons were incapable of doing anything right. Alexandria thought about doing it herself but quickly realized some outside force told her to stop. Rather than continue down a clearly not working path, Alexandria focused on rebuilding her business the old-fashioned way — through hard work and resilience.

Frustrated beyond belief, she tried to concentrate on a different future for herself and her business that would not include her brother. Alexandria did not want any connection between herself, Ashton, and Dereck. The two crossed the line too many times, and she planned to distance herself from the imminent fallout that would result once law enforcement caught on to them.

Realizing she had to do something, Alexandria decided to shut down her business in San Antonio. She planned to sell it, move to another town, perhaps even a different state, and start over. After the dust settled, Alexandria hoped no one would suspect her involvement. She never intended for anyone to suffer physically. Her brother took things too far. Murdering an innocent man was the worst-case scenario.

Sadly, she could not undo what he had done. That is why she was adamant about releasing Maddie unharmed. In a way, she worried about how much Maddie figured out about her location and captors.

Alexandria hoped they had been careful enough that Maddie was clueless and unable to help the police figure out who kidnapped her and why. Alexandria felt many regrets but remained unwilling to destroy her life for Brexley.

In New Braunfels, approximately thirty miles from San Antonio, Devvyn rolled over in bed and picked up her cell phone. She had four missed calls from Brexley. Carlton texted numerous times as well. She wanted to call Brexley but was still upset with her. Maybe it was best to meet her in person to discuss the situation.

Devvyn dropped the phone on the duvet and jumped out of bed. It had been two weeks since she saw Brexley last. Their telephone conversation did not go well either. Brexley acted like an innocent victim. She loved Brexley but knew she was not as guiltless as she acted. Devvyn helped her set up the staging business ten years prior and knew Brexley could be ruthless when she wanted to be.

Now that everything in her life was falling apart, Brexley desperately hung on to everyone she trusted. Devvyn tried to distance herself from Brexley. She did not need nor want the negative press. Devvyn's business was booming and one of the most successful Medi-Spa's in the area.

Devvyn was a faithful and good friend to Brexley. She supported and loved her dearly. However, now she noticed some bothersome traits in Brexley. It was apparent she had changed. Even Carlton backed away, planning to move to Seattle to escape her. Devvyn didn't blame Carlton. He was a treasure, and Devvyn had difficulty comprehending how Brexley could toss him aside. Devvyn planned to contact Brexley soon and have a long chat about everything. They had to clear the air! She hopped back on the bed, feeling frustrated.

Lounging, Devvyn recalled Brexley and Carlton's past. Carlton waited a long time for Brexley to commit to their relationship. Devvyn met with Carlton the day he planned to propose to Brexley. She helped him pick the perfect diamond ring, familiar with what her friend liked.

Devvyn coached Carlton, suggesting what to say and avoid, knowing Brexley. Everything seemed perfectly prepared until she received his heartbreaking phone call a few hours later. Carlton had broken it off with Brexley. She refused his proposal. It was mindblowing to Devvyn that Brexley could be so heartless and insensitive. Her actions showed Devvyn a totally different view of her. Devvyn realized it was time to step back from her relationship with Brexley.

Devvyn remembered the day she first met Brexley. They literally bumped into each other at a coffee shop in town. Brexley's coffee spilled all over Devvyn, and in return, Devvyn tripped, spilling her coffee. Since the scalding hot coffee burned neither but had poured onto Devvyn's hand, they both laughed nervously. Brexley graciously offered to buy Devvyn a new coffee and pay her for the dry cleaning of her clothes. Devvyn declined, feeling awful for Brexley, noticing how desperately she attempted to fix the situation. Brexley insisted they exchange numbers to contact her later to ensure everything was okay. Devvyn agreed.

Later in the day, Brexley called Devvyn, checking up on her to ensure her hand was not hurting since some of the coffee had spilled on it. Devvyn reassured her it was fine.

The two talked for an hour, feeling comfortable with each other. The next day, Devvyn reached out to Brexley, inviting her for lunch. The two became good friends after that. They talked daily, sometimes numerous times, texting each other throughout the day. Months later, Brexley prepared a steak dinner for Devvyn. Brexley planned to ask Devvyn for assistance setting up her new staging business. The two worked tirelessly for weeks, eventually naming the company *Sinclaire Premier Staging*.

Devvyn never wanted anything in return. It was her pleasure to help a friend. She believed Brexley would become a star in her field. She had been decorating homes and staging them for years, loving the field of interior design. It seemed natural and flawless for her to transition into her own business.

Once Brexley hired Maddie, the company was on a roll, expanding quickly to accommodate the community's increased referrals from realtors and friends. Within two years, Brexley became a known name in the area.

Devvyn was proud of her friend until she noticed Brexley's attitude changing. She seemed much more driven, less approachable, and definitely less available to family and friends. It was as if she had placed her work first, discarding everything else. Devvyn hated what Brexley had become.

When Brexley confided in Devvyn about her new writing contract with a publishing house in New York, Devvyn thought it was a horrible idea. It was one more thing to take the focus off the staging business and its success.

Devvyn argued with her friend, attempting to highlight the adverse effects of her lack of attention to the company. Brexley refused to listen, headstrong and determined to do both.

There was nothing Devvyn could say or do. She eventually gave up and vowed to remain supportive of her friend, hoping in time, she would realize she could not run a successful staging company and become a well-known author at the same time.

Devvyn sighed, reminiscing about her friendship with Brexley, which slowly disintegrated. Though Devvyn wanted to remain friends with her, she knew this temporary time-out between them was necessary. It was a blessing that Brexley chose to lean on Carlton in her time of need. He was reliable and loved her dearly, always loyally by her side. Perhaps this would bring them back together, maybe permanently? It was the push Brexley needed, or so Devvyn believed.

CHAPTER 11

A shton waited impatiently for Dereck. Suddenly, he approached the van, running away from the house, keeping his face low to avoid detection. His black, hooded sweatshirt covered his face. Once he sat in the van next to Ashton, they quickly drove toward their apartment to discuss the next step in their newly formulated plan.

As morning arrived, Dereck stood in the kitchen wearing checkered boxers, making coffee. Ashton entered the kitchen minutes later, wearing shorts and a faded dark-blue T-shirt. He looked beat, sporting a stubbly face and unkempt hair. The two sat in the living room, sipping coffee, still too tired to converse.

Dereck eventually stood up, walked toward the balcony glass doors, and looked out. The city was alive. He spotted kids playing and people out and about. Dereck desperately yearned for a family of his own and to live a normal life. He had no idea living with Ashton would turn his life upside down. Dereck never thought he would become part of a kidnapping plot and murder. He supported his lover and friend but now thought it was time to separate. It was not worth it for him to be associated with this unstable family.

Alexandria and Ashton had some serious issues. He discovered that quickly enough, regretting his decision to help them out. Dereck decided the previous night was the last time he would aid them. It did not matter if they were upset. He called Karlos, his youngest brother, and asked if he could crash at his house for a while. Karlos agreed, informing him he could stay as long as he wanted without asking questions.

Now, Dereck had to let go and figure out a way to leave without threats from Ashton. Most likely, Ashton would become belligerent, implying his participation in the murder and kidnapping, maybe even going so far as to threaten him.

Dereck knew it would not be easy but remained hopeful he could convince Ashton it was time to end their relationship.

After all, Ashton pulled the trigger and senselessly murdered the man at the warehouse. Dereck agreed to work as a security guard at the warehouse to help locate the documents Alexandria wanted. Other than that, he did not want any kind of involvement. It scared him. He agreed to help out only to appease Ashton, who continuously begged him to do something.

As Ashton finally became more awake, he opened his laptop and vigorously pecked away on the keyboard. Dereck turned around to look at him. It saddened him to realize that soon, he would be gone. Dereck would live far away, in another state, nowhere near the person he loved. Their hopes and dreams as a couple were over.

Dereck walked to the bedroom, closed the door, and looked for his dark blue suitcase. He began packing. It made no difference if he did it now or later. Ashton would be furious with him no matter what.

On the other side of town, Alexandria locked the warehouse's front door. She let out a heavy sigh, feeling disappointed and sad. Never, ever, did she anticipate having to sell her company, especially under these conditions. It made her sick.

Luckily, one of her good friends, Irene von Lundren, accepted her offer to purchase the entire business, including the warehouse filled with inventory. Irene was a local stager and competitor trying to expand her business. It did not take long for Alexandria to find a buyer. She made three calls to people she assumed would be eager to take over. The third caller agreed.

After over an hour of negotiating via video chat, an agreement was reached. The official asset sale agreement papers were in the process of being drafted by Alexandria's attorney, Patricia Stormmer. The money wire transfer would be completed within a few weeks. In the meantime, Alexandria purchased a one-way airline ticket to Florida.

She planned to stay in her family's summer home near Fort Lauderdale. Once there, she would figure out what she wanted to do next with her life and whether to remain in Florida or move elsewhere.

Alexandria jumped into her luxury sedan and sped toward her home. She had an upcoming meeting with her realtor. It was the last item on her list — to sell her house. Once the house sale was complete, nothing was left to tie her to Texas or the drama surrounding Brexley

Sinclaire. She would turn her car over to Ashton and allow him to keep it. It did not matter to her what he planned to do with it.

As Alexandria Betterson approached her home, she noticed the two unmarked police cars. She recognized one of the officers exiting one of the vehicles as she parked.

"Ms. Betterson. May we speak briefly?" asked Shawn.

"What would you like to discuss, officer? I thought I had clarified that I had no new information for you. Nothing has changed. I am expecting someone to arrive shortly. I do not have time for this right now! So, can we wrap this up quickly?" Alexandria did not want her realtor to appear while the cops were present. It would raise suspicion.

"Well, we have some questions for you that we need you to clarify for us. We can do that here, or you can accompany us to the police station. That is your choice. What would make you more comfortable, Ms. Betterson?" Shawn replied snippily.

"Fine, what is it now?" Alexandria replied in a huff, pissed off at the threatening tone the cop used with her.

"Okay. So, the other day when we were at your warehouse, you stated you had not been in touch with Ms. Sinclaire in a while. You also said you had nothing to do with the issues she was experiencing. Is that still your story, or is there something you would like to add?"

"Add? Like what? What exactly are you implying? I do not care for your tone of voice, officer." Alexandria stood in front of Shawn with her arms crossed.

"I believe there is more to your story. Perhaps you left out pertinent information," Shawn responded, noticing her stand-off attitude. Brian remained in the background, observing them both, looking around. He did not plan on talking unless things got out of control.

"Officer...what was your name again? Shawn something? Anyway, I have nothing to add to my so-called 'story.' As a matter of fact, I think it would be best to conduct any further communication with me through my attorney, Ms. Stormmer. I can provide you with her phone number. I am now heading inside. As I said, I am late for a conference call. Have a nice day, gentlemen."

Alexandria picked her purse off the ground and walked to the red front door. After unlocking it, Alexandria briefly turned around one more time to see what the two men were doing. They were both in their cars, presumably getting ready to leave. She dropped her purse on the tile flooring in the entryway. Frustrated, she leaned against the closed front door, her heart racing. 'What do they know? Do they suspect me? I need to call Ashton again,' she said out loud.

Shawn left first, heading back downtown to meet with Maddie. Before leaving, he informed Brian he was done working for the day. Brian told Shawn he was returning to the office to conduct more research on Alexandria and her brother, Ashton. He also wanted to learn more about her other employees and close acquaintances. Brian figured something shady was going on and planned to expose it. Also, he wanted to confront Carlton about his relationship with Alexandria because it bothered him. Brian wanted to fill in some blanks. Things were missing, and he did not like it, not one bit.

Alexandria called her realtor twice since she had not yet arrived. It was odd. She was always early, never late. Alexandria made coffee, taking off her high heels. Her feet hurt, and she was still agitated that two police officers had made their way to her home. They were constantly showing up unexpectedly, and that could lead to disaster. It was high time Alexandria left the area. The quicker, the better.

It did not take long for Brian to return to the office. Finally, he sat in his black office chair, relaxing. Now, he scanned through some documents. Brian believed now was the perfect time to reach out to Carlton Chastain and discuss his past relationship with Alexandria Betterson. He picked up his phone and dialed Carlton's number.

The call disturbed Carlton. He was changing into casual clothes, having finished his workout and showering. He recognized the number and frowned, wondering why Brian was calling him.

"This is Carlton," he said, sounding irritated, answering the call.

"Hello, Carlton. It is Brian. Do you have time to meet me? I want to discuss a few things with you in private. I only need about an hour of your time. I would prefer we meet now, today!"

Brian wanted Carlton to get the drift this was an urgent matter. It was a demand, not a request.

"Sure, can you give me a clue what it is about?" Carlton asked, feeling blindsided.

"Absolutely. I want to talk to you about Alexandria. More specifically, your past relationship with her. I figured you would prefer not to discuss this in front of Brexley. It is better if we meet at Joe's Coffee & Bistro. Can you be there in thirty minutes?"

"Okay, Brian. I am confused as to why you want to discuss Alexandria. That is an odd request, but because I am curious, I will be there. I only have an hour, though. Brexley and I have plans," Carlton replied as he slid his wallet into his back jeans pocket.

"Great, see you in a while," Brian responded, hanging up the phone.

Carlton combed his hair, spritzed on some cologne, and walked out the bedroom door, heading to the living room to inform Brexley of the quick errand he had to run.

Brexley was dressed, reading her emails on her phone, when Carlton entered the living room. She smelled him when he entered. Brexley gave him a warm smile, standing up to kiss him.

"Hey, Luv. I have to run out for a bit. I have some files I have to pick up at the office. Janice is heading out of town for Thanksgiving and Christmas for an extended holiday vacation, and I thought it would be best to wrap things up at the office. I will be back in an hour or two, and we can go shopping and do something you enjoy. Is that okay?"

"Oh, okay. Do you want me to tag along?" Brexley quickly asked, not wanting to stay home alone.

"No. I will be back soon. Why don't you make a list of things we have to buy later and I promise to hurry back soon. Love you!" He expeditiously left the house before she could object.

Carlton hurried to meet Brian. He had every intention of making the meeting and getting it over with quickly to spend the rest of the day with Brexley. When Carlton finally arrived at the restaurant, Brian waved him down, sitting at a small, round table by a window. He sipped coffee and had a delicious-looking blueberry muffin on a plate before him. He looked serious and not at all friendly. Instantly, Carlton worried.

"Thanks for coming, Carlton. Can I get you a coffee? How about a doughnut or muffin? The baked goods are yummy," Brian offered.

"Umm, no thanks. So, what is this about Alexandria?"

Brian placed his coffee mug on the table and folded his hands. "Tell me about your relationship with Alexandria. Please start at the beginning. How you met, and how long you dated? Do you recall the last time you saw her?"

Carlton rolled his eyes. He was greatly irritated that Brian felt the need to ask these questions. But, because he wanted to get on with his day, he answered him, still curious why he wanted to know.

First, Carlton explained how they met. It was a year earlier when he attended a management meeting at work. Alexandria was a guest speaker hired to discuss an event the company held for the holidays. She chose to sit next to Charlton. After the meeting ended, she introduced herself to him, acting flirty. The two talked for a while but never exchanged numbers. Two weeks later, he ran into her at a local restaurant.

He was drinking at the bar, and she sat on the stool next to him. They picked up where they left off before—holding casual conversations. After spending hours together at the bar, Carlton asked her for a date. She accepted. The two arrived almost the same time that following Friday at the Italian restaurant she chose. Alexandria looked pretty with her long, dark brown hair pulled up with long, unruly curls dangling down the side of her face. She had amazingly long, toned legs. She showed off her cleavage in a tight, slinky red dress, strutting toward him, wearing black high heels. He was instantly attracted to her, plus he had not had sex since his break-up with Brexley months before.

They spent dinner talking and flirting, ending up at his house, having wild sex for hours. The two saw each other two more times. Unfortunately, Carlton began to notice some rather strange and disconcerting things about Alexandria. She was relentless in bringing up Brexley and her business again and again. Alexandria became ruthless, wanting details and using sex as her weapon of choice to get Carlton to respond.

However, he was not stupid. Carlton caught on to Alexandria's game, wondering why she was doing it at all. When he confronted her, she stated she knew Brexley. They shared a history all the way back to high school and college days. That was when she explained her entire relationship with Brexley to Carlton.

Brexley and Alexandria attended the same high school though Alexandria was not from a well-to-do family like Brexley. Alexandria came from a single-parent household. Her mother worked two jobs to keep her family afloat, which meant Alexandria had to work, too, in her senior year, to help out.

Alexandria had no time to socialize or have a boyfriend, which made her envious of other girls who could date and have fun.

Brexley and Alexandria knew each other but were not good friends. Years later, they both attended the same local college in Texas. When Brexley ran into Alexandria on campus one day, they talked for an hour, catching up on their lives. The two liked each other, laughing and joking the entire time.

Eventually, they spent more time together, watching movies, double-dating, etc. Then, one dreadful night, Alexandria had to help Brexley as she had never had before.

Brexley had accepted a date with a handsome, well-known student at the university. All the girls drooled over him, yearning for his attention. However, Brexley was the one he chose. So, the two started dating. On their second date, he invited her to a local motel where he scattered rose petals over the floor, a bottle of champagne chilled in a bucket, and a small box of chocolate truffles was placed next to the champagne glasses. Brexley thought she had hit the jackpot. He was handsome, attentive, and oh-so thoughtful. The two indulged in champagne. One thing led to another. They kissed and started making out on the bed. Just as he was about to remove her panties, she stopped him, insisting she was not ready to have sex.

Brexley confided she was still a virgin. Her date became aggressive, accusing her of playing games. He threw himself on top of her, ripping off her lacy white panties. While pinning her down her arms, he violated her while she whimpered out in pain, paralyzed by fear, unable to move. Once he finished, he dressed quickly and walked out of the motel, slamming the door and calling Brexley a stupid, worthless tease.

Brexley remained half-naked on the bed, curled up in a little ball, unable to speak. She rocked back and forth, hurting. After some time, she managed to get up.

Without thinking, Brexley jumped in the shower to get any part of him off and out of her body. After showering, she dressed, wondering how she would return to her apartment. She was scared and realized Alexandria was the only one she could call and trust.

Thirty minutes later, Alexandria arrived to pick up Brexley at the motel. She entered the room and saw the rose petals, champagne, and chocolates, feeling envious. Then she saw

Brexley sitting on the edge of the bed, her legs crossed, looking terrible. Her makeup was smeared, and mascara ran down her face.

Brexley's hair was wet, and she sobbed lightly as Alexandria helped her off the bed. The two quickly jumped into Alexandria's car and drove off in silence. Arriving at Brexley's apartment, Alexandria offered to come inside and talk. Brexley informed her she needed some time, thanking her for coming to her rescue. Brexley stayed away from the school campus, classes, and everyone for weeks, staying holed up in her apartment.

One afternoon, Alexandria stopped by Brexley's apartment with pizza and sodas, hoping to cheer her up. They talked for a few hours. Brexley finally confessed and told her all the awful details of that fateful night. She also shared that she was two weeks late with her period, fearing she could have gotten pregnant since she was not on birth control. Alexandria suggested they head to a local pharmacy for an over-the-counter pregnancy test. Brexley agreed.

Once seated on the toilet back in her apartment, peeing on the stick that would determine her future, Brexley cried. Alexandria remained in the living room, hearing her sob. Brexley emerged, holding the test stick in her right hand, shaking. Alexandria looked down and saw the big negative sign indicating she was not pregnant. The two hugged, and Brexley was grateful Alexandria had been by her side through this life-changing event.

Weeks later, Brexley changed schools, eager to get far away from Stuart, the man who raped her. Brexley's father never understood why she wanted to switch to a different college in the middle of the school year. Ultimately, he figured it had to be something drastic that caused her to beg him to allow such a significant change.

Brexley moved to North Carolina to attend a prestigious university far away from Texas, hoping to escape the nightmare she relived in her sleep every night. She never informed Alexandria about her expedited departure, wanting a clean break from everyone who reminded her of that night. North Carolina was also where she met Carlton Chastain.

"So, you see, their friendship was complicated. My relationship with Alexandria was brief. Once I realized she was more interested in Brexley and was using me, pumping me for information about her life, I told her we would not work out. We were too different, and I was uninterested in pursuing a relationship with her. I asked her to stay away and stop calling me," Carlton explained.

Carlton felt awful that he divulged Brexley's biggest secret, but he wanted Brian to know everything that had led up to this point with

Alexandria. Carlton assumed Alexandria felt that Brexley never fully repaid her for the kindness she'd shown her and wanted compensation. Perhaps Alexandria had kept her secret and thought it was something that deserved a reward. Brexley disclosed the rape to Carlton the night before their first anniversary together.

Carlton had thoughtfully bought a ton of roses and had placed them all over their bedroom. A bottle of champagne chilled in a silver bucket. Carlton added a round plate filled with her favorite European chocolate truffles. When she walked into the room, it elicited flashbacks from the night she was raped. She ran from the room, crying and trembling. He found her curled up on the floor in the kitchen, hiding like a child in trouble. He bent down and tried to talk with her, but she pushed him away, screaming.

Confused, Carlton left her there for a while. He finally mustered up the courage to return and speak with her. He picked her off the floor and carried her to the couch while he sat on the coffee table facing her.

"Baby, what happened? What did I do? Please, tell me. I feel awful," Carlton confessed, watching her quivering.

Brexley managed to speak, though she was still trembling. Eventually, she told him everything. Carlton was shocked and felt even worse. He wished she had told him before. He would have never decorated the room for her the way he did if he had known. Now, he felt like a complete jerk. But it was not his fault. Hopefully, Brexley would not be mad and understand it was a romantic gesture, not something meant to harm her or evoke bad feelings from the past.

Brian finished taking notes. "So, what you are saying is you broke it off with Alexandria? When was the last time you saw her? Can you recall?" He eyed Carlton, wondering if he would tell him the truth.

"I really have no clue. It has been months. She does not call me, and I certainly do not call her. Are we done? I need to get back to Brexley," Carlton insisted, hoping to end their conversation and meeting. "Also, please — let's try to keep this conversation private, if at all possible. I do not want Brexley to know I told you about the rape. It would upset her greatly, and things are complicated enough."

"Yes, we are done for now. If I have more questions, I will be in touch. I appreciate you coming out to meet with me. Thank you for your candor as well. I will try to keep the rape disclosure private." Brian stood up to shake Carlton's hand.

Carlton approached the counter and ordered two blueberry muffins to go. He planned to bring them to Brexley. Within minutes, he sped down the road, heading to his office to pick up some files. He also planned to say goodbye to Janice, his assistant, since she would be on vacation until the new year.

Carlton graciously agreed to give her some well-deserved time off. She wanted to spend time with her grandbabies in Vermont, celebrating Thanksgiving and Christmas with them there.

Brexley lounged on the couch, making a list. First, she wanted to pick up some items at the warehouse. Since the smoke and fire restoration team cleaned the building, returning it to usable space, she wanted to head there to pick up holiday decorations if the smoke did not damage them. She also hoped to snoop around the cute designer décor store in Boerne and purchase premium faux greenery sprays. Their selection was impressive.

Lastly, she figured they could stop by Michelle's real estate office to pick up a new list of available properties for sale. Brexley was determined to find a home she liked. Carlton seemed committed to moving to Seattle by March, and she would not be why he stayed in Texas. She planned to keep things uncomplicated.

Leaving his office with a box of files, Carlton set off for his home to spend time with Brexley. He did not see the man watching him through the binoculars.

Ashton hunched down in his car seat, trying to avoid being seen by Carlton. He had been following him for over an hour, hoping to figure out his daily routine. Ashton was determined to find out more about Carlton Chastain and Brexley Sinclaire. His sister, Alexandria, acted ridiculously, insisting they drop the previous plan, and he was not interested in that. In fact, he made his own plan to get the money promised to him and Dereck.

At the same time, Dereck walked out of the house on the other end of town, carrying two suitcases and a backpack. That is all that belonged to him. The other items in the household were Ashton's. Earlier in the day, Ashton left quickly, stating he wanted to run errands, implying he would be back in time for dinner.

That gave Dereck the time he needed to finish packing. His plane was on time. Soon, he would be free, far away from Ashton and his lunatic sister, Alexandria.

Carlton arrived to find Brexley ready to go. She stood by the kitchen island with her list and purse in hand. He had to laugh. "Wow, I guess you want to get out of here?" he asked.

Brexley smiled and nodded, walking toward the garage. Before she could open the door, Carlton pulled her into his arms and hugged her.

"I missed you, beautiful." Carlton kissed her

passionately. She dropped her purse onto the floor, embracing him, still holding her list.

"Want to fool around?" Carlton asked, teasing.

"As tempting as that sounds, how about we head out and run errands? We can always resume this fun later?" Brexley suggested, picking up her purse with a wide grin stretching across her face. Her eyes sparkled, and she looked happy.

The two left the house, eager to get things done. Neither spoke on the drive. Brexley acted preoccupied, scrolling through her phone, looking up only to see where they were. Carlton realized she had a lot on her mind and attempted to keep his mouth shut. He wanted to say so much to her, but he knew now was not the time, and he contemplated when the right time would arrive. Brexley seemed less interested in a serious conversation about their current relationship status.

On the other hand, Carlton was eager to find out where he stood with her, partly because he wanted to know whether or not to proceed with his move to Seattle in the spring.

At San Antonio International Airport, Dereck was checked in and sat in the terminal waiting area to board the plane. He looked out onto the tarmac. He wondered what Ashton would do once he found the note he had left behind. He would probably freak out. Dereck was glad he never told Ashton about his youngest brother. This way, hopefully, Ashton would not be able to find him. Too much had happened in the last few months. There was no way to salvage their relationship. Ashton revealed a side of himself to Dereck that changed everything.

Having grown up in a small town, Dereck was not used to the hustle and bustle of a larger town. He liked the active setting but despised the crime. Once he realized Ashton was not the person he thought he was, Dereck began plotting and implementing a plan to exit the relationship safely. It was not easy, though. Dereck adored Ashton. He was the first person he truly loved. But he knew it would never be a healthy relationship with so many lies between them.

The fact that Alexandria kept interfering in their affairs was not helping either. He was sure it would continue throughout their relationship, and Dereck was not interested in her continual meddling. Alexandria and Ashton had a strange and seemingly unbreakable bond. He realized it was best to walk away now before things became too complex.

The announcement blared through the loudspeaker. It was time to board the plane. Dereck picked up his backpack and carry-on luggage. He walked toward the plane, his head down, feeling sad and defeated. He would dearly miss Ashton. Dereck was about to leave behind everything and start a new life, which was challenging, to say the least.

Not too far away, Ashton felt bored, continuing to follow the couple until they pulled into a parking lot by the real estate office. He figured Brexley was buying a new house to replace the one she lost due to the fire.

Feeling hungry, he decided to head home. He wanted to speak with Dereck about his ideas regarding Brexley and Carlton and how he wanted to blackmail them for some cash. Ashton spent days putting together a profile on the two. He knew they both had plenty of money to spare.

Alexandria acted oddly, telling Ashton she was done with the drama and anything related to Brexley Sinclaire. She complained about the need to escape and seemed adamant about ending ties with Brexley, Ashton, and Dereck. She wanted nothing more to do with Maddie's failed and unauthorized kidnapping and the murder of George.

Alexandria planned to wash her hands and separate herself. She went so far as to inform Ashton that she demanded space between them, believing it was in everyone's best interest. Alexandria told him yesterday that she was leaving on vacation and would not return soon, refusing to share any other information with Ashton.

At first, Ashton became belligerent, yelling

and screaming at her, telling her she was selfish. Ashton insisted Alexandria stay and help him and Dereck fix the situation, finding a way to get the money they deserved.

However, Ashton soon realized she did not care about him or Dereck. Alexandria was happy to throw them both under the bus. Alexandria was in it for herself. She used Ashton and Dereck and now wanted to leave them with the mess to clean up. Infuriated, Ashton informed Alexandria to do what she wanted. He would find a way to get money out of Brexley Sinclaire.

Ashton arrived home to a quiet house. He dropped the keys on the dining room table and walked to the bedroom, wondering if Dereck was taking a nap. Immediately upon entering the room, he spotted the note propped up on the pillow on the bed.

Nervously, he walked toward the bed, grabbed the note, and looked around the room. He noticed the closet doors open, and half of the wardrobe was empty. He read the message:

"Dear Ashton. I am heartbroken, but I have to leave. I am not coming back. The situation with Alexandria is out of control. You have changed, and I can't be part of this twisted relationship you share with your sister. I hope someday you will understand. Please don't bother to try and find me. I want to be left alone to rebuild my life. You should do the same. Wishing you the best, Dereck."

Ashton dropped the note onto the dark grey, chenille comforter and sat on the bed. *'What the heck?'* He wondered, feeling frustrated. "Why the hell did Dereck leave? What a freaking loser! I have always been there for him," yelled Ashton, now crying. He punched a pillow, feeling abandoned. After minutes passed, he curled up on the bed, still sobbing, missing Dereck. He fell asleep emotionally drained.

The day quickly faded into the late afternoon. The sky turned dark blue and grey. Brexley was worn out. The time spent at the realtor's office was frustrating. Most homes Brexley liked were already under contract and off the market.

Brexley reluctantly agreed with her realtor that maybe it was time to consider building a house instead. Unfortunately, that meant a nine to twelve month wait for a home to be constructed. In the meantime, what would she do?

Carlton quickly reminded Brexley he would be happy to stay in town, postponing his move to Seattle, or if she preferred, she could live in his house until she found another place. Brexley disliked all the options presented. She preferred her own house with no strings attached. Evidently pouting, she stood up, thanked her realtor for help, and walked outside, ready to head back to Carlton's house. Brexley lost interest in shopping, too. She was hungry. Carlton followed her out of the building. Once in his car, she looked as if she would lose it. She sobbed slightly, her hands jittery. Carlton noticed instantly.

"Brexley, Luv, what is it? Listen, stop worrying about a place to live. Everything will work out. I promise." He reached over and held her hand, reassuring her all would be fine.

"I know. I feel like a lost dog right now. Everything is so upside down. I suppose we should focus on Thanksgiving and Christmas. Maybe we can shop for things tomorrow. I am not in the mood anymore. Is that okay?" Brexley asked him apprehensively.

"Sure! Whatever you want, Luv. Do you want to pick up some food? I think we should. Neither of us wants to cook, and it looks like it may rain again soon. It is so dreary!" Carlton drove off toward Gertrude's Haus, knowing Brexley would be happy to eat some hearty food.

He figured he would pick up Rouladen for dinner, one of her favorite meals. The Rouladen *"Dinner for Two"* included two Beef Rouladen, two German dumplings, a large container of red cabbage with apple, and four small buttery dinner rolls. An extra-large slice of cake called Bienenstich (Beesting) finished off the meal for dessert. Brexley loved the cake's fluffy cream filling.

Forty-five minutes later, they arrived home

with their meals. Carlton placed them on the kitchen counter and suggested Brexley change into more comfortable clothing.

She agreed. Brexley also wanted to take a pain pill. Her hand was hurting more than usual, seemingly irritating her more.

Carlton assembled the food on plates, rushing to make the dinner table look presentable for Brexley. She was distraught, and he wanted her to enjoy the evening. It was again raining outside, and the booming thunder overhead was quite loud. Carlton started a fire in the fireplace to warm up the living room. He figured they could curl up on the couch after dinner and watch a television show or movie.

Brexley appeared a few minutes later wearing pajamas. Her long, blonde hair was braided and hanging down the front of her right side, and she had removed her makeup. She smiled, but Carlton knew she was unhappy. He hoped dinner would lift her spirits.

He pulled out the dining room chair for her and pushed it back in once she was seated. She thanked him, reaching for the wine glass Carlton filled with Chardonnay. She sipped it, looking outside, noticing the pouring rain. It depressed her even more. Carlton placed the dinner plate in front of her. She nodded as she looked at the meal, though she wasn't all that hungry. She would have preferred to stay in her room, feeling anti-social.

Yes, Carlton was attempting to make the evening pleasant for her, but she thought about the fact that he was leaving soon. It seemed pointless to her that he continued to act friendly and accommodating despite planning to move on with his life, which did not include her. She contemplated speaking with him about it but changed her mind.

The two ate dinner, listening to the whistling wind outside, getting noisier. Carlton began to speak a few times and then noticed her face. She seemed out of it. *'Maybe she took a painkiller?'* He wondered. Brexley moved food around on her plate, acting disinterested. It did not go unnoticed by Carlton. Finally, he had enough.

"Brexley, Luv…what is going on tonight? I thought you were hungry. You are acting very distant and strange. Are you hurting? Please, tell me what is happening. What can I do?" Carlton offered, looking at her with worry.

Brexley thought about his questions. She pondered which question she should answer. Her head was spinning.

"Carlton, I know you are doing everything in your power to make my stay welcoming. I just feel melancholy. My life has turned upside down. You are leaving soon, and I have not heard a word from Devvyn in quite some time. Maddie is keeping to herself, not returning my calls or texts. I am not sure what is going on with that. I cannot find a house I like, and I feel like the clock is ticking. You will be moving soon, and I will be alone." Brexley finished her glass of Chardonnay and looked directly at him. Her words stung. Carlton felt helpless. He knew she was overwhelmed with uncertainty. However, he repeatedly offered to help her.

Every time Carlton suggested something, she refused. She acted hell-bent on saying NO to everything! After the continued rejections from Brexley, he stopped asking or attempting to assist her.

Apparently, she wanted to work things out independently, and he was happy to let her try. Carlton was speechless, something that was very unusual for him. He pushed back the seat, away from the dining room table, staring at her, unable to identify the right words to say.

CHAPTER 12

Maddie sat on the chair in the corner of the bedroom, watching Shawn as he slept. He looked peaceful and passed out to the world. She, unfortunately, could not sleep. The continual nightmares, recalling the kidnapping, caused her restless nights. The previously dreadful conditions she had been subjected to made her cry in her sleep. Often, she woke up whimpering in her slumber.

After the latest episode, she jumped out of bed and quickly ran to the bathroom, closing the door. She did not want to wake Shawn.

On the toilet seat, she wept. The nightmares were always the same. She was in the freezing warehouse, and Cat-Face stared at her as she peed in her pants tied up on the chair. She felt helpless and disgusted. Other times, she dreamt of crying on the uncomfortable, rickety cot with the wimpy, smelly cover draped over her body. Maddie was thankful to be home, safe and sound, but the bad dreams continued. She wondered if she should seek professional help. Maybe she had PTSD?

Maddie was reluctant to share with Shawn what she was experiencing. It made her feel vulnerable like she could not handle her life. However, deep inside, she figured he would want to know. Perhaps, he would even be angry with her if he knew she had kept this secret from him. Maddie felt torn. She had no idea what to do.

To make matters worse, she could not force herself to respond to Brexley's calls or texts, unable to think of things to say to her. Feeling guilty, Maddie called Carlton the other day, and from their conversation, it sounded as if Brexley was not physically or emotionally stable. The house fire and problems at the warehouse caused her a lot of grief, which she was not handling well. Carlton made it clear he worried about her mental state and felt clueless about how to help Brexley further. Maddie decided to stay away and let them work out the matters. Maddie had enough to figure out in her life. Frustrated, she crawled back into bed, curling up against Shawn, praying she could fall asleep without experiencing the terrorizing dreams.

The rain briefly stopped. The evening was chilly, and it was now dark outside. Carlton suggested they head to the living room to relax and watch television. Brexley quickly declined his offer but thanked Carlton for dinner and excused herself. She was eager to get back to her room.

Carlton reassured Brexley that he would put away the leftovers. She thanked him again, then hurried to her room, ready to sleep. Brexley was hopeful that the next day would be better.

Carlton watched Brexley exit the room. He was tired and lacked patience with her. She was moping and starting to act like a spoiled child. Carlton was not unsympathetic. However, Brexley had many options available to her. The problem was that she refused them all. Instead, she acted headstrong and stubborn, declining help and suggestions. Brexley needed psychological help. Maybe everything that had happened was affecting her too much. She was clearly not coping.

Instead, she rejected everyone and made a point to keep to herself as much as possible. It was very unlike Brexley to act in such a manner. Carlton knew he had to speak up. So, he put away the dinner leftovers, snuffed out the fire, and locked up the house, heading to Brexley's room for a serious and much-needed discussion with her.

Far away, on the east coast of the United States, Dereck arrived at his brother's apartment. Karlos greeted him by opening the door and allowing him to enter. Once inside, he escorted Dereck to the guest bedroom. The two exchanged a few words, and then Dereck showered and changed into boxer shorts and a T-shirt. When Dereck entered the living room, Karlos lounged on the L-shaped couch, eating a peanut butter and jelly sandwich.

"So, when will you tell me why you left your boyfriend? I thought you two were inseparable. I assumed you would get married. What the heck happened?" Karlos asked, worried, looking at his brother.

"Do we have to do this right now? Man, I am tired. I just want to chill. Can we talk later?" Dereck begged. He knew the questions would begin quickly but hoped they would wait until morning.

"Sure, but I think you owe me an explanation. I told Jill to be gone for a week. I informed her my brother had an emergency and was coming to town. So, how long do you plan to stay?"

"You did not have to tell your girlfriend to leave. I need a place to stay for a while. I also must find a job and get an apartment or a roommate. I left Texas because Ashton and his sister, Alexandria, got themselves into some serious shit, which we can discuss at another time — not tonight. It is a long story. I refuse to be part of their drama. All I will say is this — I had to get away from them both. I think they are crazy. I saw a side of Ashton that I hate. We are definitely done. I am not ever going back to Texas."

Karlos nodded but decided to keep the questions to himself for now. He could tell his brother was hurting and not ready to discuss everything that had led up to this moment. So, Karlos thought it was best to leave it alone. He would wait a few days before bringing it up again. Dereck needed to get settled and clear his head. Karlos would not push him.

Dereck got up and walked to the kitchen, opened the refrigerator, and withdrew a beer. Once he was back on the couch sipping it, he closed his eyes, wondering if Ashton had found the note he left on the bed and what he was planning to do about it. Dereck prayed Ashton would not come looking for him. It was the last thing he wanted or needed.

It was late, a Thursday night, and Brian was in the office, scouring through the Sinclaire files. He wanted to discuss a few things with Shawn in the morning but contemplated whether or not it was a good idea. Shawn was too close to Ms. Sinclaire.

Maddie's kidnapping was also too personal for him. Shawn had been good about staying out of the investigations, but he still wanted to be kept in the loop. For a while, Brian thought it was okay. Now, he felt it was time to let Shawn know he was off both active cases altogether. Brian would document everything to cover his butt. Cameron felt the same way he did. Shawn had to be kept out of everything from now on.

Brian opened Maddie's folder. He pulled out several pieces of paper. Reading them, he sat back in the uncomfortable, old rolling desk chair. The light above his head was still not fixed, buzzing and annoying the hell out of him. He pulled out several photos from the file folder.

One picture was of two men talking near Maddie's apartment building, taken by a detective. The photograph was of Ashton Betterson and his boyfriend, Dereck. Brian had met both men before at Alexandria's warehouse on several occasions when he visited her to ask her questions. Both men seemed too nosy and insisted on listening in on the questioning. Though there was no need for them to be present, Alexandria insisted her brother, Ashton, stay. *'He was a strange man,'* thought Brian.

A few times, Ashton interrupted their discussions, asking odd questions, seemingly attempting to divert the line of questioning by Brian. However, Brian knew what he was doing and quickly redirected the line of interrogation, visibly irritating Ashton. Eventually, Ashton gave up, excusing himself to head to the back of the warehouse. Dereck followed behind him like a puppy dog. The two men were a strange couple, for sure.

Now, Brian wondered what was going on. He heard Alexandria was not staging homes or businesses or working at the warehouse. Ashton and Dereck were also not around. Brian previously informed the three not to leave town until the investigation was over and closed. Yet, all three were unavailable when he reached out to them, attempting to arrange a formal interview at the police station. It raised suspicion for Brian. He planned to locate all three and bring them in for more questioning.

He closed the large file and turned off his computer, planning to head home for the night. Just as he was about to leave, Sergeant O'Conner stopped him. "Hey, Brian...I need a minute with you, please. One of my friends, Cassidy, who is in the Staging business, informed me that one of your suspects, Alexandria, has sold her business. Did you know that?" He waited for a reaction from Brian. He assumed he did not know.

"I thought I heard something about that, yeah. What does that have to do with you? I am confused," asked Brian. He lied about knowing about Alexandria's business sale. Brian was not about to let Peter know this. It would make Peter feel superior, and he was cocky enough already.

"Well, rumor has it, she up and left town last night because she and her brother had a huge fight. Supposedly, something went down. I thought you might want to check it out. It seems strange how suddenly Alexandria is leaving town after everything that has happened. We both know in our line of work that it is suspicious behavior. Plus, Cassidy is friends with Ashton or used to be. She said Ashton has been very moody lately and acting strangely. His boyfriend has been MIA for a few days. You may want to conduct a little fact-finding mission on that one," he commented snarkily.

"Okay. I appreciate the information. Have a good night." Brian walked away, curious as to why everyone was suddenly so interested in his cases. Peter O'Conner was a brown-nosing, stuck-up guy. Brian could not stand him and made a point of avoiding him as much as possible. O'Conner had a reputation for getting involved in other people's cases, hoping he could take over and shine a light on himself. Brian had no clue how this man had made the rank of sergeant in a short amount of time. He was not the best police investigator by any means.

Brian left the building at 10 p.m. on the dot. He drove down the wet streets of San Antonio, hoping to arrive home before the weather turned worse. Another storm was forecast and was due at any moment. Brian had an odd feeling he was being followed. He looked in his rear-view mirror but did not see anyone right behind him. Before heading home, he pulled into the gas station to fill up his truck. Once he was pumping gas, he looked around for anything suspicious.

Brian did not know why he felt something was wrong. He just did. Minutes later, he was back on the road, heading toward his home in Stone Oak. When a car pulled in behind him, he approached the gate to punch the security code to the gated community where he lived. Not thinking, he punched his code, 9688, and drove through the open gate.

As Brian made a right turn, the car followed. Unaware, a car followed him. He pushed the garage door opener. The garage opened, and Brian immediately pulled his truck into the building, clicking the button and closing the double garage door.

He stepped out of the truck and opened the door leading into the house. He punched in the alarm deactivation code and turned on the overhead light in the hallway. Brian walked toward the front door to ensure it was still locked. Something was not right. He could not shake the strange feeling. Apprehensively, he touched the weapon strapped on the side of his waist, wondering why he was worried.

The evening was about to change drastically for Brexley. She had no idea as she slept curled up on her bed, still hungover from drinking too much Chardonnay.

Carlton sulked, wondering why she was acting so erratic and strange. It was becoming a pattern, one that he did not enjoy. He hoped to take her shopping in the morning, making her more cheerful. Carlton pounded on her bedroom door. He had a plan, one which seemed perfect. She did not answer. He turned the knob on the door and opened it. The room was dark, and he heard noises coming from the bed. She was in a deep sleep. He felt bad about waking her but knew it was necessary. There was no way he would wait for her to wake up in the morning and then confront her. It was happening tonight!

"Brexley, hun, wake up. I need to speak with you. Can you hear me?" Carlton asked.

"Oh, for goodness sake, what is it now? Who is dead? Someone better be dead. I am tired and not in the mood," Brexley yelled, getting irritated.

"No one is dead. I know you are tired, but

you left rather quickly tonight to head to bed. Luv, we need to talk."

"Now? In the middle of the night? Really, Carlton? What the hell? I promise I will be attentive in the morning. I need sleep. I cannot hold a civil conversation when I am angry and tired." Brexley turned over onto her side, her back facing him.

Carlton sat on the edge of the bed. "And, while you are at it, please turn off the bright light on the way out."

"Brexley, I am not leaving. We are doing this. Tonight. You will not continue to run away from this. What is going on with you lately? You are not yourself," Carlton bellowed. He was furious.

Brexley turned around to face him. She looked awful. Her eyes were red and puffy. Reluctantly, she sat up in bed, glaring at him.

"Luv, I realize so much has happened. I know you are having a difficult time. What I do not understand is why you are pulling away instead of leaning on me. What have I done to upset you? I have repeatedly tried to comfort and help you. What is it you need that I am not providing?" Carlton asked, feeling concerned.

She thought about his words and actions. Yes, he had been quite attentive lately. He also seemed interested in pursuing a stable relationship with her. However, Brexley overheard his conversation with his realtor the other night. He informed Becker he was still on track to move in the spring. The house would still be put back on the market after the holidays.

So, that left Brexley no choice but to make alternative plans. Carlton was not honest with her. He informed her that he was not in any hurry to leave for Seattle on numerous occasions. But, his conversation with Becker said otherwise.

Brexley was reluctant to tell Carlton she overheard their conversation, but he was the one insisting they have this talk tonight. So, it was best she confronted him. She felt betrayed. Brexley loved Carlton and knew, without a doubt, he was the one for her, a soul mate.

"You say you want communication. You say you want honesty. Okay, be honest. WHY did you tell Becker, your realtor, you were still planning to sell the house in spring and move to Seattle? That tells me you are ready to move on and not work on our relationship. You are lying to me!" Brexley now squinted her eyes, looking furious, speaking loudly.

Carlton took a deep breath. He did not realize she had overheard that discussion. Carlton did attempt to reassure Becker the sale of the house was still going forward, only to appease him because he was acting pushy. For Carlton, things were starting to feel different. His relationship with Brexley was changing.

Carlton honestly felt that he could not abandon her and leave for Seattle. Minutes after his quick chat with Becker, he thought it was best to cancel the house listing. That would get Becker off his back. Carlton planned to inform Becker that if he did move to Seattle in the future, he would enlist Becker's help to sell the home. That is all he could do. Hopefully, Becker would understand.

Brexley did not know Carlton texted Becker twenty minutes later, informing him to send the paperwork to terminate the listing agreement. He intended to pull the house off the market. Furthermore, Carlton planned to wait and see how things progressed with Brexley before making any more rash decisions.

Becker claimed he understood and emailed him a document to sign, which Carlton digitally signed and emailed back. So, the house was officially off the market. Carlton had not yet informed Brexley of the change, which is why she was probably so upset, feeling blindsided.

"Well, what do you have to say?" Brexley asked sarcastically, her arms crossed.

"Brexley, I have a lot to say. First, Becker and I came to an understanding. Twenty minutes after our conversation on the phone, the one you overheard, I texted him and asked him to terminate the listing. I pulled the house off the market. It is no longer for sale. I felt it was best for now. He agreed and said he understood. I planned to tell you tomorrow. I should have told you sooner. For that, I am sorry." Carlton smiled, hoping she would calm down. He hated to see her upset and acting nasty.

"Really? You are not selling the house?"

"Nope. I am not. I would prefer it if you officially move in with me, and while you are at it…" Carlton knelt, looking up at her, nervously licking his lips before shouting, "Marry me!"

He pulled out the turquoise-colored box and popped the lid open, exposing the beautiful ring he had purchased before. Carlton hoped this time that she would say YES! Carlton came up with the idea to pop the question of marriage earlier in the evening and hid the box. Now, he pulled it from the back of his pants pocket. Carlton wanted her to know that he was in this relationship forever, all in, no matter what. He would not leave her.

Brexley saw the look in his eyes. He was so darn handsome. She could hear her heart beating fast as she stared at the box in his hand. She jumped out of bed and kissed him. "Yes, I will marry you. Yes, yes, yes!!!!" This time, she did not hesitate. It felt right. The timing was perfect. She knew Carlton was the one and would not let him get away.

"Oh, my God. Are you serious?" That is all he managed to say as he slid the massive rock onto her hand. He reciprocated the kiss, elated she finally agreed to marriage.

It was not how Brexley thought she would accept his marriage proposal a second time, but she refused to say no. For weeks, she thought about building a life and future with Carlton. She also wondered how to broach the topic, scared he would feel the timing was wrong. So, she waited impatiently, praying he would eventually come to his senses and ask again, which he did. Brexley stared at her left hand, smiling. Carlton looked delighted and in love. It was the perfect moment, one she hoped they would never forget.

Carlton pushed her down onto the bed. He stripped off his clothes and kissed her, starting with her legs and working his way upward, stopping only when he gazed deeply into her eyes. She leaned back, enjoying his touch as he gently caressed her. She felt him hard against her, making her ache with desire for him. She whispered, "Make love to your future wife, babe." Carlton smirked, ready to oblige.

Devvyn had always adored the bustling tourist town of New Braunfels, Texas, as it brought it quite a bit of business. As she locked the doors to her Medi-Spa, she cautiously looked around. It was getting dark, and the rain began again.

Devvyn hated the rain more than anything. She loved the hot and dry weather. That is one reason she moved to Texas — to escape the awful weather she experienced in North Pole, Alaska.

On occasion, she visited friends, but always during the summer when the nights were bright and the weather warm. North Pole was a unique place to live. The fact it stayed light during the nights in the summer was strange to some. Natives of Alaska did not mind—most used blackout curtains to sleep.

As a child, Devvyn loved seeing the northern lights dancing across the sky. The gorgeous colors inspired her to paint growing up. She still painted, and some of her art was proudly displayed throughout her business on the walls.

Devvyn thought about Brexley. She watched the news report on television about the warehouse fire. The authorities confirmed Brexley's warehouse fire was arson. Devvyn felt sick thinking about how much Brexley was going through.

However, Devvyn was not ready to speak with Brexley. Devvyn leaned against the door outside her building and texted Carlton, hoping for an update. She wanted to know how things were proceeding with Brexley and if he still planned to move to Seattle. Devvyn hoped and prayed he would stay in Texas.

If Carlton left, Devvyn would feel obligated to step up and be there for Brexley, something she was not eager to do now. Devvyn had no idea why she was so opposed to helping her. Maybe it was their last conversation about the stupid book.

Devvyn had been quite angry with her. The two friends agreed to meet up for lunch. Brexley had some exciting news she wanted to share with Devvyn. Brexley sat across from her, looking chipper. She shoved the contract toward Devvyn, smiling. Devvyn looked it over and frowned.

"You are not seriously considering this, are you?" Devvyn asked, frustrated.

"Of course. Why wouldn't I? It is a great opportunity for me. I thought you would be happy for me. You know how much this book means to me." Brexley was hurt. *'Why does Devvyn think this is a bad idea?'* Brexley had worked hard for three years, repeatedly trying to get someone to pick up her book for publishing.

"Hmmm, let me think. How about you have worked your butt off to get your staging business off the ground for a few years now? Plus, your business is finally making some good money. Why risk that? If you put your energy into something else, you may risk your staging business failing. Really, Brexley. What the heck?" Devvyn pushed the contract back to Brexley, then crossed her arms, looking irritated.

It was not the reaction Brexley had hoped for from her best friend. Devvyn acted like a royal bitch. "What is your problem, Devvyn? When I asked you in the past if I should try to get my book published, you encouraged it. Now that it is happening, you are saying NO? Can you please tell me what changed your mind? You are supposed to be my best friend and mentor. I am getting mad!"

"Brexley, as I told you before, stop spreading yourself so thin. You are just one person. You cannot run multiple businesses successfully on your own. I know you think you can, but you can't. I would hate for you to lose the thriving staging business. You have worked hard and made a name for yourself in the industry. If you start focusing on the book, what will happen to that?"

Brexley contemplated Devvyn's answer. "Well, I have already made a plan. I am placing Maddie in charge at Sinclaire Staging. George can run the warehouse, and everything will be okay. I am not worried. Plus, I will still go into the office every day. I am still the head of the business and the company's face. There is no problem."

Devvyn thought about those words made by Brexley months ago. Now, George was dead. Maddie endured a kidnapping and acted strangely, unable to work. How would Brexley manage? Devvyn doubted things were okay. Even Carlton informed her things were not great. Carlton tried very hard to help Brexley but realized he wasn't a superhero, and his abilities were limited.

Thinking about how much things had changed, Devvyn shook her head, feeling heartbroken for Brexley. Noticing how hungry she had become, she decided to head to her favorite bistro downtown for a late evening dinner. It was a great little place with fabulous European foods. She loved their coffee and pastries.

Not much later, she devoured a pastry, looking out the large glass window. It was raining and pitch dark. The restaurant was closing soon, and Devvyn hoped to get home before the weather worsened. As she drove toward her house located on the northern side of New Braunfels, she noticed a car following her. She spotted it in her rearview mirror.

The vehicle swerved several times from side to side behind her, making her nervous. She continued to drive home, hoping she was just paranoid. *'Why would someone be following me?'* Suddenly, they honked, not just once but several times. Getting scared, she looked for a place to pull over, allowing them to pass.

Devvyn took the next exit, getting off Interstate 35, hoping the car would move along. As she drove slowly and cautiously down the access road, she noticed the rude driver and their vehicle had disappeared. She sighed, feeling relieved. Then she laughed, feeling silly that she had been so worried about nothing. Her phone pinged, and a new text came through.

Her car's Bluetooth asked if she wanted to read the message. Devvyn responded with—yes! The text message was from Carlton. The robotic voice read the text aloud, *"Devvyn, all is great. Brexley is fabulous. We are ENGAGED! Can you believe it? She finally said YES! I know she will want to tell you, so pretend you know nothing when she calls or texts you. I hope all is well with you! Let's plan on dinner soon, okay? We miss you so much. Cheers, C."*

Devvyn was delighted to hear the happy news. Finally, something good was happening! As she made a right turn, she felt the sharp, excruciating pain. Someone rammed her car, causing her to lose control. Devvyn's car spun in a circle on the slick, wet road, smashing into a light pole. Devvyn passed out as smoke billowed from beneath the car's hood.

At the gas station nearby, a few witnesses saw the tragic accident. Some fueled their vehicles when they heard the screeching noise, followed by a loud crashing sound.

Unaware of what had happened to Devvyn, Carlton snuggled up to Brexley, feeling content. Their lovemaking celebration had been incredible, and he was tired. Carlton was excited to share the information with Devvyn but hoped she would not tell Brexley that he had spilled the beans first. Hopefully, Brexley would invite Devvyn for dinner and give her the news then. Brexley snored loudly. She was worn out.   It was getting late, and Carlton wondered what tomorrow would bring as he lovingly gazed at his fiancée. Carlton finally felt complete.

CHAPTER 13

Cameron arrived in New Braunfels and came across the accident. He was in his undercover cruiser, so he quickly turned on his lights. He jumped out of the car while the rain pelted him. Cameron attempted to open the car door. It wasn't easy since the car crashed and became wrapped around the pole. He could see someone inside. Realizing he could not help, he ran back to his car to call in the accident, asking for assistance.

Within minutes, a fire truck and ambulance arrived. Not long after, the local police showed up. One of the three police officers approached his vehicle. Cameron exited the car to speak with her.

"Hi! I am the one who called in the wreck. I did not witness it, but it happened fairly recently. The car is still smoking. There are a few witnesses across the street. Well, there were. I am not sure if they stuck around with the rain and all. Oh, darn, I forgot to say...I am Cameron McIntyre with SAPD."

"Gotcha. Okay, well, you can go. We got it covered. Thanks for calling it in. Be safe in the rain," the female cop walked away.

"Umm, don't you want to take my statement or something?" Cameron yelled, following her.

Irritated, she spun around. "You just stated you didn't see anything. What kind of statement would you like to make, Officer Cameron McIntyre?" she replied, staring at him.

"It is Detective McIntyre. Okay, I just thought maybe you wanted my name or something. Nevermind. Have a great day, Officer. What was your name?"

Annoyed, she approached, facing him closely. "Detective McIntyre, as you can see on my uniform, my name is Carver. Thank you for your time. Here, take my card in case you need anything else." She walked away quickly, heading toward the mangled car. Cameron was shocked. *'She was rude as heck, or was she?'* He supposed she was correct. He had no information to share, so there would be no statement. He shrugged his shoulders, feeling like an ass.

Cameron jumped back into his car and drove off, glad the local police and EMS were on the scene. Hopefully, the person inside the vehicle would be okay. The accident scene looked terrible. From his previous experience, he assumed the person did not survive that. *'How sad,'* he thought.

Minutes later, the firefighters managed to pop open the mangled car door using the jaws of life. Immediately, one of the EMTs ran to check on the driver. He signaled his partner, who immediately came running with a gurney and cervical collar — the neck brace — to stabilize the woman.

Less than five minutes later, they managed to extract the victim. They quickly placed her into the ambulance, zooming off down the road to head toward the local hospital, hoping to save her life.

Carlton's phone rang numerous times. He finally decided to pick it up. After spending a few minutes on the call, he looked at Brexley nervously. He saw her facial expression, and her lips quivered. She twitched.

"Brexley, I know you heard that. Yes, Devvyn has been in an accident. Let's head to the hospital, shall we? She will be okay. I am glad Devvyn had my number in her purse as an ICE — In Case of Emergency contact. Hun, let's get dressed and head to New Braunfels. Come on. We need to be there for Devvyn."

As if in a trance, Brexley walked to her room to throw on some clothes. He followed her, watching her as she robotically dressed, remaining quiet. He knew this was it, the one thing that could finally drive her to madness. She looked dazed. He wondered if she needed medical attention. Maybe having her see a doctor in the Emergency Room was a good idea.

They pulled out of the driveway twenty minutes later and headed north on Interstate 35 to New Braunfels. Brexley's eyes were closed, and she made huffing noises. As they were about halfway to their destination, she began sobbing. Carlton touched her hand, driving with little to say, feeling helpless.

It was a busy night. Alexandria boarded the red-eye at San Antonio International Airport to Fort Lauderdale, Florida. Luckily, her home sold in a record 24 hours after she listed it with her friend Kristen.

Now, she was escaping Texas as quickly as she could. She parked her vehicle outside Ashton's apartment and mailed him the key along with a long letter explaining her departure. She also provided him a bill of sale—allowing him to legally transfer the vehicle into his name for a measly $10.00 price tag. She knew it would make him happy. He needed a new car, and this would help him out. She still felt terrible about not providing him or Dereck with money. However, everything had turned to crap, and now, she wanted to start her life over, away from any possible scrutiny.

Hopefully, the police would be okay with her sudden departure. Alexandria was never formally charged with anything, so she assumed it was okay for her to leave the state. Before the planned departure, as reassurance, Alexandria contacted her attorney, Patricia, and confirmed that she should be able to leave town without any repercussions.

Alexandria felt confident she made it out of Texas without any problems, but in the back of her mind, she knew somehow it was not over!

Brexley and Carlton pulled into the Emergency Room parking lot of the four-story hospital. The rain stopped, and the sky was clear. The wind was brisk as Brexley exited the vehicle. The two walked hand-in-hand toward the Emergency Room doors.

Once inside, Carlton walked to the information desk to speak with the hospital personnel about finding Devvyn. Brexley reassured the plump, older woman sitting behind the glass enclosure that she was

Devvyn's sister, which was a lie. She also told her that she had received a call from the hospital informing her that Devvyn had been transported to this location.

Within five minutes, a nurse appeared and directed the two to the waiting area. She communicated to them someone would be back in a few minutes to provide them with an update on Devvyn. Carlton did not care for the fact the nurse looked away when she implied *'someone'* would give them an update. It seemed ominous. He feared for the worst.

Brexley, on the other hand, seemed oblivious to what was happening. He wondered if she truly understood what had happened to Devvyn. Minutes later, a tall, dark, handsome man appeared. He removed his face mask and looked down at Brexley and Carlton, who were seated. They both immediately jumped up to face him.

"Hi. I understand you are the relatives of Devvyn. Is that right?" He asked with a smile. Carlton noticed the name on his white coat: *Dr. Emmerson Morton.*

"Yes, I am Carlton Chastain, and this is my fiancée, Brexley Sinclaire. She is Devvyn's only relative and sister. Please, how is she? Will she be okay?" Carlton asked.

"Let's sit down, shall we?" Dr. Morton replied, looking concerned. Once the three were seated, he spoke up. "As you probably know, she was involved in a serious car accident. I understand EMS found her pinned between the steering wheel and the car's seat. The fire department was able to extract her from the twisted wreckage. Unfortunately, she was not breathing when they managed to get her into the ambulance, requiring resuscitation twice. In the meantime, she has coded twice more here at the hospital. Oh, I am sorry....to code means she experienced cardiopulmonary arrest—her heart stopped."

"Oh, my God! Does that mean she is gone?" screamed Brexley fearfully.

"No. Not at all. Devvyn is listed in stable condition, and yes, she is alive. She lost quite a bit of blood as a result of the accident. Devvyn has numerous breaks in her left leg, which require surgery. Her right hand has a large gash, which the plastic surgeon will address after the other surgeries. With that said, she is currently in surgery, and I do not expect her to be out anytime soon. It will be several hours."

"Carlton and I will be here, or is there another place we can wait?"

Dr. Morton guided them to the second-floor waiting area near the operating rooms. He reassured them that Devvyn had a good chance of recovery and that her heart was now considered stable. She had not experienced any other cardiac events, which was a good sign.

Feeling grateful, Carlton and Brexley

thanked Dr. Morton for the information. They returned to their seats eager to receive an about Devvyn's surgeries.

Carlton called Brian a few minutes later and told him about Devvyn's accident. Plus, he wanted to know if it was an accident or if someone caused the accident on purpose to harm Devvyn. It was Carlton's first thought. The incident seemed suspicious to him.

Cameron wondered what had happened to the person inside the vehicle. It appeared as if it was a fatal accident. He sped down the road, eager to meet Stephanie, his girlfriend. He was about to pull into the driveway of her home when his phone rang. He answered it quickly.

"Hello. This is Cameron."

"Hey, Cam. It is Brian. I just got a disturbing call from Carlton. Do you remember Devvyn? Brexley's good friend?"

"Of course. I wanted to date her for a long time. We had lunch together once. I asked her out twice after that, but she continually turned me down, haha. Why? What's up?" Cameron asked, now curious what Devvyn had to do with anything. He hoped she was not involved in the crimes.

"She was in an accident in New Braunfels a little while ago. I made some calls to NBPD. It does not look like it was anything she did to cause the accident. Witnesses stated she was turning when a truck came barreling down the street and struck her. She lost control and spun around, hitting a pole. I think this may have something to do with Brexley Sinclaire. What do you believe?" Brian hated the idea of another person associated with Brexley becoming an innocent victim. Why was this happening?

"Damn. That is awful. Will Devvyn be okay? What did Brexley say?" The two conversed for almost 30 minutes about the accident.

Cameron was shocked to learn he had been at the accident earlier, and the person inside the destroyed car was Devvyn! Cameron finally cut off the conversation when Stephanie walked out of the house, giving him a strange look since he had been in the driveway for over half an hour without coming inside. She glared at him with her arms crossed.

Cameron followed Stephanie inside the home but could not help but wonder about Devvyn. She was a great person and did not deserve what someone did to her. He planned to find out more about the supposed accident in the morning. He yearned to spend time with his girlfriend and enjoy the rest of the night.

Dereck still thought about Ashton daily. He was assimilating into his new life on the east coast. Ashton did not call or text him. Dereck was relieved but still wondered why he had never attempted any form of communication. He assumed he was mad, hurt, or both.

Dereck did not regret his decision to cut his

ties with Ashton. He only wished he had done it sooner. Now, he planned to forget all that had occurred in San Antonio and live the rest of his life without drama. His new life was stress-free.

In the hospital, the day was moving along too slowly for Brexley. She felt restless while she thought about Devvyn. Carlton sat in the large waiting area, mindlessly staring at the wall-mounted television. A holiday movie played on the screen, and Brexley wanted to pay attention but was too upset to keep her mind focused. Carlton typed a message on his phone, attempting to keep his mind off the current situation.

Forty minutes later, a short female doctor approached them, smiling. "Hi! I understand that you are the family of Devvyn." He looked at them. " Is that correct?" Dr. Kavan asked.

Carlton stood up quickly. "Yes! We are. Is she okay?" Brexley stood beside him, holding his hand, hoping to hear good news.

"Yes, she made it fine through surgery. She is currently in recovery. Once we move her to her room, you can see her briefly. She will need lots of rest, so please limit your visit today. We will come to get you in about an hour or two."

Brexley and Carlton thanked Dr. Kavan for the update, grateful that Devvyn survived the surgery without further complications.

It was a huge relief. Brexley hugged Carlton and began crying. She was happy her friend had a chance to recover. Hopefully, it would not take long for her to regain her health and resume life.

Cameron left Stephanie's house on the other side of town and headed to work back in San Antonio. He wanted to learn more about Devvyn's accident and how it could relate to the current situation with Brexley Sinclaire. His gut instinct told him the two were intertwined. It seemed likely that Devvyn became another innocent victim in Brexley's unfortunate business.

Shawn was busy researching Devvyn on his computer at the police station when Cameron appeared. "Hey, you. What are you doing here? I thought you took the rest of the week off to help Maddie?" Cameron asked.

"No, I am taking next week off for Thanksgiving. I wanted to follow a hunch I had concerning the Brexley Sinclaire case. I had to ask for a copy of the accident report from NBPD and find out more. What are you doing here? I thought you were staying with Stephanie in New Braunfels for the next few days?" Shawn looked at Cameron, speculating what would have made him leave his girlfriend to come to work.

The two worked for hours early into the morning, pouring over reports and taking notes. One thing Shawn knew for sure, Devvyn was targeted on purpose. There was no other reason why the large truck would have struck her so hard unless it was deliberate. Now, the challenge was to find out why.

Sitting in his apartment, Ashton decided to find another accomplice. Since Dereck was gone, he required help to complete his next step. One of his good friends, a private detective named Stefan Miller, was a great alternative. He was a decent guy but always enjoyed making some money on the side, even if it was not in an ethical way.

Ashton called Stefan and explained the preliminary plan, hoping he would agree. After listening to Ashton for twenty minutes, Stefan informed Ashton he would be happy to provide him with inside information and help him with his final step, as long as Ashton would agree to his fee — 45% of whatever money they collected. The agreement was made. The next move would be a doozy, and Ashton grinned ear to ear, eager to get started. All Ashton wanted was money. At this point, nothing else mattered.

On the hospital's second floor, Devvyn opened her eyes and looked around. Everything looked fuzzy. When her eyes finally focused, she recognized Brexley sitting in a chair by her bed. Behind her, Carlton leaned against the wall by the window, smiling.

"Welcome back," Brexley said, holding Devvyn's hand.

Devvyn withdrew her hand and rested it on

her stomach, wincing in pain! "What happened to me?" she asked. Her voice sounded raspy, and her head pounded loudly, making her want to throw up. " God, I have a massive headache."

Carlton approached the other side of the bed and looked down at Devvyn. "You were in an accident, Devv. But thank God, you will be okay. He squeezed her other hand gently.

Devvyn looked at Brexley. "Tell me what you know."

Brexley bit her lip, trying to figure out where to begin. Luckily, Carlton took the lead and began explaining the situation. A few minutes later, the three sat in silence. Devvyn looked shocked.

"Did someone hit my car on purpose? Were they trying to kill me? My God, why would they do that?" Devvyn shouted, exacerbating her aching head.

"We don't know, Devvyn. It may have been on purpose. I have not received confirmation from Shawn, Cameron, or Brian. Once we know, I promise to share that with you I do need to call them and let them know you are awake. They may wish to ask you some questions," Carlton elaborated. He walked out of the room to the hallway, eager to make a phone call.

Brexley stayed by Devvyn's bedside. "What can I do to help you, Devvyn?" Brexley offered.

"Would you and Carlton feed Chewwee? He

is probably starving. Plus, he probably has to go potty. I have not put him out since before I went to work! Gosh, I hope he is okay!" Devvyn worried about her brown Shih Tzu. He was an adopted pet from the local pound.

Devvyn thought he was the cutest dog she had ever seen. His snaggletooth poked out when he looked at her, and he appeared to smile. His right ear was also damaged. It looked like it had been chewed on the ends, though it most likely was a birth defect. Thus, she named him Chewwee.

"Of course. Should we go now? We can come back later to check on you?" Brexley suggested.

"Yes, that would be great — no hurry to come back. I am sure I will be sleeping. Thank you, Brexley, for taking care of Chewwee. That means a lot." Devvyn closed her eyes. Everything hurt, and she heard the nurse enter the room, asking the others to leave so Devvyn could rest.

Carlton looked surprised when Brexley exited Devvyn's room. "Is everything alright? Are we leaving?"

"Yes, Devvyn would like for us to feed Chewwee. I still have a key to her place. Let's leave. We can come back later."

Brexley reached for Carlton's hand. He was elated by her display of affection. It was not usual for her to do that. They walked toward the elevator to leave the building.

Shawn pounded his desk loudly with a fist to gain Cameron's attention. He listened to Officer Rosenthal as he shared disturbing information about Devvyn's accident.

Cameron jumped when he heard the thud noise and turned around. He had been standing in front of the whiteboard, looking a the pictures taped onto it. Shawn was making weird faces, and Cameron became curious. He sat down in the chair and rolled it toward Shawn's desk.

"So, you are sure it was no accident? It was an intentional ramming? They attempted to harm or kill Devvyn. Okay. Well, I appreciate it if you would send me a copy of the report for our records. Yes, I am happy to stay in touch with you too. I will send you what we have. Again, I appreciate your cooperation and help, Officer Rosenthal. Yes, you too." Shawn hung up the phone.

"Can you believe that? It was not an accident. All the witnesses said the same thing. The truck sped up to hit her on purpose. Can you believe that shit?"

"Yes, I can believe it. It seems like everyone around Ms. Sinclaire is becoming a victim. We need to expedite the investigation and solve this case to stop them from trying it again. Next time, it may be Carlton or Brexley!" added Shawn. He worried Maddie could still be in jeopardy as well.

The two decided to call Brian and fill him in on the new information. Now that they had a formal report with findings, they would inform Brexley and Carlton that Devvyn's accident was not an accident but rather—an attempted vehicular homicide. The perpetrator knew what they were doing. They sped up on purpose to inflict as much harm as possible. From how the accident scene looked, Devvyn was lucky to have survived.

Devvyn was grateful for the invention of pain medication. It took away some of the discomfort and allowed her to relax. She wondered how Chewwee was doing and if he missed her. Brexley would probably take Chewwee to Carlton's home to watch over him. Devvyn closed her eyes, hoping she would feel more like herself once she woke up again.

The fluffy, brown Shih Tzu greeted Brexley. He recognized Brexley and wagged his tail as he jumped up, eager to gain her attention. "I see you, Chewwee. Here, let's go outside. I know you have to go potty," she said, leading him to the backdoor.

He quickly ran out to the large tree and lifted his leg, peeing for what seemed like a long time. Brexley left him alone to sniff around the yard while she hunted for some dog food in the pantry. Carlton sat on the large recliner, closing his eyes for a few minutes, allowing Brexley to tend to Chewwee.

She gathered the dog's belongings and placed them into a tote she found in the kitchen. Brexley planned on taking Chewwee back to Carlton's home until Devvyn was ready to come home.

"Hey babe, we are ready. Let's drop off Chewwee at the house and head back to the hospital. Okay?" Brexley asked. She placed the leash on the excited Shih Tzu, leading him out of the home. Carlton locked the door.

Chewwee sat on Brexley's lap, curled up in a ball. He was sleeping soundly as they pulled up to the home. Carlton took the dog from Brexley so she could jump out of the car. Together, they followed Chewwee, who led the way into the living room. His tail wagged the entire time. He was a happy dog, that was for sure. Brexley smiled. It reminded her of Jovanna.

Observing the dog evoked feelings she had pushed aside. She tried desperately to forget about Jovanna, missing her dearly. Now, she had Chewwee for a while. It made her happy to have a dog in her life again, even if she was just a temporary mommy to Chewwee.

After a few minutes, Carlton let Chewwee out so he could explore the big backyard. She excused herself and headed to the bathroom. Brexley was exhausted and wanted to bathe. She sat on the tiled bench in the shower, contemplating why someone would want to harm the people she loved. It seemed crazy. She was not a horrible human being and treated others with respect. Only a few people she could think of would potentially want to harm Brexley or her family and friends.

One was Marsha Wingard. She ran a successful school teaching staging. In the past, she had asked Brexley for help to spread the word about her business. When Brexley read through Marsha's books and checked out her online courses, she knew she could not recommend her. There were too many bizarre ideas that were inconsistent with the staging world. So, she decided not to endorse her. Shortly after, Marsha threatened Brexley and informed her she would be sure to trash her company's name out of spite.

The other person that openly disliked Brexley was Karmen Kittenhoff, known as KeeKee by her friends. She recently became a well-known staging star on a national television channel specializing in airing DIY- (do-it-yourself projects) and real estate shows. KeeKee felt Brexley was a competition because she was the runner-up to receive the television contract.

Though Brexley never intended to accept it if she did win, feeling it was not her cup of tea — too time-consuming and showy. KeeKee went out of her way to discredit Brexley and make her look incompetent so she had a better chance of winning the show's contract.

After hearing the horrific lies spread by KeeKee, Brexley quickly withdrew her name from the contest, sealing the deal for Karmen Kittenhoff.

Brexley could honestly not think of another person who held a grudge against or wanted to harm her. She was at a loss. After a few minutes, she stepped out of the shower, feeling better. She dressed quickly in a maxi dress and headed to the living room to chat with Carlton. Brexley wanted his feedback on her thoughts about her potential enemies.

Brexley found Carlton on the couch asleep with Chewwee in his arms. Both were passed out. She smiled and thought they looked adorable.

Quietly, Brexley covered up Carlton with the blanket on the couch. She tiptoed out of the room and headed to his study. She wanted to conduct some research on stagers in the area. Brexley felt confident a stager was behind all the horrible things that had happened, and she wanted answers of her own. Everything that had happened seemed very suspicious to her.

Brexley moved aside a pile of papers on Carlton's desk so she could work when a notepad caught her attention. It had a bunch of things scribbled on it. The first line read: *WHY?* Underneath the line, there were ten reasons identified.

1)   Revenge
2)   Jealousy
3)   Ex-Lover
4)   Ex-Co-worker
5)   Ex-Boss
6)   Money
7)   Dealings gone bad
8)   Staging competition
9)   Staging contracts
10)   Her

The following line was labeled THINGS WE KNOW:

1)   Kidnapping
2)   Maddie involved
3)   B's house torched
4)   B's Warehouse burned
5)   George Murdered
6)   Notes left at numerous locations

The first thing Brexley questioned was number 10 on the list – HER? Who was HER? Why did Carlton not identify the person by name? Did he know HER, or was it just someone he suspected? Either way, Brexley planned on asking Carlton about HER. It seemed very suspicious.

Brexley stared at the paper, contemplating why Carlton made these lists. *'Was he attempting to solve the case on his own? Was he looking for clues because he was scared for his fiancée's life and his own? Did he know something that no one else knew? Did he suspect someone!'*

Aha...he must have a feeling about someone. Maybe it was HER? Brexley could not wait for Carlton to wake up. She jumped out of the chair and strutted to the living room to confront him.

"Carlton, wake up," Brexley yelled. Chewwee looked irritated at her high-pitched voice and jumped off the sofa, curling up by the fireplace.

"My goodness, Brexley. Must you yell? I am right here," Carlton snapped, irritated.

"We need to talk," she demanded.

"Okay, and it can't wait?" Carlton rebutted.

"No, it most certainly cannot. I was in your study. I wanted to conduct some research on the computer when I found your Suspect List...or whatever it is. Who the hell is HER—number 10 on the list of WHY?"

Carlton sat up and ran his fingers through his hair. He never intended for Brexley to see the lists. It was his personal attempt to rationalize the events and who may be involved.

Now, Brexley would force him to divulge who he named HER. He specifically put HER because he worried Brexley might find the list someday. He did not want her to know it was Alexandria.

"Her? Her who?" he asked, pretending to

forget who she was supposed to be. He refused to get into a huge fight with Brexley.

"Haha. Good try, Carlton. You know darn well who she is. So, spill it. WHO is HER? I want answers."

"Brexley, the lists are assumptions with a few facts. I am no detective. I made them for reference purposes only. It is nothing. Stop the nonsense," Carlton insisted, hoping she would stop pursuing the issue. He sat up, rolling his eyes with impatience. She was acting crazy.

"NO. I want to know who HER is, and I want to know right now. Why did you not list her name? Do you not know it, or did you purposely leave it off?" The second she finished the sentence, it hit her. Carlton used the code of HER to specifically keep the person's real name off the list. He did not want Brexley to know. It infuriated her even more.

"You do know," she screamed angrily, squinting her eyes.

"Yes, calm down. I do." Carlton confessed.

"Okay. Is it someone I know? Please. Just tell me. After everything…who is it!??"

"Alexandria."

Brexley stared at Carlton. She could not believe her ears. Had he just said Alexandria? *'He better not mean Alexandria Betterson.'* She thought. *'NO, it cannot be her. There is no way!'*

"Brexley, I did not want you to know. Honestly, I am unsure if she is involved, but she is a suspect. I had a meeting with Brian. He wanted answers on my relationship with her and how you fit into all of it. I explained things as best as I could. I am sorry, Brexley...I told Brian about the rape and how you and Alexandria were involved in the past. Please forgive me." Carlton tried to reach out and grab Brexley's hand, but she quickly swiped his hand away, then wrung her hands.

"How dare you! How could you tell him about my business? Who gave you the right to interfere like that? Screw you, Carlton. I cannot believe you. And what the hell did happen between you and Alexandria? Huh? You were always so evasive about the topic. Did you screw her?" She observed him. "Oh, my God! You did, didn't you? You are unbelievable."

Before Carlton could respond or elaborate further, Brexley ran to her room. She grabbed her purse and keys. Within a few minutes, she pulled out of the driveway in the SUV. Carlton heard her leaving and came running out to stop her.

"Brexley, please. Let me explain. Honey, please don't leave. Let's talk about it," he begged, yelling. He noticed Mr. Villegas across the street staring at him as he moved his garbage can to the curb. Carlton gave up as Brexley peeled out of the driveway.

Feeling defeated, Carlton reluctantly walked back into the house and closed the garage door.

He wondered where Brexley would drive to this time of day. Carlton sighed, frustrated with himself for not being more transparent with Brexley and telling her about Alexandria earlier. He never meant for her to find the list or about his intimate relationship with Alexandria. He hoped it would remain his secret. Now he knew the secret could very well have just destroyed all he and Brexley had rebuilt over the last few months.

Brexley could barely see. She was bawling her head off, and the tears pouring down her face made it difficult to see. Frustrated, she pulled off the side of the road to calm down. Sobbing, she turned on the flashers on her SUV, staring at the road. She remained there a few more minutes, wondering about her destination. She had not thought that far ahead.

Instantly, she thought of the only place where she could hide out—her dad's house. Within less than an hour, she walked through the front door of Harrison Sinclaire's massive estate. He greeted his daughter with open arms, not asking questions. He knew better. It was best to be supportive and allow Brexley to share why she chose to visit him on this day, at this hour.

"Darling, I am so happy you are here," he joyfully exclaimed, kissing her cheek. "Come in. Your room is ready, and I have snacks on the kitchen counter. I must say, I was delightfully surprised to receive your phone call." Harrison was very thoughtful. He adored his daughter and loved her visits. Though, lately, they were scarce.

"Dad, all I want is wine. Do you have Chardonnay?" Brexley gave him a crooked grin.

"Of course, come on, follow me to the den. Let us chat." Harrison knew she would open up quickly. Brexley never held back her feelings from him. They had a great relationship, and he felt blessed.

After a few minutes, Brexley relaxed on the fluffy, white sofa. The long sofa faced the beautiful lake. Brexley had forgotten how much she missed the view. She sipped her glass of Chardonnay while Harrison watched her, hoping she would tell him why she was there. He swished around his glass of whiskey in his hand, then quickly took a big swig. She seemed mesmerized by the lake.

CHAPTER 14

Carlton stayed in the living room for hours. He watched Chewwee as he peacefully slept by the fireplace. After a while, he fed the dog and put him outside. Carlton figured Brexley was not coming home. It was after 9 p.m., and she disliked staying up late. Even more, she hated being out late. He wondered if she checked into a hotel or drove to her dad's home.

After Chewwee ate and did his business outside, Carlton secured the house and walked toward his study. He sat down behind his big, messy desk, staring at the paper that had caused so much upheaval. He was still pissed at himself for leaving it out in plain sight. Why had he not put it inside the desk or in his briefcase? His carelessness cost him. Brexley was furious with him and was now staying away. He contemplated calling her but thought she would not answer the phone.

Reluctantly, he decided to head to bed. If he did not hear from Brexley in the morning, he planned to text Harrison to see if she was there. If not, he would ask Shawn what to do. Maybe he could try to locate Brexley.

In Florida, Alexandria entered the hotel room. She sat down on the comfortable bed and looked out. It was a beautiful night, and she was delighted to be far away from Texas. She wondered if Ashton had found the car. She wanted to call him but felt it was a horrible idea.

In the morning, she planned to find an apartment to rent. Hopefully, she would be able to find a job or start a new business to bring her one step closer to moving toward her new goal of rebuilding her life. As far as she was concerned, her new life had just begun, and she was ready to live it to the fullest.

Ashton listened to his new confidant suggesting how they could kidnap Brexley. He felt it was the easiest way to get the money they sought. Carlton would pay big bucks to get Brexley back. Ashton wasn't thrilled at the thought of having to kidnap someone else. It did not work out so great the last time. He figured there had to be a better way to extract money from Ms. Sinclaire.

"We need to dig up dirt on Ms. Sinclaire. There has to be a secret out there we can use against her. It would be easier than trying to kidnap her. What ya think?" Ashton asked, feeling clever.

"Sure, we can do that, but it may take some time. Do you want to waste more time on this crap?" Stefan asked, not happy about the blackmail idea. He preferred to get down to it. Kidnapping was easy and guaranteed a payout. People wanted their loved ones back, unharmed.

"I guess we could try blackmail first," Ashton concurred. "But we have to find something to use against her first. Where do we start?"

"Well, I have an idea. How about with your sister? She knows her well. I bet there is some juicy gossip and skeleton's in the closet too."

"Yeah, well, that is not gonna work. She is gone. She sold her business and ran away like a coward. I have no clue where she is, and I don't really care," commented Ashton. He was deeply hurt that Alexandria high-tailed it out of town without letting him know about her plans. It was pure betrayal as far as he was concerned. Then, his lover made a quick exit too. Both were cowards, as far as he was concerned, and he honestly did not care about either anymore. He was done with them.

"That complicated things. We will be on our own to dig up some things from Brexley's history," complained Stefan. " I am telling you, we need to rethink this and choose the kidnapping gig." Ashton rolled his eyes at him, unwilling to consider the kidnapping. It was too much work.

For some inexplicable reason, Brexley felt more at home at her father's house than anywhere else. She loved Carlton's home but felt safe and secure here, in her father's place. Harrison and Brexley sat silently in the den while she sipped her wine, staring at the darkness outside.

"Brexley, as much as I love seeing you, why are you here? Did something happen between you and Carlton? I just spoke with him yesterday. He implied things were going well between you," Harrison stated.

Brexley contemplated her father's words. She disagreed. Things were not okay. Carlton lied to her. He disguised information to make it difficult for her to decipher. Obviously, the two still had unresolved trust issues.

"Dad, you know how much I adore Carlton.

However, he did something, and I am baffled. I am not sure how to handle it. I could not stand being around him. I had to leave. I knew you would welcome me without interrogations." Brexley smiled at her dad. She began sobbing when he sat next to her, hugging her tightly. He loved his daughter and hated seeing her this unhappy.

"What shall I do, Dad?" Brexley asked. She hoped he would have a magical answer for her. He usually did. His words of wisdom soothed her.

"Well, what did Carlton do, honey? You have not shared that with me."

Brexley spent a few minutes explaining everything that had occurred over the last few weeks and ended with the most recent event. Brexley concluded by telling him about Carlton's withholding of truth.

"I see. So you believe Carlton is lying to you? Brexley, he is attempting to protect you, as always. I am sure he did not want to upset you further. Come on. Carlton is the nicest and most sincere man I know," Harrison insisted. He moved away from Brexley so he could look at her face.

"I suppose," she responded, agreeing.

"Maybe you should call him. Tell him you are safe at my house. I would hate for him to worry! Please, Brexley! Stop being so darn stubborn," Harrison begged. He disliked the idea of Carlton driving around town searching for Brexley this late at night.

"Okay, Daddy. I will."

Harrison stood up and walked to the big windows admiring the lights around the lake. He closed the blinds while Brexley called Carlton.

The phone rang a little after 10 p.m. Carlton stared at the phone number, reluctant to answer. However, he realized it was better to speak with her than let it roll over to voicemail. It would irritate her and cause more problems.

"Brexley, are you okay?" He asked apprehensively, answering the call.

"I wanted you to know I am at Dad's. I am fine. I need some space and time to think about things that have happened. Do you understand, Carlton?" Brexley replied, sounding a bit snippy.

"Yes, I do. Thank you for calling, Brexley. Please say HI to Harrison and take all the time you need. Please realize that I never meant to hide anything from you."

"Whatever, Carlton. I will speak with you some other time," she abruptly hung up the phone, not allowing him a chance to respond.

Carlton stared at the phone. *'WOW, she is pissed,'* he thought. *'She is also overreacting!'*

Harrison overheard the conversation. "You were not very kind, Brexley." He scolded her.

"I informed him I was here, safe and sound.

That is all he needs to know for now."

"Okay, if you say so. Well, I am tired, and it is late. I have rounds in the morning at the hospital. You have a key. Come and go as you please. I love you, Brexley." Harrison kissed his daughter on the forehead and walked toward the bedroom. He was exhausted and upset with her, feeling she handled the situation poorly with Carlton.

In his opinion, she should have apologized for her blatant rudeness. Harrison hated it when they fought. They were meant to be together, and Harrison wished they would come to that conclusion sooner rather than later!

Brexley remained on the couch. Feeling restless, she opened the doors and walked out onto the deck. Lights reflected off the lake from houses, which looked magical to her. She loved the glow bouncing off the lake, sparkling in the night. Brexley leaned against the railing, feeling the cool breeze. She missed Carlton and suddenly felt awful about how she had reacted. She wondered if it was too late to call him back and apologize.

Carlton was terribly upset. He thought about jumping into his car and driving to Harrison's home to speak with Brexley in person. However, he knew she would not appreciate his unexpected visit, especially since it was late. As Carlton jumped into the shower, he could not help but continue to reminisce about his argument with Brexley. After his quick shower, he dressed in sweats and a T-shirt, walking to his bedside table to pick up his phone. He figured she might answer the phone.

At the same time, Brexley walked inside the house and locked up. She felt it was best to call Carlton and apologize. She missed him and realized she had acted impulsively and childishly.

Just as she was about to dial his number when he called. She stared at the phone and took a deep breath before answering.

"Hi, hun. I am so thrilled you called," Brexley started. "Before you say anything else, please hear me out." Brexley spent almost five minutes explaining her erratic reaction and apologized, hoping to fix the rift between them. Carlton smiled, listening to her. He knew it was difficult for her to admit fault but was happy she chose to do so.

After a few seconds of silence, he spoke up. "Honey, come home. I miss you. We have both said and done some things we regret. I am so sorry for my part. I promise to communicate more effectively. I never want you mad at me."

Brexley was elated. She immediately responded. "Of course. You are right. We can both be hotheads at times. I am so sorry, baby. I will return in the morning. I am too tired to drive this evening. Please, don't be mad." The two remained on the phone for almost an hour.

It felt good to Brexley that she had made up with Carlton. He was her true love, and she wanted to move ahead and forget about their fight.

Harrison was standing in the hallway. He had been heading to the kitchen to retrieve a water bottle when he overheard the conversation and was ecstatic that the two lovebirds had finally come to their senses and made up. There was no reason for them to remain apart. Harrison knew how much they adored each other.

As night turned to day, Brexley awoke, yawned, and stretched. She was feeling quite refreshed. She was also happy to be heading home, eager to see Carlton.

Back in New Braunfels, Devvyn received the news that she could head to a step-down unit and no longer required the ICU. It made her happy. She had not heard from Brexley or Carlton, which seemed odd. She looked around and finally located her cell phone on the table beside her bed. She dialed Brexley's number, and she immediately answered.

"Hello, Devv. How are you feeling? I am planning to visit you later today. What may I bring you?"

"I am okay. I am feeling much less sore. My leg hurts the most. My stomach aches, but it is okay. How is Chewwee? Thank you for taking care of him." Devvyn worried about Chewwee.

She was less concerned about Brexley and her drama. The two spoke for a few minutes, and Devvyn shared the news she was changing rooms, moving out of the ICU, which seemed like a significant change in the right direction for her recovery. Devvyn also insisted Brexley not visit for a few days, as she wanted to rest.

Brexley understood but was hurt, given that the two women had been so close in the past. However, she refused to argue with Devvyn. She would respect her request. Brexley hung up the phone, planning to head back to San Antonio to see Carlton.

It was almost Thanksgiving, and Brexley wanted to ensure they had all the food they needed for a small celebration. They could run to the grocery store, stocking up on essentials if need be. She also planned to invite her father for dinner. Brexley could not imagine Thanksgiving without him.

Carlton was up and checking the fridge for food. He had already picked up a turkey and other items for the festive meal. He planned to cook and hoped Brexley would bake some pies. He wondered if Harrison would join them.

Carlton heard his cell phone making a noise and looked down at the counter. It was a text message from Brexley informing him she was returning to the house. Carlton felt relieved.

Not far away, Stefan left the building and jumped into his car. He laughed, finding it funny that Ashton had reached out to him. Stefan felt sorry for Ashton, who was an incompetent fool. After listening to Ashton, Stefan made the decision not to help him. At this point, he had enough information to get the job done without him.

In the meantime, he would need to find a way to get Ashton out of the picture. There were too many loose ends, and it was better to start fresh.

Unfortunately, Ashton believed he had made the right decision to call Stefan. He felt the two would find a way to extract cash from Ms. Sinclaire or Mr. Chastain. Either way, Ashton knew he was about to get some money, and the idea thrilled him. Everything was about to turn out in his favor. Once he had cash in hand, he planned to jump on a plane to the Maldives, where he hoped to live out the rest of his life. Little did he know Stefan was not planning on becoming his accomplice.

Brexley pulled up in front of Carlton's home. Before she could jump out of the vehicle, the garage door opened, and he greeted her with a smile.

Carlton opened the door for her, allowing her to jump down. "Hello, my Luv. I am so happy you are home." Once she stood before him, he pulled her into his arms, giving her a long and passionate kiss. Brexley's heart raced with desire for him.

The two walked inside, chatting happily, unaware of the man watching them in the dark navy SUV across the street. The man had a plan, and now that he knew where to find Ms. Sinclaire, perhaps he could move on to step #2. Though, he was getting bored of the entire Ms. Sinclaire affair. Maybe it was time to scrap the project.

Devvyn woke up and felt so much better after her nap. The doctor had already been in to speak with her that morning and informed her that she could go home in a few days if she continued to improve. He felt her recovery was nothing short of a miracle. The doctor advised Devvyn to hire home health personnel to aid her during her recovery.

She also required physical therapy, which would allow her to regain her walking ability. Devvyn was thrilled at the idea of going home. She worried the hospital would recommend a rehabilitation facility and was not keen on the idea. She preferred to recover at home.

As she was about to watch the news, there was a knock on the door. He grinned at her as he entered the room, holding a massive bouquet of flowers in a clear vase and two balloons. He approached the bed. "Hello, friend. How are you feeling?" asked Cameron. "I hear you have been through quite the ordeal. Gosh, I am so glad you will be okay." He stared at her.

Devvyn was surprised to see Cameron. They

had been friends for a while, but she had not talked with him in months. She had also heard rumors he had a girlfriend, and they were in a serious relationship. So, why was he here to visit her? It seemed a bit odd.

"Well, I have to tell you, this is quite an unexpected visit. What are you doing here, Cameron?"

"I am here to see you, silly. Why else would I be here? I heard about the accident and wanted to see you. I care about you. You know that!" He smiled as he placed the flowers on the table and tied the balloons to the back of the chair in the corner of the room.

"It is very nice to see you, Cameron." Devvyn managed to smile, but she was utterly confused. The last time they spoke, he informed her he wanted to date her. However, she had turned him down. They had just finished lunch at the diner, and he seemed hurt by her choice of response. She informed him it was better they remain friends. It wasn't that she did not like him or wasn't attracted to him.

On the contrary, Devvyn found him charming, handsome, and very kind. Once she discovered he was best friends with Brian and Shawn, she worried. They were known to be party animals. However, now that Shawn was supposedly dating Maddie, he calmed down. Nonetheless, at the time, she felt it was in her best interest to remain friends with Cameron with no strings attached. Now that she looked at him, she wondered if she had made the wrong decision. Devvyn pondered if he still had a girlfriend. She hoped not.

Cameron stayed for over an hour. Once he noticed she was dozing off, he informed her he would leave, allowing her to rest. He promised to return the next day if that was okay. She nodded with a huge grin.

He bent down, kissing her on the cheek, and she whispered into his ear, "Thank you for coming. It was great to see you, Cameron." He stood up and winked as he walked out of the room. Suddenly, she felt hot. He still made her heart beat fast. Maybe that was a good thing!

Cameron walked down the hospital corridor, whistling. He was delighted she was receptive to his visit. It made him even more optimistic that she had whispered into his ear, telling him she was glad he had visited. As he approached the elevator, his happiness dissipated. He thought about Stephanie. Guilt hit him. It was not a good idea for him to reconnect with Devvyn while he was still in a committed relationship with Stephanie. It was unfair, and he did not want to hurt anyone.

In the elevator, he thought about Devvyn and decided to wait and see how things played out tomorrow once he returned to visit her. If she appeared interested in rekindling their friendship, he would be happy to do so.

Cameron had always felt attracted to her, wishing to be with her.

In the meantime, he planned to stay away from Stephanie. It was better to wait and see how things progressed before he made any decisions one way or the other.

Devvyn scooted down into the bed and pulled up the blanket. Though she was sore, she giggled. It had been a while since she felt wanted. Devvyn was excited at the prospect of his visit tomorrow. *'Everything happens for a reason,'* she said to herself, falling asleep happily.

A few days later, Brexley woke up feeling refreshed and happy. The day was beautiful. Brexley admired the large turkey in the refrigerator. "Goodness. Why would you buy such a huge bird? We are only two people! How are we ever going to eat that thing?" she joked.

"I called Harrison and invited him to dinner. He accepted and asked if he could bring a plus one. I said of course. Do you know who he plans to bring? I was surprised that he mentioned a date."

"What? Is Dad dating? Are you sure?" Brexley looked shocked.

"All I know is that he asked if it was okay if he brought someone. I said yes! He did not elaborate, and I did not feel the need to snoop."

"Aha. I see. Well, I will call him now to find

out what is going on," Brexley declared.

"Not so fast." Carlton grabbed her arm, keeping her from calling her dad. "Stop it. We will see him tomorrow. Let it be. Your dad deserves companionship. If he found someone who makes him happy, you should be okay with that. In fact, it is good for him." Carlton released her. She nodded.

"I suppose you are right. That is why I love you. You keep me grounded, and I need that." She kissed him, holding him tightly. Brexley could not wait to become his wife and spend the rest of her life with him. He truly was the perfect match for her.

They spent hours in the kitchen preparing for the next day, prepping all the food. Brexley baked an apple pie and a pumpkin pie. The house smelled divine. Carlton made the green bean casserole ahead of time and placed it in the refrigerator in the garage.

Carlton also wanted to make the sweet potatoes, but Brexley reassured him they had time in the morning to get it done. She planned to swing by the hospital and check on Devvyn in a bit, even if she insisted she stay away.

Chewwee slept by the backdoor on the floor, snoring away. He was content. Brexley was happy he seemed okay. She could not wait to return him to Devvyn. Brexley knew how much he meant to her. Brexley informed Carlton she was heading to the hospital. He did not want to join her. He had a few things he wished to finish at the house.

Carlton planned to set the table and make a few phone calls. He knew he could not talk Brexley out of going. Though, he felt she should stay home. He was still worried someone could try to kidnap her or, even worse, harm her.

Twenty minutes later, she pulled out of the driveway, intent on speaking to Devvyn. There was a lot that needed to be said. Brexley felt the time had come. With Devvyn in the hospital, it was perfect timing. She would not be able to get up and leave, forcing her to hear what Brexley had to say.

In a way, Brexley felt guilty about having this conversation under these circumstances, but too much had changed between them. Since Devvyn's near-death experience, Brexley felt rattled. She wanted to make amends and fix the problems between them. She loved Devvyn and hoped they could finally get everything out in the open today, once and for all!

Simultaneously, on the other side of town, Stefan pulled away from the house. He headed to tie up loose ends. Nothing worried him more than someone who knew too much about him. In a way, Stefan was grateful. Thanks to a nosy friend, he was about to make some righteous money. The door was unlocked as he turned the handle. He entered the house with the gun behind his back. Snooping around the home, he

343

wondered if he was there. Instead of calling out his name, he quietly walked from room to room, searching for him.

As he approached the bedroom door, he stopped. If he were inside, there would not be much time to explain his presence. He placed the gun in the back of his belt for a second while he pulled the ski mask over his head. Then, he reached for the gun and aimed it ahead. He pushed open the door with his foot, which stood ajar. Sadly, the victim never knew what hit him. It was fast and quiet. The silencer ensured that no one else heard anything.

The news broke a few hours later that a body was found floating in the river at the famous River Walk in San Antonio. When authorities fished the man's body from the water, he had two bullet holes in him — one to the head and one to the chest. The San Antonio Police Department (SAPD) confirmed his identity was still unknown as the victim was discovered without identification. His face was cut up as if he had been dragged along rocks or other sharp objects.

A local news channel called it a tragic murder with very little to go on. However, since the River Walk was a public place with many security cameras, it was speculated that a surveillance video could show the murder or the dumping of the body. Hopefully, someone would come forth with information to help solve the case.

Brian, Cameron, and Shawn met at the crime scene. None of the three men recognized the dead man. His body looked awful. Once the victim was removed and sent to the morgue, they would have to wait to see what the medical examiner could discover, hopefully aiding the police in finding the next of kin.

"It is so sad when we find a John Doe. I wonder if anyone has reported him missing. Hopefully, they can lift prints. The body was not in the water that long. Maybe we can get some hits on the DNA or dental records. I hate to deliver bad news to a family right before the holidays," Cameron complained. The other two nodded in agreement. No one liked to be the bearer of bad news, especially during the season of celebration.

Cameron excused himself and left to head to the hospital in New Braunfels to visit Devvyn. He was officially off-duty and wanted the opportunity to spend time with her. He still had not called Stephanie. Oddly, she had not reached out to him either. It was quite strange and unusual. It was as if she sensed something was wrong.

Devvyn was pissed off when Brexley walked through the door. She held a vase with soft pink roses, Devvyn's favorite. Brexley placed them on the window sill and walked toward the bed.

"Hello, dear. How are you feeling? You look

good, considering what happened. Your cheeks have color again. You were looking quite pasty for a while. I was worried," Brexley said, pulling up the chair next to the bed.

"I am okay. I thought I had asked you not to come for a visit for a few days. I need uninterrupted rest," Devvyn looked mad. The scowl on her face was apparent.

"Well, I figured you would enjoy some company. After all, we are friends, and I love you. What is wrong? Besides, it has been days! By the way, you look great!"

"This is not the time to get into a fight, Brexley. I am tired, hurting, and not in the mood. I would assume that you understand," Devvyn retorted snidely.

"Yes. However, this is precisely why we need to talk. You and I have drifted apart for a while. I am sorry, and I feel horrible about that. You mean the world to me. I was upset with you when I told you about my book contract, and you dismissed it as if it were nothing. Again, this isn't about me. How can I fix this between us? I do not want to go through the holiday season with us apart. Please, tell me what I can do," Brexley pleaded.

Devvyn contemplated Brexley's plea. She felt the same. She hated how things were between them. Worse, she missed her best friend. Devvyn allowed pride and jealousy to interfere with their friendship.

"You are not the only one to blame, Brexley. I have not been kind to you. I was mad at you for how you treated Carlton. He is a treasure, and I was hopeful you would see that. Also, I am thrilled for you about the book contract. I was jealous and angry. I'm angry because I thought you would stop staging. You worked so hard for all the successes in your life. I did not want you to throw it away. I should have let you do what you wanted without acting like a spoiled brat. I am sorry." Devvyn held out her arms.

Brexley stood up and hugged her friend gently. Both began crying, then laughing.

"We are so dumb," declared Brexley.

"Yes, we are. Forgive me, Brexley."

"Only if you forgive me, Devvyn."

The two chatted for almost thirty minutes until an unexpected knock disturbed them. The door opened, and Cameron appeared with a box in his hands.

He wore tight-fitting faded jeans with a white dress shirt and cowboy boots. His thick, dark hair looked shiny and was combed to one side. His blue eyes sparkled, making him look sexy as hell. Instantly, Devvyn smiled in a flirty way. It became pretty apparent that something was happening between them.

"Hey, Cam. What are you doing here?" Brexley interrogated him.

"Just visiting a friend, same as you,"

Cameron replied calmly, with a cheesy grin.

"Aha…I see! Well, I am heading home. Devvyn, I love you. I will call you in the morning."

The two women hugged, and Brexley exited the room swiftly. She felt odd, like a third wheel. She could smell the cologne on Cameron as she walked past him. *'Whew, who is he trying to impress,'* Brexley said to herself.

"Well, wasn't that just as uncomfortable as can be," joked Cameron. He smirked, showing off his pearly white teeth.

"Don't worry about it. It is good to see you, Cameron. What's in the box?"

"Here, let me show you." He opened the box and placed it on her lap.

"Is that what I think it is?" Devvyn inquired with a smirk.

"Oh, yes. It is your favorite, as I recall. You devoured the last piece of Chocolate Cheesecake with peanut butter cups. I bought this one at the same bistro where we had lunch. I remember how much you loved the dessert."

"Oh, my gosh. You are too thoughtful. Do you know that? I will only eat it if you share it with me," Devvyn insisted.

"Unfortunately, I only brought one fork," Cameron explained. "So, you eat it."

"No, we will share. I don't have cooties. Besides, we have swapped spit in the past, haha," Devvyn reminded him of their one kiss.

It was the afternoon they left the bistro. Cameron offered to walk her to her car after their lunch. She wanted a hug, and Cameron went in for the kiss. Devvyn did not resist. Both appeared shocked at how lovely the moment felt. They immediately pulled away, pretending nothing had happened. Devvyn leaned up against her car, looking down at the street. Cameron fidgeted with his jacket.

"I supposed I better head home," Devvyn said.

"Yes, me too," Cameron agreed.

Cameron helped her into the car and then closed the door, smiling at her. The two waved goodbye with a sense that more could be between them. She zoomed off without another word.

He called a few times to pursue another date, which she declined. She felt unsure how to handle her feelings when she was near him. That kiss was heavily on Cameron's mind today as he purchased the large piece of cheesecake for her. It elicited feelings he had forgotten. As his mind spun with memories, he tried to focus on the now. He picked up the fork, scooped up a chunk of the cake, and fed it to Devvyn. As she chewed it, licking her lips, he finally took a bite. The two grinned at each other. Five minutes later, the cheesecake slice was gone, but the spark between the two was definitely increasing.

Once Brexley returned home, she wasn't sure how to feel about Cameron showing up at the hospital. *'Devvyn is dating Cameron?'* Brexley recalled hearing from Shawn that Cameron was dating someone in New Braunfels, but it never occurred to her it was Devvyn. *'Why would Devvyn keep it a secret?'* She wondered. But then again, they were not on the greatest terms until today.

She walked into the house, and Carlton embraced her. He took the purse out of her hands and dropped it on the floor, taking her into his arms. Surprisingly, he picked her up and carried her toward the sofa.

Once he gently placed Brexley on the couch, he took off his shirt and slowly unbuttoned his pants with a sexy smirk. "I missed you, beautiful," he teased, pulling off her shoes and kneeling before her. Brexley quickly pulled off her shirt, tossing it at him, giggling.

"Show me," Brexley responded.

"You don't have to ask twice, Luv."

CHAPTER 15

Devvyn assumed Brexley would demand details about Cameron. Sadly, she had no idea what to tell her friend. She was confused. It seemed as if there was a definite attraction between them. She clearly felt it. However, she failed to ask Cameron if he was still dating someone else. One thing was for sure, Devvyn would not be the *'other woman.'* She refused to settle.

If Cameron were still attached, she would not even entertain the idea of moving forward and trying to see where things would lead. The doctor appeared as she stared out the window, daydreaming about Cameron.

"Good morning! How are you feeling?"

"Oh, good morning, doc. I am feeling much better, thanks. I wish I could go home. I am not getting much rest here. The nurses are constantly in my room, checking on me," Devvyn complained.

"I have looked at your chart and believe we can release you. Under most circumstances, we would keep you longer. However, it is Thanksgiving, and I realize you wish to be home. You must utilize Rehabilitation Services and hire some home health aides, but if you agree to that, I can release you today. I am sure you have other places you would rather be right now," the doctor announced.

"That is fantastic. Thank you! Yes, of course. Whatever you want," Devvyn instantly responded. She wanted to head home as quickly as possible.

"Great. While you arrange transportation, I will sign your discharge paperwork and provide information about Rehabilitation Services and everything else you need. I can send a Patient Representative to speak with you if you wish."

"No, that will not be necessary. I will follow

all instructions, and I have plenty of people in my life who will ensure I do what is needed," Devvyn said, agreeing to his requests. She realized Brexley would become a hover Mom, keeping a watchful eye on her.

The doctor left the room, and Devvyn immediately picked up the phone to call Brexley. Once she held the phone in her hand, she had a change of heart.

"Hi, it is Devvyn," she said quietly.

"I know it is you! How are you feeling? What time will you be up for company?"

"That is why I am calling. I can leave shortly to return home, but I need a ride. Would you have time to pick me up? If you can't, it is totally okay. I can call someone else," she explained. She hoped he would agree. There were things she wished to discuss with him in person.

"Of course. What time do you need me? Now?" He questioned, happy she had called him and asked for his help.

"You could come in thirty minutes or so. I am unsure how long the staff will take to finish my release paperwork, but I would love to see you now." She spoke with him for a few minutes and then hung up the phone with a smile. Then she wondered if she should call Brexley and inform her about her release from the hospital.

Ultimately, she decided against it, feeling

Brexley would rush to her aid, and she did not want to see her right now. Devvyn was much more interested in visiting with him, plus she figured Brexley and Carlton had plans for Thanksgiving.

Unexpectedly, her phone pinged. It was a text message from Carlton. He was extending an invitation for dinner at his house. He apologized for the late notice but informed her that they would love to have her join them if she was released today. Dinner was at 5 p.m. They would be happy to pick her up if need be. Devvyn decided to hold off on a response, pending her conversation with Cameron.

Cameron was in his car, about to pull out of the driveway, when Stephanie called. He picked it up, apprehensively, curious as to why she called. She had a lot to say, asking many questions. He answered honestly. Twenty minutes later, he said goodbye to her for the last time. Interestingly, she did not seem surprised or upset that he wanted to break up. In fact, she sounded relieved.

Shawn and Maddie RSVP'd with a 'YES.' They planned to attend the Thanksgiving dinner since neither had extended family. Shawn insisted they join in the fun. He knew Maddie wasn't keen on spending time with Brexley, but she reluctantly agreed.

Brexley and Carlton worked in the kitchen. Christmas music blared throughout the house.

During the previous night, Carlton brought out the Christmas tree, placing it in the living room near the fireplace. Though it was not yet decorated, it looked pretty. It was a tall, full, faux tree illuminated with thousands of tiny, warm white LED lights. It made the living room look festive. It was the beginning of the decorating season, and Carlton knew Brexley would be thrilled. She was eager to begin decorating the tree right after Thanksgiving.

The fireplace roared as the day was cold. It was only 29 degrees. By San Antonio standards, that was downright freezing cold. Most Texans did not appreciate the chilly weather. Chewwee was stretched out before the fireplace, taking advantage of its extra warmth.

Brexley smiled as she heard Carlton singing. He was in a joyous mood. He stopped for a moment and glanced at Brexley. She blew him a kiss. Her heart overflowed with love for Carlton. Their lives were finally on track, and she couldn't be happier.

Harrison was the first to arrive at the house at 3 p.m. He had previously informed Carlton he wanted to come early to allow them some private time to become acquainted with Carmella, his new love.

Harrison and Carmella brought several bottles of wine and a Cheesecake. Brexley graciously took it from Carmella and guided her into the living room. She smiled at her Dad, asking if they wanted something to drink. Minutes later, the four sat in the living room, chatting.

Carmella was a tiny woman. She was 5 feet tall and weighed no more than 100 pounds. She had shiny, long, black hair dusted with a few gray strands. Carmella chose to wear her hair down, which was quite long, almost touching her bottom. She dressed in black slacks, a dark red blouse, sensible black shoes, and carried a small black Gucci purse. She had amazingly long eyelashes, and Brexley wondered if they were real. Carmella's light brown eyes were large and gorgeous.

"So, Carmella, how did you and Dad meet?" Brexley grilled her right off the bat. Carlton rolled his eyes with displeasure. He had hoped she would hold off on the interrogation. But Carmella was quick to answer.

"Your dad and I both work at the same hospital. I am also a Neurosurgeon, like your father."

"Oh, I see. That is wonderful." Brexley was surprised. In the past, her father had been adamant it was a bad idea to date in one's work circle. Therefore, Brexley was astonished to hear they were work acquaintances.

"Carmella moved here from Austin about six months ago. She wanted to be closer to her only sister, Josephine," added Harrison.

"Where is your sister today? You could have

invited her!" Brexley offered.

"Oh, no. She is on a Mediterranean cruise with her partner until after the new year."

The four conversed for a while longer. Brexley took an instant liking to Carmella. She seemed kind, attentive to her father, and funny. The women chatted in the kitchen as Carmella offered to help prepare the rest of the meal. The men remained in the living room for a few minutes before they joined them.

In New Braunfels, Cameron helped Devvyn into the SUV as she finally left the hospital. He chose to utilize the larger vehicle instead of the car, realizing it would be easier on her.

Once they entered her home, he helped her dress in casual but comfortable clothing before heading to Carlton's place. Devvyn had asked Cameron if he wanted to accompany her to Brexley's Thanksgiving Dinner. He thought it was a fantastic idea.

Devvyn also finally got up the nerve to ask Cameron about his girlfriend, hoping they were no longer a couple. He responded right away, informing Devvyn they had broken up. He had made it clear that he had feelings for someone else.

"Gosh, I hope you did not break up because of me," Devvyn gushed, flattered but apprehensive.

"Of course I did. I have been attracted to you for a very long time. I am thrilled you finally admit you feel the same." He gently took her and held it as they drove toward San Antonio. Maddie and Shawn arrived not long after Harrison and Carmella. They joined everyone in the large kitchen. Before too long, Cameron and Devvyn appeared. She sported crutches, as she hobbled through the doorway.

Once everyone was seated around the long table, Carlton stood up. He glanced at the attentive group. Maddie and Shawn sat next to each other. Devvyn sat next to Shawn. Brexley was seated at the end of the table.

Carlton sat at the head of the table. On the other side of the table, Harrison sat next to Carmella, and Cameron sat next to her, facing Devvyn.

"Thank you, everyone, for joining us for this Thanksgiving meal. This year has brought us feelings of gratitude. For one, Devvyn is on the mend after a horrible accident. Second, Maddie is safe and sound after a horrendous kidnapping. Third, my beloved Brexley has survived losing her house, a fire at the warehouse, and dealing with the tragic loss of her good friend, George...may he rest in peace. Finally, Brexley and I have an announcement to make: We are engaged!" The crowd clapped, overjoyed at the fantastic news. Harrison teared up as he lovingly observed his daughter.

"I propose a toast," Harrison announced, immediately standing up and holding his wine glass. "To Brexley and Carlton. Wishing you a life filled with love, happiness, understanding, and respect. May you make beautiful memories. And while you are at it, how about a grandchild or two?" He joked, sitting down.

Brexley jumped out of her seat, ran to her father, and hugged him. She was grateful for his love. She kissed him on the cheek, feeling elated.

The meal was superb, and the group enjoyed their time together. After the food was devoured, the guests took their leave. Before Devvyn and Cameron departed, Brexley handed Chewwee to Cameron. He held the dog and his bag of goodies.

"Thank you both for caring for my baby while I remained hospitalized. It means the world to me. I am thankful to you both. Also, congratulations on your engagement," Devvyn said, smiling as Chewwee licked her across the face. Minutes later, Cameron, Devvyn, and Chewwee headed to New Braunfels.

The last ones to depart were Harrison and Carmella. They stayed behind, hoping to learn more about Brexley and Carlton's wedding plans.

Once Brexley's father and girlfriend left to return home, Brexley closed the door and looked around. The evening was quite memorable. Carlton invited her to join him on the couch. He was drinking a glass of wine, happy to see her smiling.

"Well, what do you think, Luv? I believe that was an excellent get-together. Your father seems quite enthralled with Carmella. She is a lovely lady. Maddie and Shawn looked blissfully in love. Devvyn appeared to be quite smitten with Cameron."

"Yes, babe. I am still feeling overwhelmed with emotions. I do not even know what to say. It was a day I will not forget. Now, we should make plans for Christmas. What do you think?" Brexley snagged the wine glass from Carlton and swiftly drank the Pinot Noir. He hoped she would agree.

"Absolutely. Let's invite the same couples. You can decorate the house. I will help...of course."

"Sounds terrific. Let's clean up the kitchen and head to bed. What do you say, my sexy fiancé?" She turned toward Carlton and kissed him, elated they had publicly announced their engagement. They realized this evening would end with a fabulous celebration in bed, and both were eager to get started!

Devvyn and Cameron arrived at her home about forty-five minutes after departing Carlton's house in San Antonio. The two chatted during the commute, Cameron holding Devvyn's hand, smiling, while Chewwee napped on her lap blissfully.

Though Devvyn was still in pain, she was

happy with her life. Once they arrived at her residence, Cameron escorted her into the home and ensured she was comfortable and could take care of herself before departing. He dreaded leaving her, but she insisted, stating she was tired and needed rest. One of the home health nurses was due to arrive early in the morning to help her. Thus, she would be okay.

Though, to make Cameron feel better, she offered to call him in the morning with an update on her condition.

Harrison and Carmella walked through the front door of his home and headed to the den to look out onto the lake. He held her hand lovingly as he reminisced about the dinner. Harrison was delighted Carlton and Brexley were engaged. He could not wait to help with the wedding plans, ready to watch his one and only daughter walk down the aisle, marrying the man of her dreams.

Thanksgiving meant nothing to Stefan. He was more interested in taking care of business. After leaving his home, citing he had to work, he approached the warehouse. No one was around. The building was locked up, and everyone had been sent home until after the new year. However, he planned to see if he could break into the building.

After his previous conversation with Ashton, he knew there was excellent blackmail material in the hidden wall safe. He hoped to extract it and use it against Brexley, knowing she would pay money to keep him from releasing the material. If that did not work, he would resort to kidnapping Carlton.

What Stefan did not know, however, was that someone had beaten him to it. The elusive individual now held a stack of papers in her hands.

It did not take long for Stefan to break into the warehouse. Ashton had provided him with access before his tragic demise. Now, Stefan planned to find documents in Brexley's office. If everything went as expected, he would have enough on Brexley to blackmail her.

When the kitchen was clean, Brexley and Carlton headed to bed. Earlier in the day, Carlton had taken all of Brexley's clothing and other items out of the guest room and placed them in the large walk-in closet in his bedroom. He hoped she would be happy about the change.

As she walked toward the guest room, he pulled on her arm gently. "Where are you headed, beautiful? That is not our room," Carlton declared.

"What do you mean, Carlton?" Brexley asked, perplexed.

"It is time we share everything. That includes the bedroom. I don't want you in the guest room! I have moved all your things into the primary bedroom. Come on, let's go," Carlton announced. He led her to the bedroom, hoping she was in the mood for a bit of playtime. He was aroused and wanted to make love to his fiancée.

The night was quiet as Brexley and Carlton slept soundly. It wasn't until 4 a.m., when Carlton received a phone call informing him the warehouse had been burglarized that they woke up.

"Did I hear you correctly? I thought we still had security people in place. What time did it happen?" Carlton shouted into the phone.

Five minutes later, he hung up the call and looked at Brexley. "Sorry, babe, someone managed to get into the warehouse again! It looks like your office was the target. Let's head over there. Cameron is there with Brian and Shawn. None of them are too happy either."

Reluctantly, Brexley agreed. The repeated break-ins were becoming ridiculous. 'Why does this continue to happen?' She wondered.

Twenty minutes later, Brexley and Carlton drove toward the warehouse, furious about the situation. Carlton wondered how someone managed to break into the warehouse. The alarm was set, and two security guards had been hired. Carlton concluded it had to be an inside job. There was no other rational explanation. Of course, they would have to hire a different security company immediately and change all the codes to the alarm system.

Once Stefan was home, he opened the big black plastic bag he used to transport the papers and other items he took from Brexley's office. Stefan found a few things he believed were important and potentially helpful, but he was losing interest in this job. It seemed as if most valuables remained secure and locked away. He could not access them. Frustrated, he figured at this point, it was time to cut his losses and forget about Brexley Sinclaire. She was a waste of time and energy. He wished Ashton had never involved him in this absurd situation. Stefan walked to the shredder and, one by one, fed the papers into the machine. As it destroyed the documents, he smirked. Finally, there was nothing else to tie him to Ms. Sinclaire. It was done. He could go on with his life with zero regrets.

Cameron looked around. Shawn, Brian, and Officer Knight worked to lift fingerprints while the rest of the team took photos of the destroyed office. It looked as if a tornado had blown through it. Pictures were smashed, and there was quite a bit of broken glass on the concrete floor. Brian felt horrible for Brexley. He knew she was tired of it all. He hoped she would consider closing her business. It did not seem like it was worth it to keep it running under these tragic circumstances.

Brexley approached the office, and Carltons shook his head. "Brexley, maybe you should wait in the car, Luv," he suggested as he peeked through the doorway. His heart sank. It was worse than he had anticipated.

Shawn appeared, holding a set of keys. "Hey, you two. Do these keys belong to either of you? I found these near the window." He held the keyring in his right palm.

Brexley looked at them and shook her head. Carlton shrugged his shoulders. "I have never seen them before," responded Carlton, curious about who had left the keys behind.

"Okay. I will bag them as evidence," Shawn stated as he walked away.

"This is so weird. Did someone have the keys to get into the building? They must have had the alarm code as well, right?" Brexley confirmed, staring at Carlton.

"Yes, that would be my assumption as well. I wonder how someone managed to get ahold of a set of warehouse keys? Unless the keys Shawn found belong to the security guards? I gave the security company silver keys on a gold keyring to the warehouse. Maybe these are someone's personal keys?" Carlton explained.

Brian overheard Carlton and intervened. "We need to check with the security firm you hired. I need a list of employees tasked to work here. Then, we can see if any of their fingerprints match."

Brexley almost cried. The office was a disaster. She glanced at the corner of the room and noticed the tall palm tree knocked over.

That seemed downright stupid. 'Why do that?' Brexley walked toward the large picture and removed it from the wall, eager to check the wall safe.

Once it was open, she noticed every item from before was still inside the box. Brexley secured the wall safe again. Carlton assisted Brexley in replacing the artwork on the wall, covering up the safe.

Twenty minutes later, Carlton begged Brexley to return home, insisting there was nothing they could do at the warehouse. Law enforcement would do their part. Carlton noticed how much it pained Brexley to see the warehouse office in such disarray. Reluctantly, she agreed. They said goodbye to Shawn, Brian, and Cameron, walking toward the SUV. Brexley stopped briefly and looked around.

"Hun…do you think I should sell the business? So much bad stuff has happened. I am not sure the company can withstand all the negative publicity."

Carlton took Brexley's right hand into his as he looked her in the eyes. "Luv, whatever you want to do, I will support you. I hear what you are saying, but I doubt we should give in to the criminals. That is what they want you to do. However, I understand you are worn out and tired of all the horrible events. Let's think about it through Christmas and then make our decision. What do you think? It is ultimately up to you. I am just here to provide you with love and support."

Brexley wept. She pulled him against her. He felt terrible. Carlton knew she was ready to call it quits. It would not be an easy decision to make. But it was something Brexley needed to do. Carlton doubted she wanted to return to staging after all that had happened. Many of her regular clients, primarily realtors, had already notified her they chose to utilize other staging companies for their listings.

Their cited reasons for leaving *Sinclaire Premier Staging* were the warehouse fire and unreliable staffing. Most claimed they required a steady staging company, which *Sinclaire Premier Staging* currently was not. The early holiday shutdown hurt Brexley and her business. There was no denying it. Carlton hated it. He knew the temporary holiday shutdown was making it easier for Brexley to move toward closing down the business permanently.

Brexley released Carlton and opened the SUV door. She slid into the passenger seat and closed the door. Carlton walked around the front of the vehicle and joined her. Once in the driver's seat, he turned his head to look at Brexley. She leaned her head against the side of the vehicle. Her eyes were closed, but tears ran down her cheek. Seeing her so vulnerable made him feel emotional. He hated witnessing the hurt on her face while she attempted to remain stoic.

Carlton turned on the SUV and backed out of the parking lot, planning to drive home. The temperature dropped, and it was getting frosty. There was a slight chance for a dusting of snow in the next few days, which was quite rare for the San Antonio area. Brexley kept her eyes closed. Carlton assumed she was trying to calm down or possibly falling asleep from exhaustion.

Arriving at home, Carlton pulled the SUV into the garage. He walked around and opened the door for Brexley. She was now awake, her makeup smeared from the tears.

"Come on, Luv. Let's get inside. It is freezing in the garage, "Carlton urged. She followed him inside, devasted that her life continued to be a surreal nightmare.

Devvyn was hurting. Her leg throbbed, and she had a massive headache. The home health nurse left, ensuring Devvyn had plenty of pain medication. As Devvyn lounged in the recliner, her legs up, she thought about Cameron. She felt the urge to call him but did not want to appear too eager. Lucky for her, he called her ten minutes later, asking if he could come by for a quick visit. Devvyn was thrilled.

It was a little after 5 p.m. when Cameron rang the doorbell. He could hear Devvyn yelling from the living room, asking him to enter. He assumed she was resting in the recliner, unable to answer the door. He turned the door handle and let himself into the home. Cameron held the large bouquet in his right hand when he entered the living room. She sat up, smiling.

"Hi, Cam! So glad you are here! Thanks for the visit," Devyyn stated, noticing the flowers. He walked up to her and handed her the bouquet. "For you, babe." He leaned down, kissing her on the mouth. She reciprocated the kiss, almost dropping the flowers in the process.

Surprised by the kiss, she quickly said, "Would you mind putting them in water? There is a pink vase on the counter, near the stove."

He nodded, walking toward the kitchen to do as she requested. Devvyn giggled, feeling desired. Cameron was undeniably interested in her, and she was beyond thrilled. She was eager to spend more time with him.

Brian and Shawn left the police station a little after 8. p.m. It was a long and unexpectedly horrible day. Neither was in the mood to remain at the office, figuring it was time to relax and forget about the newest Brexley Sinclaire tragedy. It seemed as if there was one catastrophic event after another.

Shawn wondered if Brexley was ready to sell the staging company. He noticed how much it hurt her to see the business trashed. Someone had it out for her, that was for sure. The messages were clear. Shawn was keenly aware Brexley was strong, but he believed she was at her wit's end, probably ready to stop all of this. He did not blame her. If Brexley were his fiancée, he would suggest selling the business and letting it go. It hardly seemed worth the hassle to keep it running. Shawn planned to call Carlton in the morning to discuss the plans for *Sinclaire Premier Staging*.

The night was cold, and Brexley sat on the couch, curled up under the fluffy faux fur blanket. The fireplace was warm and cozy, but she felt hopeless about her company's current situation. Brexley overheard Carlton's conversation with her dad earlier.

He had informed Harrison they would decide by Christmas how to proceed with closing the staging business. Harrison wanted Brexley to sell the company and warehouse. He hoped she would regain her safety and have a bright new future with Carlton by doing so. Harrison worried if she kept the company open, the threats would resurface again and again until the perpetrators were caught. He was concerned that it could take months or longer for any arrest to happen. He doubted that Brexley had the stamina to keep going through it all.

CHAPTER 16

Brexley had enough. She dreamt about the various break-ins, the repeated violent attacks against her, the business, and her friends. Though the thought of closing the doors of her staging company once and for all saddened her, she knew it was the right decision. Maybe she was giving in to the criminals by doing so, but at this point, she did not care. Her mind was made up. Brexley knew what she had to do, and she was ready to discuss it with Carlton.

She also planned to ask Maddie to come to the house to inform her of the decision. Maddie would need to find a new job. Brexley wanted to offer her a hefty severance package to help her reestablish her life away from *Sinclaire Premier Staging*.

The only thing that pulled at her heart strings was that it was almost Christmas. She did not like delivering such awful news right now. However, she was keenly aware it would never be the right time. She had to do it now while she still had the courage. The new year would be a fresh slate and a new beginning!

She remained hopeful that everyone would find a reason to celebrate the changes. Brexley walked to the kitchen and made breakfast. She heard Carlton walking toward the kitchen. He appeared freshly shaven, wearing jeans, a sweater, and loafers. He rubbed his eyes as he approached her. Without speaking, he kissed her on the cheek, grabbing a mug to pour himself some hot coffee.

"My, my...don't you look tired. Are you okay, honey?" Brexley asked, flipping the eggs.

"Sure," he gruffly responded, taking a sip. "Shit, that is hot," he complained, burning his tongue on the coffee. Irritated, he grabbed the plate off the counter. "Thanks for making breakfast," he headed to the dining room.

"Are you okay?" Brexley slid the eggs onto a plate and stared at Carlton. It was unlike him to be bitchy first thing in the morning. Brexley remained in the kitchen, wondering what had happened.

She overheard him talking in the dining room on the phone, which seemed strange. He never liked to talk while eating. She tried to listen to the conversation to figure out who was on the phone with him. It did not take long. It was her father. Immediately, she knew they were plotting something. She took her plate and walked into the dining room, ready to discuss it with Carlton.

Carlton frowned when he saw her. Brexley looked irritated, and he knew why. She probably overheard his conversation with Harrison. They had discussed the holidays and upcoming events, nothing too secretive. However, Carlton hoped to surprise Brexley with a few things. He was hoping she did not overhear their entire conversation. It wasn't easy to surprise her. She seemed to know everything and was particularly good at finding things out beforehand. Carlton realized this a long time ago.

The weeks flew by quickly. Brexley admired the Christmas decorations as Carlton appeared with two cups of hot chocolate. The house sparkled with lights and festive décor. Brexley loved everything about the decorations, and even Charlton beamed with pride, admiring how the home looked.

It was warm and inviting, with just enough bling to make a statement. Brexley had chosen to use metallics for her color palette, staying with platinum, light gold, and silver. She threw in touches of cream and white. The 10-foot-tall Christmas tree was breathtakingly gorgeous. It was primarily decorated with white, silver, and cream ornaments. It looked ethereal and frosty.

"Can you believe Christmas is a few days away? I watched the news last night, and a winter storm is coming. I hope it will not be too bad. Your dad and Carmella plan to arrive the day before Christmas and stay at the house. I think that is great. It gives us a chance to get to know her better. After all, it seems that he may be considering proposing to her!"

"What? Did he share that with you? He did not say that to me!" Brexley complained. She placed the hot cocoa mug on the coffee table and plopped down on the couch.

"Don't be mad. He wants to keep it a secret. I think he is worried you will try to talk him out of it. They have only dated six months."

"Listen, he is an adult. If he loves her, he should do it. Life is short. I want him to enjoy the rest of his life, and if that means marrying Carmella, then so be it!"

The two discussed the winter storm approaching, and Carlton decided to head into town the following day to stock up on essentials. Brexley planned to stay home and bake Christmas cookies. She was elated her favorite time of year had arrived.

At the police station in San Antonio, Shawn frowned as he found the large manilla envelope on his desk. It read: Shawn Johnson. The red lettering below stated: *CONFIDENTIAL* in all capital letters.

"Hey, Brian, did you see who dropped this off?" he asked, waving the envelope in the air.

"No, why? What is it?" he responded.

" I have no idea. Let's open it and find out. Shall we?"

The look on his face instantly worried Brian. "What is it, Shawn? Are you okay?"

"No. We have to run to Carlton's house and have a chat with Brexley Sinclaire. I knew she was hiding something." He threw the envelope contents on the desk and pointed to two pieces.

Shawn shook his head. Brian knew this day was about to become a royal pain in the butt, and he was less than thrilled.

Carlton answered the phone, sounding chipper. "Hello, Shawn. Happy Holidays! How are you? I cannot wait to see you at Christmas. What's up?"

"Ummm, Carlton, I need to see Brexley tonight. What time is good for you?" he asked apprehensively.

"It is almost 8 p.m. Can it wait until the

morning? We are getting ready to watch a movie and head to bed," Carlton responded.

"No. What time?"

"Can you tell me what this is about...you are worrying me."

"What time, Carlton?" Shawn insisted, now sounding stern.

"Okay. Thirty minutes. I will let her know you are on your way." Carlton hung up the phone. Brexley overheard the conversation.

"What happened? Something is wrong. Oh my gosh! " she whined.

"Calm down. We do not know what Shawn wants. He was very insistent he speak with you tonight. Is there something you suspect he is coming to discuss with you? Please, if you know anything, give me a heads up!"

"Hell no! Come, on, Carlton. I thought we were over the trust issues! I have no clue what he wants or why he is coming over to chat this late at night." Brexley crossed her arms. She felt hurt that Carlton would insinuate she knew why Shawn insisted on speaking with her this evening. She was over the drama, wishing to enjoy the holidays without strife.

"Okay."

Carlton stood up and walked upstairs to change out of his pajamas. He figured it would look odd. Brexley stayed on the couch in her leggings and a long-sleeved shirt. She stared at the flames in the fireplace, contemplating what

Shawn had uncovered. Instantly, she became nervous, standing up and pacing around the room. She wondered if she should speak with Carlton before Shawn arrived.

Carlton strolled into the living room, holding his phone and a glass of Pinot Noir. He did not look happy.

"Carlton, I may know why he is coming to speak with me. Don't be mad," she began.

Immediately, Carlton became angry. His nose flared, and he ground his teeth, seething. "Okay, what is it, Luv?" Carlton said contemptuously, attempting to remain calm in her presence. He wanted to scream but held back. *'How could she lie to me?'* He wondered. *'What has Brexley been hiding this entire time?'*

"Well, it has to be the short version since he is on his way."

"Fine, Brexley, get on with it...what the hell?"

It did not take long for Brexley to reveal what she believed Shawn had discovered. Carlton stared at her, unable to think clearly. *'Why would she keep this from me? It is not that big of a deal!'*

Shawn knocked on the door just as Carlton was about to respond to Brexley's revelation. However, he knew that now was not the time. Instead, he walked to the door and greeted Shawn and Brian.

"Come on in. Brexley is in the living room waiting." Carlton led them into the large room.

Brexley stood by the fireplace, unable to sit still. Shawn approached Brexley and handed her a document. She looked down at the paper and nodded.

"So, let me guess…this is one of the things the thieves were after. Tell me why! It seems straightforward, but I am sure there is more. Please, explain it to me, Brexley," Shawn shouted.

"Yes, I signed the document a few years back with KeeKee, I mean, Karmen Kittenhoff. We were both in the running to become a television host for a DIY- Do It Yourself Design show. KeeKee seemed nervous and wanted to ensure she had exposure. So, she asked me to sign the document agreeing to a joint venture if I won. After negotiating through our attorneys, we reached an agreement. Part of the agreement was I had to drop out so she would receive the contract. Once she was in the position, she was supposed to hire me as her assistant, allowing me on the set with her. Unfortunately, she wanted the document back once I dropped out, worried I would try to enforce the notarized and legally binding papers. I stopped responding to the numerous threats she made against me. Eventually, she stopped contacting me. I figured she was happy since she received the contract with the cable television station, and I was out of the way. I never planned to pursue enforcement of the documents until she informed me she wanted to reopen her San Antonio staging company and offered to buy me out of mine. I refused. She began threatening me again."

Shawn was furious with Brexley for withholding such vital information. "So, if you suspected she may have been involved with the kidnapping and such, why did you not tell me about this?"

"Umm, ask Maddie. She knows why."

"What does that mean, Brexley?" Shawn asked defensively.

"She was in the room when I video-chatted with KeeKee. She overheard the information. She knew about KeeKee and the threats."

"Bullshit! Maddie would have told me," Shawn argued.

"Whatever! I did not think it was relevant. I heard KeeKee changed her mind about the staging company in San Antonio and opened a new business in Los Angeles. So, why does any of this matter?"

"It matters because I still do not know who kidnapped Maddie and why. I also have no idea why someone delivered these documents to me. There was a reason they wanted me to know. Is there something else you are hiding?"

"NO. Nothing. I have no clue who kidnapped Maddie. I do not know why my house was torched, or my warehouse was subjected to arson. I had nothing to do with any of it," Brexley vehemently declared, now sobbing out of frustration.

The doorbell rang, and Carlton walked to the door to find out who was there. She walked in with her head down.

"I need to speak with Brexley, " she said. Immediately, she stopped in the doorway. She spotted Shawn and Brian having a discussion with Brexley. She felt the urge to turn around and leave but knew it was too late.

"What the hell are you doing here?" Shawn screamed as he saw her. "Did you put the envelope on my desk?"

"Yes. I did. I was hoping to help Brexley. I knew she would never confess to the documents, especially since a money trail is involved."

Carlton looked at the woman. "What money trail?" He stared at Brexley, wondering what else she was hiding from him and everyone else. He was furious.

"I think you need to fill them in, Brexley," she responded as she sat close to Brexley.

"Really? Did you provide him with the documents? You are the one who destroyed my office?" Brexley shouted, pointing at her.

"No. When I left, the office was intact. I did not destroy anything. Shawn told me about the mess, and I can tell you someone broke into the warehouse after I found the papers. They were probably looking for the same thing," Maddie explained.

Shawn could not look at Maddie. He fumed. Brian told him to sit down as he planned to interrogate Brexley about what else she knew.

"So, who kidnapped Maddie? Why would someone burn down your house and warehouse? What money trail?" Brian stared at Brexley.

Brexley explained, attempting to remain calm. She outlined the initial contract agreement, which included $100,000 in cash to help establish a new business venture between the two. The money portion of the deal was verbal, and Brexley agreed to pay it even though she had nothing in writing. When Karmen Kittenhoff refused to ante up her part, also $100,000, Brexley called her and demanded her money back. KeeKee said it was part of the deal and non-refundable.

Outraged, Brexley called her attorney. He informed her any agreements, not in writing, would be difficult to enforce, especially since Brexley did not identify the reason for the payment to KeeKee.

The attorney said it could be considered hearsay, a gift, a loan, or just about anything without written communication between them. So, Brexley decided to cut her losses and let it go, hoping KeeKee would disappear with the cash and leave her alone. Yes, there was a money trail of the check, which was the second piece of paper in the envelope that Shawn received. Brexley denied knowing that Maddie knew where she kept the documents. She also had no idea why Maddie would provide a copy of them to Shawn.

Shawn stood up. "Well, how does Alexandria fit into any of this? I would have bet my next paycheck she was involved. I thought she was responsible for Maddie's kidnapping. Maybe not the fires, but definitely the abduction. She was very defensive each time I spoke with her, and her brother was strange, to say the least."

Maddie looked away. Instantly, Brian noticed. "What do you know, Maddie?"

"When I conducted research at home, I located an article in a newspaper with a photo. In the picture, Alexandria stood beside Brexley, handing her an award. I saw the dragonfly tattoo!"

"What the hell, Maddie? You should have told me sooner," Shawn complained.

"You cannot hide information. It is against the freaking law!" Shawn continued to yell.

"I know. I uncovered it earlier today while riffling through the rest of the papers I took. I planned to return them to Brexley's office. However, when I saw the tattoo, I knew I had to tell you. Yes, Alexandria is the woman in the cat mask, or Cat-Face, as I call her. She may be partially responsible for my kidnapping. I say partially because I overheard her telling her brother numerous times she did not agree to a kidnapping and wanted to return me unharmed. She reiterated it on several occasions, apologizing for everything. She said Brexley was the only one that should pay the price. I was an innocent victim, and she was dreadfully sorry that I was involved."

Brexley cried. She was angry that Maddie had given the papers to Shawn. She was also furious with Alexandria for kidnapping Maddie. "So, where is Alexandria now? Do we know?" Brexley asked, still sobbing.

"No. Alexandria sold her business and home, leaving the area. I have not been able to locate her. I assume she hightailed it out of the state, maybe even the country. I know if I were her, that is what I would do," Brian added.

"What about her brother?" asked Maddie.

"No idea. Never saw him again. His landlord stated he abandoned the apartment with all his belongings still in the home. It is very odd. I wonder if he is hiding out with Alexandria or if something happened to him?" Shawn announced.

"Okay, call me dumb, but how are Alexandria and KeeKee connected?" Brexley asked, staring at the group.

"I can answer that," Maddie confessed. "When I located various documents, I noticed a paper that identified KeeKee and Alexandria as co-owners of a staging business. They originally opened a staging company together. I assume Karmen Kittenhoff and Alexandria discussed Brexley, sharing their grievances. Each must have had some kind of disagreement with Brexley or held a grudge. Maybe that is how they conspired to work against her. Of course, I have no actual proof. These are assumptions based on the LLC Formation paperwork I found."

The group appeared stunned by the revelations. None of them had tied KeeKee to Alexandria. Now, it became clear. The two had been working together for a while.

"I am shocked. I never thought Alexandria would stoop so low. KeeKee, well, that is another story. She always seemed quite unethical," Brexley declared.

"That leaves George—my wonderful friend. He was an unfortunate victim, caught off guard," Brexley added. She placed her hand over her mouth, devastated.

Carlton shook his head. It was too much information all at once. Brexley sobbed on the couch, looking ill. She rocked back and forth, still in shock.

"Hey, I wanted you to know something I discovered the other day. I forgot to mention it before. I traced the number from that nasty phone call you received, Brexley. We were right. It is a burner phone. The number is one tied to a phone carrier that sells pre-paid phones. So, unfortunately, we will never find out who made the call to you. Sorry!" Brian explained.

Shawn heard enough. He rose to his feet. "Well, okay then. I suppose you did nothing wrong, Brexley, and I cannot think of anything to charge you with at this time. I will leave you alone to sort things out with Carlton. Maddie, come with me, please." Shawn left quickly, taking Maddie roughly by the arm and dragging her out of the house. He pushed her into the back seat of the police cruiser, waiting for Brian to join them.

"I am sorry, Brexley, for all of it. I know it has been difficult for you. I will help Shawn with the report." Brian walked out the door to head to the car.

Carlton closed the door, moseying toward the couch. Brexley sat expressionless on the edge of the seat.

"You know, you could have told me everything. None of it was your fault. Why did you feel the need to hide it from me?" Carlton asked. He felt blindsided. It was difficult to comprehend why she did not trust him enough to tell him the truth. That stung.

"I did not want to upset or involve you. I thought I had it under control," Brexley explained. She saw how he looked at her. Trust was broken. Would she be able to fix the situation in time for Christmas? She refused to have this hanging between them.

"That is a lot of money, Brexley. I do not blame you for wanting it back. What I do not understand is why Alexandria kidnapped Maddie. Explain it."

"Maddie was aware of what had happened between Alexandria and me. Alexandria wanted money and prestige. She asked me numerous times to help her with her business, but I refused. I had my hands full and was busy keeping my company afloat. Alexandria threatened to tell everyone about the rape and lie about the circumstance, embellishing the story to make me look like an unethical and horrible person. She wanted nothing more than to tarnish my reputation. Once I outright refused to help her, she said I would be sorry. She reminded me of all the times she had been there for me and stated I owed her! I never thought she would do anything. Honestly, I did not associate her with the kidnapping. I cannot believe she had it in her to do that to Maddie!"

"I am sure she hired her brother to help her with the kidnapping. Most likely, that is why he has vanished as well. Brexley, Luv, you need to learn to trust me. How can we get married if there is no trust?" Carlton announced. He wondered if this was the first time she had hidden something like this from him.

Brexley tried desperately for over an hour to explain to Carlton she never meant to withhold the information. She hoped to avoid this exact situation! After all, she was the victim, losing her home, car, and potentially her business. Yes, Maddie suffered too. She felt horrible about the situation but knew Alexandria was to blame for all of it. Now, she wondered if Alexandria and her brother were responsible for the fires. She doubted Karmen Kittenhoff could pull off arson.

"I wonder if Alexandria and KeeKee worked together. It seems like they were both out to get you. The way the clues unraveled it points to a joint venture."

Carlton was devastated and wondered how Brexley would cope. After what seemed like an eternity to Brexley, Carlton sat beside her and reached for her hand. "Luv, I am not mad. I was shocked and confused. I know none of what happened was your fault. You are not to blame for the fires or kidnapping. I get it. Please promise me that you will be 100% transparent about everything in the future. I need to know I can trust you!"

"Of course. I am sorry. I should have shared all of it with you before. I am responsible for that. I cannot change it. I promise never to do that again!"

Brexley leaned over and kissed him on the lips, tears running down her cheeks. She loved him dearly and wanted him to understand her point of view. She also planned to make it up to him for the rest of their lives.

Brian left Shawn and Maddie alone to talk in the interrogation room. Brian turned off the cameras in the room so they could speak privately. He knew Shawn was pissed and demanded answers.

"So, tell me…why did you bring the papers to the office? You left them on my desk! You could have shared them with me at home without all the drama. I am freaking pissed. I really am!"

"I know!"

"So? Why did you not disclose the discovery of papers and the association between KeeKee and Alexandria before all of this happened? You look like a fool, and so do I. Brian is livid. I promised him he could trust me, but now I doubt he will."

"I am so sorry. What do you want me to say? I thought I was helping," Maddie insisted. She was on the verge of crying.

"No. You made it worse. Now, I have to figure out what to do about you. Brian was there. He knows you lied. You also tried to cover your lie. I am sure he wants to press charges against you for concealing evidence related to the kidnapping. What am I supposed to do now? Do you know what you have done?" Shawn screamed. His face was red, and he was breathless from shouting. Shawn's head pounded, and he felt sick to his stomach. He had no clue what to do.

After spending hours in discussion, Brexley and Carlton agreed they would work on their trust issues. It would take time. In the meantime, they would hold off on the wedding. Maybe they could begin planning it but postpone the date announcement. There were too many reasons to wait, and the holiday season was not the time to work on them.

Two days after the fiasco, Harrison arrived with Carmella. They were thrilled to spend the holidays with Brexley and Carlton. Neither of them was aware of what had taken place before, and Brexley wanted to keep it that way until after the new year.

In the apartment across town, Maddie faced Brian and sobbed. She knew he was there to arrest her. She had broken the law.

Brian stood up. "Maddie, I have decided that I cannot find a reason to charge you with any crime. You were a kidnapping victim, and I am so sorry. I hope we can find the perpetrators in the future, ensuring you see justice. I wish you and Shawn a Merry Christmas." He hugged her and marched out of the house, leaving the couple in shock. They had just received the biggest Christmas present ever! Maddie was not planning on wasting the one free get-out-of-jail card. Maddie would never lie to Shawn or hide anything from him again.

Cameron received the shocking information

pertaining to the Brexley Sinclaire case from Shawn. Initially, he planned to keep it to himself. However, after speaking with Shawn, he decided to inform Devvyn about the situation. He figured she had a right to know.

The assumption was that Devvyn had been targeted by either Alexandria or her brother to specifically send a message to Brexley Sinclaire. They wanted her to know she was responsible for anything tragic that happened to those she loved the most, including Devvyn. It was brutal retaliation for refusing to help Alexandria with her business dealings.

Devvyn shook her head, unable to comprehend why someone would be so malicious. It turned her stomach. She felt sad for Brexley. Her life had been turned upside down.

Shawn, Cameron, and Brian agreed there was little they could do at this point to bring in Alexandria without knowing her whereabouts.

They would put out an alert, making her a WANTED person/person of interest in the cases. They still could not tie Alexandria or her brother to the murder of George Hernández. Even worse, they had zero leads on the arson cases.

The criminals had been very careful covering their tracks. Lastly, they would also ensure Ashton Betterson became a WANTED person in all the cases. It was all they could do to try and bring about justice for Maddie and Brexley.

The only other person of interest, Dereck, could not be charged with anything. He worked at *Sinclaire Premier Staging* the night George was murdered. However, there was nothing to tie him directly to any of the crimes. So, investigators dropped him off the suspect list.

KeeKee, Karmen Kittenhoff, was found dead in her bed three days later by her lover. Her death left behind a long list of unanswered questions. Was she murdered to cover up crimes? Weeks later, the coroner's report identified high levels of fentanyl in her system. No one knew if she had taken the opioid willingly or if someone had given her the drug, hoping she would overdose and die. Her death has remained an unsolved mystery.

Christmas Eve finally arrived. Harrison and Carmella relaxed on the couch facing the fire. He sipped scotch while Carmella enjoyed a glass of Cabernet. Both appeared blissfully in love.

Brexley placed the food on the table while Carlton answered the door. Devvyn and Cameron appeared. She was seated in a wheelchair, which instantly caused a commotion in the room.

"Goodness, what happened?" Brexley asked as she approached Devvyn.

"I tripped over Chewwee and broke my foot. Can you believe it? Now both of my legs are damaged. I am such a clutz," Devvyn complained. She felt embarrassed.

"Oh my gosh! Are you okay?? Here, let me wheel you to the table," Brexley offered. After helping Devvyn get seated at the table, the doorbell rang. Brexley opened the door and welcomed Maddie.

"I am so glad you agreed to come to dinner. I thought you would stay away. Get in here," Brexley said with a grin on her face. Shawn entered the house, handed Brexley a large Poinsettia plant, and kissed her on the cheek.

"Thank you for having us," Shawn declared as he walked into the dining room with Maddie by his side.

The group of friends sat around the large table. Carlton stood up to make an announcement. "I wanted to say that Brexley and I are grateful you are here to share Christmas Eve with us. We have so many blessings, and you are one of them. I realize it has been a difficult few months, but we can make it through anything together. Thank you for your love and friendship. Oh, and Brexley would like to say something, too." He sat down quickly, allowing her to speak.

Brexley stood and nodded, thanking Carlton. "I am thrilled we are together tonight. I am grateful that my dad has found love again! Carmella, welcome to the family! I want to thank Maddie for the friendship we share.

Lastly, I am eternally indebted to Carlton for his unconditional support and love. He has put up with me for a long time. And now....I have one more secret, Carlton, that I need to share with you." She approached Carlton, gently took his hand, and placed it on her belly. He looked at her, confused, shrugging his shoulders.

"Yes, we are expecting a baby! I am pregnant!" Brexley shouted excitedly.

"Are you serious?" Carlton scooped her off the ground and spun her around, almost hitting Harrison in the process. He kissed Brexley and sobbed, realizing this day was a momentous occasion he would never forget.

The group of friends clapped, thrilled for the couple. Harrison stood up and hugged Carlton and Brexley.

"Well, you finally listened to me. However, I hoped you would be married first," Harrison winked at his daughter. "Brexley, we have to plan that wedding!" Harrison boldly announced. He chuckled. It was a relief the two love birds would finally have their happily ever after!

"Merry Christmas, everyone! Let's eat," declared Carlton enthusiastically. He walked Brexley to the chair and held her hand, hopeful their baby would look like her!

The holiday season was one they would remember for the rest of their lives. It brought unexpected surprises, closure, love, and a baby.

Brexley Sinclaire knew, without a doubt, she was the luckiest woman alive.

Brexley and Carlton agreed to an intimate but expedited destination wedding in Paris, France. Carmella and Harrison accompanied the future Bride and Groom. Shawn and Maddie declined to fly to Europe to participate in the wedding as she was still in therapy for her PTSD. However, they planned to witness the nuptials through video chat.

Devvyn was part of the wedding as Brexley's Maid of Honor. Luckily, all her injuries healed in time, allowing her to fly to France. Harrison was Carlton's Best Man, which was not unexpected. Cameron was along for the fun and to support his fiancée, Devvyn.

It was a beautiful wedding. The bride wore a pale blush pink gown, with her hair pulled up. Instead of vail, she tucked tiny roses and baby's breath in her hair. Her bouquet overflowed with white Peruvian lilies, icy pink roses, white lilacs, white freesias, and baby's breath.

The groom wore a dark navy suit, white dress shirt, and pastel pink bow tie. Carlton stood nervously by the pergola in the garden, waiting to see his bride walk down the stone pathway. After the ceremony, the couple flew to Italy to enjoy their honeymoon for two weeks.

Returning to the U.S., Brexley worked feverishly to prepare for the child on the way. She attempted to finish decorating the nursery before the wedding, but other things got in the way.

Carlton insisted he did not want a gender reveal party. He preferred to wait and find out during the birthing process if they were having a boy or a girl. Brexley was forced to keep the nursery's colors neutral, not to give away any clues about the baby's gender, because she already knew.

Four months after their honeymoon, Carlton watched as Brexley gave birth to their daughter. He held her hand and praised her hard work as she pushed to bring their child into the world, suffering through almost twelve hours of excruciating labor.

Brexley and Carlton named their child Charlotte Hope Chastain. The baby entered the world with curly dark brown hair, like her father. She had her mother's beautiful, full lips. Charlotte weighed 8 pounds, 7 ounces, and measured 20.5 inches long. Their lives would never be the same, and Brexley felt intense love. She held her precious little girl, sweaty and content. Brexley proudly gazed at her loving husband. Carlton rested his hand on hers protectively. He vowed to care for his wife and child until his last breath.

Brexley published her book three months after giving birth. Though it did not make the New York Times Best Seller List during the first week of publication, her book managed to snag the third spot a few weeks later, helping propel her writing career.

Brexley eventually sold her staging business to a friend to focus on her writing. She agreed with her friend, Devvyn, that it was best to concentrate on one job, not two!

Writing novels gave her a new sense of purpose, and she felt zero regrets about prioritizing it.

In the end, it was not about fame and fortune for Brexley Sinclaire, but rather the true love right in front of her. Carlton's steadfast love for her helped chisel away all her doubts about love and trust. He gave her unconditional love, something unfamiliar to her. Ultimately, Brexley allowed herself to be happy, and her future was bright.

~The End

ABOUT THE AUTHOR

Addilyn Prescott is an American author living in the beautiful state of Texas. Addilyn was born in the United States of America but raised in Europe. She holds degrees in Psychology (minor in Criminal Justice) and Victim Survivor Services. She enjoys writing about mysteries and romance.

www.ingramcontent.com/pod-product-compliance
Lightning Source LLC
Chambersburg PA
CBHW051313250626
47155CB00007B/2308